Four Funerals and Maybe a Wedding

Four Funerals and Maybe a Wedding

RHYS BOWEN

BERKLEY PRIME CRIME
New York

BERKLEY PRIME CRIME
Published by Berkley
An imprint of Penguin Random House LLC
375 Hudson Street, New York, New York 10014

Copyright © 2018 by Janet Quin-Harkin
Penguin Random House supports copyright. Copyright fuels creativity, encourages
diverse voices, promotes free speech, and creates a vibrant culture. Thank you for buying
an authorized edition of this book and for complying with copyright laws by not
reproducing, scanning, or distributing any part of it in any form without permission.
You are supporting writers and allowing Penguin Random House to continue to
publish books for every reader.

BERKLEY is a registered trademark and BERKLEY PRIME CRIME and the B
colophon are trademarks of Penguin Random House LLC.

Library of Congress Cataloging-in-Publication Data
Names: Bowen, Rhys, author.
Title: Four funerals and maybe a wedding / Rhys Bowen.
Description: First edition. | New York : Berkley Prime Crime, 2018. |
Series: A royal spyness mystery ; 12
Identifiers: LCCN 2017061359 | ISBN 9780425283523 (hardcover) |
ISBN 9780698410268 (ebook)
Subjects: LCSH: London (England)—History—20th century—Fiction. |
Aristocracy (Social class)—England—Fiction. | Women spies—Fiction. |
BISAC: FICTION / Mystery & Detective / Historical. | FICTION / Mystery &
Detective / Women Sleuths. | GSAFD: Mystery fiction.
Classification: LCC PR6052.O848 F68 2018 | DDC 823/.914—dc23
LC record available at https://lccn.loc.gov/2017061359

First Edition: August 2018

Printed in the United States of America
1 3 5 7 9 10 8 6 4 2

Cover art by John Mattos
Cover design by Rita Frangie

This book is dedicated to the memory of
Katherine Kellgren
who was the brilliant reader
of the Audible audio version of my Royal Spyness books.
She passed away far too young.
Katy was beautiful, vivacious, gracious and enormously talented.
She brought every character in my books to life.
Her reading earned the books almost annual Audie nominations,
and one year she won Best Female Narrator,
beating out Meryl Streep.
I can't imagine the audiobooks without her.

Acknowledgments

Thanks, as always, to my brilliant team at Berkley: Michelle, Roxanne, Jennifer and the marketing and social media gurus who make my life so smooth and simple. Thanks to John for being my first editor and to my sister-in-law Mary Vyvyan, who lets me stay every summer in a home not quite as grand as Eynsleigh (but almost).

Also, thanks to Hank Phillippi Ryan for sharing her hilarious bird story that inspired a scene in this book.

Four Funerals
and Maybe
a Wedding

HAMISH HECTOR ALBERT EDWARD,
DUKE OF GLENGARRY AND RANNOCH,
AND HILDA ERMINTRUDE,
DUCHESS OF RANNOCH,
INVITE YOU TO THE WEDDING OF HIS SISTER,

Victoria Georgiana Charlotte Eugenie

to

the Honorable Darcy Byrne O'Mara

SON OF LORD KILHENNY
OF KILHENNY CASTLE, IRELAND

AT 2 P.M. ON SATURDAY, JULY 27
AT THE CHURCH OF THE IMMACULATE CONCEPTION,
FARM STREET, MAYFAIR

AND AFTERWARD AT
RANNOCH HOUSE, BELGRAVE SQUARE, LONDON S.W.1

Chapter 1

WEDNESDAY, JUNE 12, 1935
16 EATON SQUARE, LONDON, S.W.1

Things are actually going smoothly for once. I can't believe it. Here I
am, staying at the house of Polish princess Zamanska (known to
her friends as Zou Zou) while Darcy is away and I prepare for my
wedding. I didn't think I'd ever write those words, certainly not
about someone as wonderful as Darcy. It seems only yesterday that
I fled from Castle Rannoch and arrived alone in London, penniless
and without a friend in the world. But it's actually going to happen
in a few weeks' time. Golly. Mrs. Darcy O'Mara. As Jane Bennet
would say, "How shall I bear so much happiness?"

I was standing at my window on the top floor of Princess Zamanska's
lovely Georgian house on Eaton Square (which, in case you don't know,
is one of the poshest addresses in London). It was another glorious
summer day. We had been blessed with a long dry spell, so unusual in
English summers. In fact my whole spring so far had been a delight,
ever since I returned from lending support to my friend Belinda in

Italy. In May there had been the king's Silver Jubilee, with a triumphant procession to St. Paul's Cathedral, the king and queen riding in an open landau. I had been part of the congregation at St. Paul's and it was a moving experience.

This afternoon I had been going through my clothes and seeing which ones might be good enough to take into my future life as Mrs. Darcy O'Mara. Yes, I know, I'm going to be an ordinary missus, rather a step down for a cousin to the king, but Darcy is actually an honorable, the son of a lord, and because I'm the daughter of a duke people will still have to address me as Lady Georgiana—unless they habitually forget like my maid, Queenie!

I stared at the items hanging in a rather grand French wardrobe and winced. Aging tweed skirt, a couple of white blouses, cotton frocks made for me by the gamekeeper's wife at home in Scotland. Hardly haute couture! Actually it wasn't as if we were going to live anywhere grand. Darcy's father, Lord Kilhenny, had made it clear he wanted us to consider Kilhenny Castle our home, and that was very nice, but it wasn't the sort of place you'd want to spend the whole year. (Too cold and dreary, like Castle Rannoch, for my taste!) Also there were times when Darcy needed to be in London for his work—which is rather hush-hush.

But occasionally we did move in quite grand circles, ranging from an invitation to Buckingham Palace to Princess Zou Zou's international playboy set (which included my cousin the Prince of Wales and his lady friend from America). I was constantly reminded that my wardrobe was sadly lacking when compared to every other lady's Paris models. Still there was hope on the horizon in that department too. My mother, the former duchess and now about to marry a very rich German, had promised that she would come to London and we'd shop for a trousseau. She was very grateful to me for saving her from an embarrassing situation in Italy. I didn't dare count on this, as my mother was the most fickle of creatures and I hadn't been able to count on her since she bolted from my father and me when I was only two. Still, this time

I really had saved her bacon, so she jolly well should be grateful enough to pay for some decent clothes for me!

I decided that if Mummy came through, I might abandon most of my schoolgirlish and boring wardrobe and become a new and fashionable woman. I'd certainly turned some heads in a borrowed backless dress in Italy. Svelte and sexy, that's what I would become. My picture in the *Tatler: Lady Georgiana, dressed in Chanel at Ascot . . . Lady Georgiana, looking rakish at opening day at Cowes . . .* I broke off, grinning at this absurdity. My husband-to-be was as penniless as I was.

The square below basked in afternoon quiet. The breeze that came in through the window was warm and scented with the sweet smell of honeysuckle and roses. A thrush was singing madly in the garden at the center of the square. A nanny in a smart uniform was pushing a very grand pram. Next year, I thought . . . but I'd want to push my own pram. In any case we probably couldn't afford a nanny.

I had just turned away from the window when I heard the doorbell jangle below. Zou Zou wasn't actually in residence at the moment, having flown over to Paris in her little two-seater plane to do some shopping. I leaned out as far as I dared but there was a porch over the front door and I could see nothing. I stood, listening and wondering who might have come to call. Obviously someone who didn't know Zou Zou was away. Then I heard the light tap of feet coming up the stairs, a knock on my door. I opened it to see Clotilde, the princess's maid.

"My lady, zere is a visitor for you," she said. (Her French accent was still rather strong.)

"Who is it?" I asked. For a moment I had a wild hope that Darcy had returned earlier than expected. But then he wouldn't be a nameless visitor. He'd have bounded straight in past Clotilde and up the stairs.

"A lady," Clotilde said. "She did not 'and me 'er card. She merely says, 'I understand you 'ave Lady Georgiana Rannoch staying 'ere at zee moment. I wish to speak wiz 'er.'"

Oh dear. That sounded serious. I glanced in the mirror to see if I looked presentable. Not very. It was a hot day and my cotton frock was crumpled. Clotilde must have noticed this because she said, "I recently washed and pressed your green silk, my lady. I will tell zee visitor zat you will be down shortly."

"Thank you, Clotilde," I said. "And please see that my visitor is offered tea or lemonade or whatever she wishes."

"Of course, my lady." Clotilde was a perfect maid: she always knew the right thing to do on any occasion, from turning a blind eye when the princess invited a male friend up to see her etchings to mending holes invisibly in velvet burned by my maid, Queenie, who was about as un-perfect as one could imagine. But Queenie, the disaster-maid, was not with me at the moment. She was still with Darcy's relatives in Ireland, where she was learning to be an assistant cook. I couldn't decide whether I should summon her back when we moved into a place of our own. The problem was that efficient maids cost money and of that we had little. Maybe I could ask Mummy to supply me with a maid as a wedding present. But as we had both found out, too-perfect maids aren't always desirable!

Hastily I scrambled into my green silk dress, brushed my hair and went downstairs trying to look cool, calm and collected.

"Zee visitor is in zee small sitting room, my lady," Clotilde said. I pushed open the door. My visitor was sitting in a chair by the window with a cup of tea in her hand. She looked up, frowning, as I entered.

"Ah, there you are, Georgiana. I wondered where on earth you had got to," she said. "We hadn't heard from you in ages. We thought you might still be in Switzerland but Binky suggested you might be staying with that foreign princess woman, and he was right, clever old thing."

My heart sank. It was my sister-in-law Hilda, Duchess of Rannoch, usually known as Fig.

"Hello, Fig," I said as pleasantly as I could as I pulled up a chair beside her. "What a surprise. How lovely to see you. I thought you'd be up in Scotland for the summer. That's why I didn't come to call."

Her scowl deepened. "We were but we came down for a doctor's appointment. It makes a change from bloody Scotland, where it has rained incessantly this spring. And Binky has taken up golf. Does nothing but hit a stupid little ball over miles of heather into little holes. What a waste of time."

"A doctor's appointment?" I said the words cautiously. "You're both in good health, I hope? Oh, don't tell me it's another baby on the way?"

"God forbid," she said, rolling her eyes. "No, I told Binky we have the heir and he can do without the spare. As if anyone would want to inherit that cold and drafty white elephant that is Castle Rannoch."

"So it's just a routine check?" I asked.

"Actually it's Binky's toenails," she said, with supreme distaste in her voice. "He has ingrown toenails and they are spoiling his golf game. Apparently it requires a small operation to make them right again and he thought it had better be done in London, just to be on the safe side. And I said if I was being dragged to London for his toenails the very least he could do was to take me to Ascot for once. We have so little opportunity to dress up at home. I might buy a new hat."

"How jolly," I said. "Shall you be going on opening day? I might see you there."

"You are going to Ascot?" She sounded quite vexed, as if I'd arranged this deliberately to spite her. "On opening day?"

"Yes, the queen invited me to join her party."

"You're going on opening day with the queen?" Fig really did wince now. She had never forgiven me that Queen Mary had actually become quite fond of me and invited me regularly to the palace—also that I was of royal blood and she wasn't. To smooth this over I added, "I'm going to borrow one of Zou Zou's hats. She has some quite outrageous ones."

Fig frowned as she looked at the silk dress. "That dress you are wearing looks rather chic. Did you borrow that from your foreign princess?"

I was dying to say, "What? This old thing?" but I couldn't pull it off without grinning. "It came from my mother," I said. "It was one of her few castoffs that actually fit me. On her it came to her ankles and just hung loosely. On me it's short and formfitting, but at least it's silk."

"One thing I can say for your mother, she does have good taste in clothes."

She took a sip of tea before adding, "Of course the same thing can't be said for men. Who is her particular beau at the moment, dare one ask? A polo player? A racing driver? A Texas oilman?"

"They are all in the past," I said. "It's still Max von Strohheim, the German industrialist. I think you've met him. He's nice. She's been with him for a couple of years now, and what's more, they are planning to marry next month. Big wedding in Berlin. I'm going to be a maid of honor."

"Good God," Fig said. "It seems that everybody in the world is getting married this summer, including you, one gathers. One saw the engagement announcement in the *Times*. So it's actually about this wedding that I am here. We haven't yet received an invitation. . . ."

"That's because the final details have not been put into place yet, Fig. We only just heard that I had been given permission to withdraw from the royal line of succession. Until that we couldn't go ahead. We've chosen the date, July 27, and we just have to have invitations printed and mailed."

"That was a big step to take, Georgiana," Fig said. "One does not reject one's place in society and one's obligations lightly. I'm sure Binky would never have renounced his place in the line of succession to marry me."

I tried to keep a straight face. I didn't think that any man in his right mind would have renounced anything to marry Fig. I'm not normally so uncharitable, but Fig has been utterly beastly to me since she came to live at Castle Rannoch, making it plain that I was no longer welcome at my childhood home.

"I was only thirty-fifth in line, Fig. Your children would be on the throne before me if a meteor strike or plague wiped out the rest of the royal family."

"That's true, but all the same . . ." Fig took another sip of her tea, then put down the cup and saucer with a clatter on the little glass-topped table.

"I intended to marry Darcy whatever happened," I said. "I would have run off to Argentina if Parliament had said no."

"So are we to expect that you will be married from the family seat in Scotland?"

"Castle Rannoch? Good heavens no," I said, rather more emphatically than I had meant. Then I remembered it was her home and she was stuck there for most of the year, so I added, "I do want my friends to attend my wedding, and Castle Rannoch is in the middle of nowhere, isn't it? Besides, they'd all have to stay at the castle. You'd have to entertain them, Fig. And think of all the Rannoch family members—those hairy cousins with the big appetites. It would cost a pretty penny."

I knew I had hit a nerve there. Fig is the stingiest person I have ever met. I saw her face twitch. "Of course you are not wrong there," she said. Then she paused. "I mean, how would they all get to Castle Rannoch? There is no bus or train."

"My point exactly," I said. "And of course there is no Catholic church within miles."

Her eyes blinked up and down rapidly now. "A Catholic church? You are planning to marry in a Catholic church?"

"That's because I'm marrying a Catholic, Fig."

"You're not planning to convert, are you?" She sounded as if I'd just said that I was planning to marry a pygmy and become a cannibal.

"I haven't decided yet. I'm supposed to be taking instruction from a priest in London—to let me know what I'm getting into. I have to promise to bring up the children as Catholics."

She actually reached out a hand and laid it over mine. "Oh, Georgie. Are you sure you want to go through with this? I mean . . ."

"Fig, let's get this straight," I said, still trying to remain calm. "I love Darcy. I want to marry him. His religion means something to him, whereas mine means going to church occasionally because it is expected of me."

"You couldn't have a proper Church of England ceremony and just a Catholic blessing at the end?" she suggested.

"Then it wouldn't be a sacrament."

"A what?"

"A holy wedding in the eyes of the church. I wouldn't be considered properly married. But I really don't mind where we marry as long as we do marry."

"So where is this ceremony to take place? In London?"

"Yes, I think so. That way it's easy for Mummy and Max and other friends to come from the Continent. Darcy worships at something called the Farm Street Church when he's in town, so I wouldn't mind holding it there."

"The Farm Street?" Fig's eyebrows rose in astonishment. "Where in heaven's name is that?"

I did smile now. "On Farm Street in Mayfair, actually. That's how they always refer to it. Its real name is the Church of the Immaculate Conception or something terribly Roman like that. It's where posh Catholics attend church in London."

"Are there any posh Catholics?" she demanded, looking down her nose at me.

"Well, yes. There's the pope for one. And the Duke of Norfolk. The premier duke in the peerage of England, therefore one rung above you, Fig. His family is Catholic. And of course Princess Zou Zou. You can't get much posher than a princess."

"A Polish princess, Georgie. In countries like that they hand out titles like certificates on sports day at school. And she is only a princess because one presumes she married a prince."

"You're right. She was a mere countess before." I grinned. "Anyway, take it from me that there are enough posh Catholics to fill a church."

"And you will be staying with this princess until your wedding? You will be married from her house? What about the reception?"

I took a deep breath. "Actually, Fig, I'd really like to be married from our London house, if you and Binky would be willing to come down for the wedding. And I'd like Binky to give me away."

She shifted uncomfortably. "I don't know what he'll say about walking you down the aisle in a Roman Catholic place of worship, Georgiana. But he is very fond of you and we know how softhearted he is, so I expect he'll agree." She paused, then could hardly bring herself to say, "And I suppose you expect us to fund the wedding?"

"Mummy is providing my trousseau and Belinda is making my wedding dress," I said. "I'm sure Zou Zou would be happy to provide the wedding breakfast here, but it would be nice if it could be at my family's London house. Nothing too fancy, of course. Champagne, a cake and a few nibbles. You and Binky could manage that, couldn't you?"

She had gone quite pink. "Yes, I suppose we could," she agreed. Then she wagged a finger at me, looking almost animated. "Binky can wear his kilt and Podge can be a page boy and I wonder if Addy is old enough to be a little bridesmaid?"

I could see her warming to it by the minute.

"Binky looks spiffing in his kilt," I said, encouraging her.

"And bagpipes," she added. "You know how Binky loves his bagpipes. We'll bring down old Mr. McTavish."

"Oh golly," I said. I know the sound of bagpipes should be in my blood, but I can't stand them, having been woken by them at dawn on regular occasions. "Do we really have to have bagpipes?"

"A Rannoch wedding with no bagpipes?" She sounded shocked. "It simply isn't done, Georgiana. Binky would insist if you want him to give you away."

I decided that bagpipes for five minutes at the end of my wedding ceremony was a small price to pay for keeping my brother and his wife happy.

"Of course," I said, giving her a winning smile. "Definitely bagpipes."

$\mathcal{C}$hapter 2

Tuesday, June 18
Opening Day at Royal Ascot

I'm off to Ascot with the king and queen. Could there be anything
more terrifying? Having to look chic and not put my foot into a
rabbit hole with all those people watching me. Every time I think I
have overcome my girlish clumsiness, something new and
embarrassing happens. But not today, please! Not in front of the
royals with the world watching!

I spent hours agonizing in front of the mirror, deciding which of Zou
Zou's hats looked chic rather than ridiculous on me. Clotilde had
hatboxes open all over my bed and handed me one after another. I
could tell from the look on her face which were duds and which weren't.
Certainly not the bright pink feathers. I looked like a flamingo in a
windstorm. I was rather taken with a white straw with a very broad
brim that hid my face in deep shadow, thus making me look mysteri-
ous. But then I decided I'd bump into people every time I turned
around. Probably knock the queen forward into her prawn canapé. In

the end I opted for a stylish little blue pillbox. Clotilde nodded to let me know it was the right decision to go with a blue-and-white linen suit.

At ten o'clock I took a taxi to Buckingham Palace. I must have looked presentable for once because the driver didn't ask me if I wanted dropping at the servants' entrance. I wasn't actually supposed to be there until ten thirty, but knowing His Majesty's fetish for punctuality and the fact that he keeps the clocks at Sandringham half an hour forward, I thought it wise to show up early. It was a good decision. Their Majesties were both sitting, dressed and ready, in the area at the top of the stairs. His Majesty was in a gray morning suit and top hat and Queen Mary was in gray silk and a broad-brimmed hat topped with a swirling ostrich feather. They looked formidable and I swallowed hard as I went up the staircase to greet them.

"Ah, young Georgie, there you are," the king said, and I noticed he glanced at the ormolu clock in the niche. He gave a satisfied nod. "Splendid day for it, isn't it?"

"The weather is very fine, sir. Not too hot," I said as I curtsied. Yes, I know he is my cousin, but he is still the king, and one curtsies and calls them "sir" and "ma'am."

"You look very nice, my dear," the queen said as I curtsied to her and kissed her cheek. (Thank heavens I hadn't opted for the broad brim. I would have poked her eye out.) "Quite suitable."

I took the seat I was offered and there was a moment's awkward silence, since one is not supposed to initiate conversation with royals. I was conscious of the clock ticking loudly and felt I had to say something.

"How is your health, sir?" I asked the king.

"On the mend, I hope," he said.

"He has been basking in the glow of the jubilee last month." The queen glanced at him fondly. "What a wonderful occasion. All those people lining the Mall. We'll treasure it forever, won't we, my dear?" She reached across and covered his hand with her own. I noticed the concern in her eyes. He had never quite recovered from a bout of pneumonia.

"A lot of fuss and getting dressed up," he muttered, but he looked quite pleased.

"I thought it was absolutely splendid," I said.

The Daimler was announced fifteen minutes early and off we went with the king's equerry and the queen's lady-in-waiting making up the party. "Shall we be meeting other members of the family there, ma'am?" I asked.

"The Kents are coming. You are great friends with Marina, of course. Bertie and Elizabeth said no, although young Lillibet begged to be taken. The child is mad about horses. But her father couldn't be wrapped around her little finger for once. You know how Bertie hates big gatherings with that stutter of his."

"If the boy would just practice," the king stormed, "he'd get over the blasted stutter. I keep telling him, 'Take a deep breath and then spit it out, boy.'"

I could see why the Duke of York stuttered every time he faced his father.

"And David?" I asked cautiously, as the Prince of Wales was giving his parents headaches by flaunting his American lady friend.

"David? One never knows whether he'll bother to turn up or not," the queen said brusquely. "Apparently royal duties are not high on his list of priorities. And if a certain woman snaps her fingers he'll go running in her direction. One hopes he would not dare to bring her to Ascot. We shall certainly not receive her if he does."

"That blasted boy will be the death of me," the king said. "What he sees in that harpy I do not know. It's not as if she's young or pretty. God knows we've tried thrusting enough attractive and suitable women in his direction. I don't know what he's thinking. As if he could marry her—twice divorced."

"We don't know if the second divorce has gone through yet," the queen pointed out. There was an uncomfortable silence as the car drove over Westminster Bridge.

"Let us turn to happier subjects," the queen said. "Your upcoming wedding, Georgiana. How are plans progressing? Have you decided on where to hold it yet?"

"Not exactly, ma'am," I said. "I gather there is a suitable church on Farm Street in Mayfair. Close to Rannoch House."

"But the Brompton Oratory is also close to Rannoch House, is it not? You should make sure the church has enough room to accommodate your entire guest list. Our family will all expect invitations, and your great-aunts at Kensington Palace would be most offended if you did not invite them. In addition to which, you are related to various European royal families. I rather think they may want to attend. The young Bulgarians, for example. You attended their wedding, did you not?"

Oh crikey, I thought. Was my royal cousin planning to invite the royal houses of Europe behind my back? Fig would not be amused if she had to provide champagne and cake for hundreds of hungry Europeans. And the last thing I needed at my wedding was to walk down the aisle and see Prince Siegfried staring at me. The family had tried jolly hard to get us married off. His nickname was Fishface. Need I say more?

"Why does the girl not want Westminster Abbey or at the very least St. Margaret's, Westminster?" the king demanded.

"She's marrying a Catholic, George," the queen said gently.

"Bloody nonsense," the king muttered. I wasn't sure whether he meant it was bloody nonsense that I was marrying a Catholic or that I couldn't get married at Westminster Abbey because I was marrying one. Actually I was truly grateful. I'd have died of fright if I had to walk down the aisle at Westminster Abbey!

"Let the girl marry properly at the abbey and then have some Catholic johnny come in and swing some incense at the end or something," the king said, getting quite animated now.

"I'm afraid my fiancé would not consider us married in the eyes of the church unless we had a Catholic ceremony." I hardly dared to speak the words because I'm sure it isn't done to contradict a king. "It's a matter of a sacrament."

"Bloody rubbish," the king said.

"Do let us know the minute the date and place are secured, won't you?" the queen cut in hastily. "We will obviously want to make sure that we can attend, and my secretary will bring you a guest list of those relatives abroad you should invite."

"Of course, ma'am," I said. "We have set the date as July 27. Darcy is away at the moment but we must attend to final details as soon as he returns."

"Now, about bridesmaids," she went on, turning to me as if the idea had just struck her. "You will be having bridesmaids?"

"A maid of honor, ma'am. My best school friend. My niece is too young to be part of a wedding, although I want my nephew to be a page boy."

"I am sure Elizabeth and Margaret would be only too delighted to be your bridesmaids, if asked," the queen said. "Little girls do so enjoy dressing up. Elizabeth would do a sterling job of carrying your train and little Margaret is now old enough to behave herself, one hopes."

"A little firecracker, that child," the king said and laughed heartily.

Oh golly, I thought. Two princesses carrying my train. And the crowned heads of Europe watching as I put my foot into the hem of my dress and pitch forward, as I did at my presentation at court! I bitterly regretted that Darcy and I had been foiled in our attempt to elope.

We left the city behind and drove through the leafy green countryside of Berkshire. There was much cheering when we arrived at the racecourse and I felt horribly self-conscious as faces peered into the car and I overheard a cockney voice saying, "'Oo the bleeding 'ell is that with them?"

I hadn't thought much about what Ascot would entail. I knew there was a royal enclosure with strict protocol and dress code. I presumed we'd sit in a shady box and sip champagne and watch horses. Now reality dawned as I saw a string of open horse-drawn carriages ahead of us.

"Thank heavens it's not windy today," the queen said. "Remember last year, when it was hard to keep our hats on? If Lady P had not had a vast supply of hairpins in her handbag, my hat would have sailed away."

Lady P, the lady-in-waiting, turned back from her seat at the front of the car. "I have a supply ready today, Your Majesty. In case of sudden breezes. Shall we double-check the hat before you get into the carriage?"

"Hand the hatpins to Georgiana," the queen said. "She can do emergency repairs if necessary."

That's when I realized that I was to ride with Their Majesties in an open carriage. Oh golly.

"Ma'am, surely you won't want me in the carriage," I said. "I could wait for you in the royal enclosure. Your subjects will want to get a good view of their sovereigns."

"On the contrary, Georgiana. This may be one of the last royal events you can attend as a family member," she said. "I want you to enjoy every minute of it."

I saw then what she was doing. I had just renounced my claim in the line of succession. She was reminding me that I'd no longer be even a very minor royal. Presumably I would no longer be invited to dinners at Buckingham Palace or other royal weddings. I'd be Mrs. Darcy O'Mara. Housewife. Well, actually that didn't bother me too much. I was always terrified at Buckingham Palace anyway. And Mrs. Darcy O'Mara sounded pretty good to me!

We were helped into the carriage. I didn't stumble or pitch forward onto the king's lap. I was proud of myself. Other carriages behind us were occupied by various family members, and we set off down the main straight—the straight mile of the racecourse—to loud cheers. It was indeed an experience and my cheeks were glowing pink as I followed Their Majesties up to their seats in the royal enclosure. How very odd to have people curtsying to me! I was very grateful to find myself sitting behind the king and queen, next to Princess Marina, now Duchess of Kent. She smiled and squeezed my hand.

"How lovely to see you, Georgie. I thought that was you in the smart hat in the first carriage. How are your wedding plans progressing?"

"Well," I said. "I am to see the first sketches for my dress this week and my mother is coming over to help me shop for my trousseau."

"How exciting. And where will it be held?"

"That's still a matter for debate," I said, realizing the queen was within hearing distance. "We'll be sending out invitations as soon as everything is in place."

I looked around but couldn't see the Prince of Wales, nor Binky and Fig, which was a relief. The races started. A young equerry placed a bet for me. I knew nothing about horses or form and chose blindly . . . and I won. Then I promptly lost at the next race. I had been to point-to-point and steeplechasing before, as Darcy's father ran a racing stable in Ireland (now owned by Princess Zou Zou). But I had never seen a flat race with this much glamour and pageantry and the absolute thrill of the pounding hoofs flashing past us. Between races I was invited to watch the horses being led around the paddock.

"I like the look of number seven," the young man who had been escorting me said. "Good solid legs. What do you think, Lady Georgiana?"

I was about to say that I preferred number five when I froze. I blinked, not sure if what I was seeing was a trick of the light. But the sun moved out from behind a small cloud and it wasn't. Darcy was standing down in the paddock next to a gorgeous olive-skinned woman wearing a skintight dress and an amazing hat covered in daisies. They were standing very close together, as close as her hat would allow, leaning toward each other in what was clearly a private conversation. Then she looked up at him, smiled and nodded. I couldn't breathe. Part of me wanted to be calm and grown-up and call out to him. "Yoo-hoo, Darcy," I'd shout. "What a surprise. It's your fiancée." Then he'd be surprised and embarrassed that I had caught him out. But I couldn't do it. All I wanted to do was to run away, go home. Hide.

"I think I need to sit down," I muttered and stumbled back to my seat. My head was reeling with thoughts I couldn't stop. I had thought he was on business abroad. If he was in the vicinity of London, why hadn't he come to see me first? And who was that woman? And why was he standing so close to her as they shared a private joke? The hurt was almost physical.

I stumbled into my seat and sat down.

"What is the matter, Georgie?" Marina asked. "You're looking awfully pale. Are you all right? Should I send for a glass of cold lemonade for you?"

"Nothing, thank you. I'll be fine. Just a little warm," I said. I stared straight ahead at the back of the queen's head and out to the racecourse. I wanted to tell somebody. I wanted somebody to hug me and tell me that it was going to be all right. What had I been told so many times before? "Bed hopping is the major sport of your class, isn't it?" And Darcy and I were staying chastely away from beds until our wedding night. Maybe he missed warm flesh too much and had found a willing partner. Who wouldn't be willing with someone as gorgeous and suave as Darcy?

For a moment I thought I might be sick. All I wanted to do was go home, but I was trapped here until the royals decided to leave, and I had no home to go to. I was staying at Princess Zou Zou's house, alone with a maid and a housekeeper. I had nobody nearby whom I could turn to. Except . . . I glanced across at Marina. Her husband, Prince George, the king's fourth son, had been known as the worst sort of playboy before his marriage. Had Marina known that and married him anyway? Was it considered normal for people of our rank to keep a mistress, to sow wild oats?

"Marina?" I lowered my voice. "When you married, did you expect your husband to be faithful?"

She turned to me, looking almost amused. "I'm sure all healthy young men like to be playboys before they marry," she said.

"But do you expect him to be faithful now?" I asked. "Or is it simply a case of don't ask, don't tell?"

"What an extraordinary question," she said and I realized I had overstepped the bounds of propriety.

"I'm sorry. I should never have asked," I said. "But I'm to be married soon and I know that my future husband has not actually been a monk all his life, so I wondered . . ."

"Whether George was being faithful to me?" she finished. "As to that, he is quite devoted so far, but then we've only been married six months. And if he says he's going to his club—well, I trust that he is going to his club. One has to or life becomes miserable. There is nothing worse than living a life of suspicion."

"No, I suppose there isn't," I agreed. But I continued to stare out at that racecourse. Did I want to be married to a man, knowing I couldn't trust him? Worrying every time he went away that he was meeting another woman? Could I be brave enough to walk away before the wedding or did I want to take Darcy on any terms? At this moment I truly didn't know.

Chapter 3

TUESDAY, JUNE 18
BACK AT EATON SQUARE

I should never have written in my diary how well things were going. I
should have known it was tempting fate! Darcy hasn't even been to
see me yet, and he was only thirty miles from London. Perhaps he
doesn't really want to marry me and is trying to find a way to get
out of it. Oh gosh—what am I going to do?

I had a good cry when I arrived back from Ascot. I don't think I've
ever felt more utterly alone. I tried to tell myself that I could be misinterpreting what I saw. Perhaps Darcy had just met an old chum, a
long-lost cousin. But the questions always remained: why was he at the
races when he told me he had to go abroad on business, and why had
he not even been to see me when he was that close to London? I couldn't
come up with any logical explanation.

There was a letter waiting for me when I arrived back at Eaton
Square. It had an Italian stamp and it was from my old school friend
Belinda. I opened it eagerly.

Darling Georgie!

I know you've been waiting to hear from me but frankly I've been plucking up the courage to come back to my old life in England. Also it is rather lovely here by the lake and Francesca is still spoiling me. But I realize I should not stay any longer. I have visited Camilla and the baby several times. He's growing into a sturdy little chap and they adore him. But I realize it's not healthy for me to stay, and another thing . . . I caught Paolo looking at me, that flirtatious sort of glance he used to give me, and I realized I couldn't possibly let him show any interest in me again. I might just be too tempted. I did adore him once, you know.

So I'm packing up and coming home. Dying to see you, darling! I've been craving your company ever since you went away. And you'll be pleased to know that I have not been idle. I shall be arriving with sketches for your wedding gown, and once you approve, we'll go shopping for fabric. I'm almost as excited as you are.

Returning on the 18th. I trust you are still at the princess's house? I'll give you a tinkle as soon as I'm back at the mews.

Hugs and kisses,
Your friend, Belinda

She was returning on the eighteenth. That was today! I found myself smiling as I put the letter down on the table in front of me. Dear Belinda. She would be somebody I could talk to. She would understand how I felt. After all, she had been betrayed by a man herself—with even more dire consequences. I had only recently returned from keeping her company on Lake Maggiore. And as a thank-you she had offered to design my wedding gown. I was dying to see her sketches. I wanted to feel excited, but a voice in my head whispered, What if she has designed it for nothing?

But I was not going to listen to that voice. I was going to be strong and brave. Belinda had been in a horrible situation and it all turned out well, I reminded myself. "I'm going to give Darcy the benefit of the doubt," I said out loud. "He'll show up and explain everything and I'll feel silly that I ever mistrusted him."

I half expected him to come that evening, but he didn't. Nor the next morning. I was anxious to see Belinda but didn't want to leave the house just in case. I was hunting in my address book for her old telephone number when the doorbell rang. I froze. "Please don't let it be Fig again," I whispered.

Clotilde's light feet came up the stairs and there was a tap on my door.

"A visitor for you, my lady. She 'as brought a suitcase wiz 'er."

"Did she give you a name?"

"Yes, she is a Miss War-somsing. War-zone?"

"Warburton-Stoke?" I asked.

"I believe so. She spoke razzer quickly. A fashionable young lady."

I didn't wait to hear any more. I was already running down the stairs. I pushed open the door of the morning room and there was Belinda, looking exactly as she always had before. . . .

"Darling!" she exclaimed and rushed toward me, arms open.

"How are you? You look wonderful," I said. "How was the train journey?"

"Bearable, only just. It's so annoying traveling without a maid. The moment I got home I summoned my former maid Florence and it turns out she has found another position. Another position! With someone else! How's that for loyalty?"

I had to smile. "She had no idea how long you'd be away or whether you'd be returning, Belinda. So now what will you do?"

"Go to one of those dreadful agencies, I suppose. Oh, I hate starting from square one again and training a new girl. At least she won't be in a constant state of shock when she finds men creeping out of my bedroom in the morning."

"You've renounced men, have you?" I asked.

She made a wry face. "Absolutely. I'm going to live a life of chastity and keep cats."

"Do you even like cats?" I was laughing now.

She laughed too. "Actually I can't stand them, but it's what spinsters do, isn't it? Who do you have as a maid these days?"

"Right now I'm borrowing Clotilde, Zou Zou's maid," I said. "She is beyond wonderful."

"And the awful cow-faced monstrosity? You've finally let her go?"

"I left Queenie in Ireland, training to be a cook," I said.

"Thank God. She's probably poisoning half of Ireland by now."

"No, actually she's quite good at it. A few accidents, one gathers, but she hasn't set the kitchen on fire yet as far as I know."

"So you won't be bringing her back when you marry?"

"I haven't decided yet. I have to make decisions about so many things. I don't even know where I'll be living."

"Well, speaking of weddings—" She lifted the suitcase onto the sofa and opened it. "Are you dying to see how I'm coming along with your wedding dress?"

"Oh yes. Rather." In spite of everything I was excited.

"Well, darling, here are the preliminary sketches. I thought you'd want plain and simple, no frills or froufrou."

She produced a sketch, handing it to me. The dress was indeed simple—cut almost straight down to the ankles with a train going out from the floor. The arms were bare, cut away at the shoulders, and at the neck was a ruffle of white feathers. Oh crikey! I swallowed hard but managed to look hopeful as I caught her eye.

"It's very—um—modern, Belinda. Don't you think it might be too sophisticated for me to pull off?"

"That's precisely the point," she said. "People tend to think of you still as a young country girl, fresh from the Highlands of Scotland. We want to show the smart set and your royal relatives that you are just as fashionable as any of them."

"It looks awfully tight," I said. "How do I walk?"

"The skirt will have a slit in it, darling. A concealed slit that won't be noticeable until you walk down the aisle. And that lovely long train will slither behind you as if it's alive."

"And the feathers at the throat?"

"Well, it shouldn't be too plain, should it? We'll make it in a heavenly raw silk or something, but it does need a touch of adornment, and feathers are so in this year."

I didn't know what else to say. I could see that it could look stunning, when worn by the right woman. Mrs. Simpson, with her boyish figure, would look good in it. But me? Tall, thin and a little gangly— Georgie who tends to trip over things in a skintight skirt? Asking for disaster.

"Wait till you see it on," Belinda said. "I've run up a sample for you to try, so that you get the effect." She produced a white garment from the suitcase and shook it out. "It's only a cheap satin but it will give you an impression."

"We'd better go up to my room to try it on," I said. "People can see in through the window down here." I headed up the stairs, followed by Belinda carrying the dress. I slipped off my cotton frock and Belinda helped me step into the new creation, easing it up over my hips and then hooking it down my back. I turned to look at myself in the mirror. I looked like a long white tube with feathers about to stick up my nose.

With all the stress of the past day, I could no longer be tactful. "I look as if I've just been swallowed by a boa constrictor!" I blurted out.

"Well, if you want to look frumpy like your dowdy duchess cousin, then anyone can make you layers of fluff and froth," she said in a hurt voice. "Designer gowns are always impossibly chic and startling, but if you're not willing to take the risk . . ." She started unhooking the back and almost yanked it off me.

"Belinda," I said, putting a tentative hand on her arm, "I'm sorry if I hurt your feelings, I really am. And I can see it's a lovely dress, but not on me. I want to feel like a princess, not like a walking drainpipe. And Darcy would take one look and laugh, I know he would."

She gave a sigh. "I suppose it's back to the drawing board, then," she said, her voice still stiff and huffy.

"Don't go to too much trouble, because for all I know there might not even be a wedding," I said, and to my horror I burst into tears.

Then, of course, she was comforting me, leading me to the bed to sit down.

"Georgie, my darling. I didn't mean to upset you. And I'm sorry I was snippy. Only I thought you'd be surprised and thrilled and you weren't."

"I'm sorry too," I said, between sobs. "I wanted to like it, but it's just not me and everything seems to be going wrong right now and I meant what I said that there might not even be a wedding."

Belinda sat beside me and held my hand. "Darcy is getting cold feet?"

"I don't know," I blurted out. "Maybe I'm getting cold feet."

I recounted the incident at Ascot.

"Aren't you jumping to conclusions?" she asked when I had finished. "Darcy is the naturally friendly type. And he enjoys chatting with beautiful women. And he often puts a hand on a shoulder or arm when he's talking to someone."

"But he told me he had to go away on business. If he's now within an hour of London, why hasn't he been to see me? Isn't that the first thing a dutiful fiancé should do?"

A frown crossed Belinda's face. "Well, yes, you do have a point there. But there must be an explanation. I bet he'll show up and when you question him he'll say he'd met an old friend and was asking for her suggestions for honeymoon hotels."

"As long as he intended to take me with him," I said gruffly. "Oh, Belinda." I looked up at her. "I really don't know if I can go through with this. I mean, what sort of life will it be if I worry about him every time he's away? I don't think I'm overreacting if I don't want a husband who might be having fun with another woman, am I?"

"Most of our set would say that you are. I think most society women are prepared to turn a blind eye to unfaithful husbands, and certainly aren't above the occasional roll in the hay themselves. It's an accepted sport of our class."

"Not for me," I said. "I have too much of my great-grandmama's blood flowing through my veins. There was no other man for her than Prince Albert."

"Not true." Belinda gave a wicked grin. "What about all that talk about Mr. Brown and the times they went off together into the heather?"

"Malicious gossip, I'm sure. But anyway, that was long after Albert died. They were both devoted during his lifetime."

"Then you have to sort this out with Darcy before you marry," Belinda said. "You have to tell him how you feel and tell him you can't marry him if he plans to have a roving eye."

"Oh golly." I put a hand up to my mouth. "I can't see myself saying that."

"You have to establish the rules, Georgie; otherwise, you're in for a miserable life."

"You're right." I sighed. "I expect I'm just being silly. Darcy will turn up any moment now and explain everything."

"That's the girl." Belinda stood up, giving me a friendly pat. "Now we have work to do. How long until the wedding?"

"We have sort of agreed on July 27. I have to be in Berlin for Mummy's wedding at the end of this month and it has to be before the king and queen go to Balmoral."

"Good God. Are they coming?"

"The queen said she wouldn't miss it."

"So it's going to be a bloody great shindig, is it?"

"If the queen has her way, it is. Now she's talking about inviting the crowned heads of Europe. Your relatives will expect an invitation, she said."

"Is that what you want?"

"Gosh no! I'd like a little church in the country with just a few close friends if I had my way."

"Then tell them that. It's your wedding. It's not as if the king and queen are paying for it, is it?"

"I suppose not."

"So you can do anything you want. Small church. Close friends. Regret not enough space for crowned heads."

She smiled at me and I returned the smile. "Oh yes, that sounds much better. Can you imagine how nervous I'd be walking up the aisle with crowned heads watching me? But there's another thing, Belinda. The queen hinted that Princess Elizabeth and her sister would love to be bridesmaids."

"Holy merde," Belinda said. "Do you even know them?"

"Oh yes. Quite well. Elizabeth and I had an adventure together once. But can you imagine . . . walking down the aisle with two princesses holding my train?"

"And does that mean I'd have to make bridesmaids' dresses for two princesses?" Belinda asked, looking quite pleased. "An awful lot of extra work, Georgie, but it would put me on the map, wouldn't it?"

"I suppose it would. But no drainpipes for them, please. Dresses that make them look like . . . well, little princesses."

"And who will pay for these dresses? I planned to give you mine as a wedding gift, but if you end up with a whole gaggle of bridesmaids . . ."

"Mummy has promised to fund everything," I said. "And it won't be a whole gaggle. I don't think I know any more little girls. My niece Adelaide is too young and unpredictable."

She sighed, running her hand through her dark, sleek bob. "I'll see what I can do, Georgie, but this does complicate things. I'll have to hurry up and get that workshop in Mayfair if I'm to fit princesses for dresses."

"You'll probably be summoned to their place on Piccadilly, I expect," I said. "Gosh, Belinda, this is all getting so complicated, isn't it?"

"Well, your dress comes first, whatever happens. You want to look like a princess too, I gather."

"Simple but elegant," I said.

"But you don't want frills, do you? You don't want to look like a bloody great meringue."

"No, of course not."

"Come over and we'll go through wedding pictures and you can see if any catch your eye."

"Yes. Let's do that."

I went to the front door with her and waved as she walked down Eaton Square. I was feeling more hopeful now. I'd have a dress that I wanted and I'd sort things out with Darcy and all would be well. As for the crowned heads and princesses, I shut them firmly from my mind.

$\mathcal{C}$hapter 4

Still no Darcy. Why hasn't he come to see me? Oh dear. I was quite
cheerful for a while. Now I'm down in the dumps again.

But I'm so glad Belinda is back. It's good to have someone to talk to,
although that dress was absolutely frightful. I hope I can persuade
her to make one that's not too fashionable. And no feathers. I
know I'd sneeze instead of saying "I do."

If I do have a chance to say "I do," that is.

Darcy didn't put in an appearance all that day or the next. I went over
to Belinda's with strict instructions to Clotilde that she should telephone me if Darcy arrived. Belinda and I sat on her sofa going through
old copies of the *Tatler*, looking at society weddings. The trend was
unfortunately long and slim—lots of women who looked like walking
drainpipes—and lots of feathers. But I did see some evening gowns
that I thought would look good on me, one where the skirt opened up

like a flower toward the floor. Belinda promised to play with some sketches for me. And her sketches for the princesses were charming. No problem there.

She had hired a new maid—Huddlestone. I tried not to laugh when she told me.

"Did you ever hear such a name?" Belinda said.

"You're not going to call her that, surely? What's her first name?"

"She won't tell me. She says proper ladies' maids are always known by their last name."

"Unless they are French," I said. "But she's right. What's she like as a maid?"

"Very proper. Very correct. She's been a maid for a countess who died. So she thinks my little establishment is shockingly lacking. She may not last. We'll probably drive each other crazy."

"When does she start?"

"At the end of the week. I'm already having second thoughts. I should have found a nice willing Italian girl and brought her over with me."

"She wouldn't leave her mama," I said. "My nice Irish girl wouldn't."

"Servants are such a pain these days. Why did our parents have such an easy time?"

I left her cleaning madly before Huddlestone arrived.

As I arrived back at Eaton Place a taxi drew up beside me. A window was wound down and a voice called, "Yoo-hoo! Georgie darling!" It was my mother. The taxi driver rushed around to open the door for her and she stepped out, looking oh so fashionable as always—navy sailor jacket, white broad trousers and a jaunty sailor hat. Only she could have worn the outfit without one expecting it to have come from the second act of a musical comedy accompanying some kind of song about "what fun we're having at the seaside." The taxi driver blushed when she paid him and told him he was a dear.

For once in my life I was pleased to see her. "When did you get into town?" I asked, kissing, as always, two inches from her cheek.

"Yesterday, darling."

"And where are you staying?"

"Claridge's, where else?" She slipped her arm through mine as I steered her up the steps toward the front door. "We tried that new place, the Dorchester, last time and it was sadly lacking. Besides, one does like to go where one is known. They even had my favorite flowers in the suite when I arrived, although it is a trifle over the top. I have a grand piano in my living room, can you imagine the absurdity? I don't even play. Perhaps they know I might entertain dear Noël."

She spoke of her friend Noël Coward. I couldn't help smiling. My mother, who had grown up in a row house in the East End of London, had taken to luxury like a duck to water. I opened the front door and ushered her into the drawing room.

"Is your hostess not at home?" she asked.

"She's in Paris shopping," I said.

"That's where I was. I'm surprised we didn't bump into each other," she said. "So you're all alone here, or are you enjoying being all alone with the gorgeous Darcy?"

"At the moment I'm all alone. He's off somewhere on business."

"I thought I caught a glimpse of him in Paris the other day," she said. "But I was in a taxi and he was going into the Ritz." She gave a delightful shrug. "I may have been mistaken. So many dark and handsome men in France."

I wished she hadn't said that. Immediately my brain put Darcy, the mystery woman and the Ritz in Paris together. I changed the subject hastily.

"Is Max with you?"

"Much too busy, darling. Factories churning away like crazy. And his father has not been too well, so he's being the dutiful son. Besides, this is girl time for us, isn't it? We're going to have such fun buying clothes for our trousseaus."

She gave my arm an excited squeeze.

"But before we discuss where we want to shop, I've something I have to show you," she said. She sank onto the sofa and opened her purse, pulling out a sheet of stiff paper. Without saying a word she handed it to me.

I read:

ALBERT SPINKS

AND

HETTIE HUGGINS

ARE GOING TO BE TYING THE KNOT
AT THE PARISH CHURCH, HORNCHURCH, ESSEX
AND AFTERWARD IN THE BACK GARDEN OF
22 GLANVILLE DRIVE, HORNCHURCH, ESSEX
ON AUGUST 17, 1935

Mummy took a deep breath and looked up, glaring. "I suppose you've already seen this?" she demanded.

"Actually I haven't. I don't suppose that Granddad knew where to send it. Or it might have gone to Rannoch House and Fig burned it. But I knew it was going to happen. They told me."

"What does the old fool think he's doing? I suppose she trapped him. He always was softhearted."

"He's lonely, Mummy. And she cooks well."

Mummy tapped her red-painted fingernails impatiently on the arm of the sofa. "So you approve of this fiasco?" she demanded.

"I can't say that I'm happy with it. I find her an awful, annoying woman who wears curlers in her hair and has a cigarette hanging out of her mouth, but if she makes him happy, then we shouldn't complain, should we?"

"Not complain? I'm to have a Mrs. Hettie Huggins as my mother?"

"Actually it's more like 'ettie 'uggins," I said, not resisting a grin.

"She's awfully common. And she's already told me I can choose whether I want to call her Granny or Nanny. Can you imagine?"

"We must go down to Essex right away and talk him out of it," Mummy said. "I wouldn't be surprised if she's only latching on to him because she knows I've got money and you've got a title."

"That may be true," I said. "She does come across as a little grasping."

"Then we should kidnap him or something. Go to church and leap up when they say 'any cause or just impediment.'"

I laughed. "What cause or just impediment? I don't think curlers in the hair are a just cause."

"We'll say he's gone senile, darling. He doesn't know what he's doing."

"There is no brain that's sharper than your father's," I said. "It's up to him, Mummy. After all, we only flit in and out of his life occasionally. He told me he was fed up with sitting alone with the wireless in the evenings."

"I could always bring him out to Berlin, I suppose," Mummy said thoughtfully. "I'm sure Max could find him a nice little cottage with a garden."

"You know what he thinks of the Germans. He never forgave them for Uncle Jimmy's death in the war."

"That's silly to hate Germans en masse. Most of them were innocent boys obeying orders, just like the British soldiers."

"Was Max one of them?"

"Luckily he didn't have to fight. He was in a protected occupation, running one of his father's factories that just happened to be making guns at the time."

"How convenient for him," I said. I paused, then added, "Mummy, do you worry that Max is awfully pally with the Nazis?"

"He's not pally with them," she snapped. "He just knows on which side his bread is buttered. He's smart enough to play along and they give him big orders for his factories."

"But what if there comes a time when he can't play along anymore?

And what about you? Will you be happy living among them as Mrs. Max von Strohheim? They seem to be becoming more and more extreme from what one reads."

"I stay out of politics," she said. "I too know on which side my bread is buttered." She picked up the wedding invitation again. "But about this ridiculous charade. Should I buy him a cottage in the country, do you think? Get him right away from her?"

"He wouldn't take your money, Mummy. He says it's German money and he's not touching it."

"So obstinate. Do you think we have to go and eat jellied eels and whelks and dance Knees Up Mother Brown?"

I laughed then. "Mummy, you are an utter snob! You grew up in that environment, remember?"

"Yes, and escaped as soon as I could. Oh, my parents were both lovely people, you understand. I'm not running them down."

"I think your father is the nicest person I've ever met," I said. "I was angry that he'd been kept away from me until I was an adult."

"As was I, darling," she said.

"You were?"

"Oh yes. When I left your father, when I couldn't take the depressing horror of Castle Rannoch for another second, I was told quite clearly that I'd given up all rights to my child and should never show my face again."

"Crikey," I said. "I had no idea."

"Oh yes. The family made sure they kept a tight rein on you. Sir Hubert Anstruther wanted to adopt you when I was married to him, you know. But the family wouldn't hear of it."

"Yes, I heard about it."

"He was so fond of you. Such a lovely man. I was quite happy married to him."

"Why did you leave him, then?" I demanded, as I'd also adored being with Sir Hubert.

"Too many mountains, darling. Always off climbing something.

And then the Monte Carlo racing driver came along and . . . well, it was all too tempting. I suppose I just like men too much."

"And what happens when you're married to Max and another racing driver comes along?"

She gave a knowing smile. "I'm older and wiser now. I realize they won't come along so frequently anymore and I should be grateful for what I have."

She stood up again. "I should be going. I've a million things to do. Hair to be colored, toenails, new shoes made . . ."

"Would you not like some tea or a cool drink first? I can ring for Clotilde."

"No time, darling. Come over to Claridge's and have dinner tonight. I thought the new chef was awfully good. And then we can plan our campaign of shopping. And strategize about how to rescue your grandfather." She turned back to me, wagging a finger. "You've been frightfully clever and solved some murder cases, haven't you? You must know how to bump off an old woman!"

"Mummy!" I gave a horrified giggle.

"Just a thought," she said and swept from the room.

Chapter 5

So many complications suddenly: Granddad's wedding, my dress from
hell, Fig wanting me married in Scotland, the queen wanting a big
spectacle of a wedding and a bridegroom who might have been
spotted going into the Ritz in Paris! And I thought everything was
going smoothly!

No more visitors, I thought. Each person who had shown up on my
doorstep had brought more disturbing news into my life. I rather
wished I hadn't promised Mummy I'd have dinner with her at Claridge's that night. That involved getting dressed up in my best evening
gown and taxis. At least Mummy had oodles of money and had promised to take care of my trousseau, so I wouldn't have to worry about
that. But at this moment I just wanted to retire to my room, curl up
and sleep. I glanced at the carriage clock on the mantelpiece. Time for
a nap before I had to change!

I went upstairs and lay on my bed listening to the noises floating in from the square. For the middle of London it was surprisingly peaceful: birdsong from the big trees in the central garden, the rustle of a breeze, the occasional slam of a motorcar door and footsteps on the pavement. I closed my eyes and drifted off.

I must have been in that deep sleep one sometimes experiences in the middle of a warm afternoon, because I was only vaguely aware of a tap on my door and someone entering my room. Clotilde has come to lay out my evening attire, I thought through my haze of slumber. Then somebody kissed my cheek. I sat up, colliding with the person hovering above me.

"Ow!" came a voice. A deep male voice.

I opened my eyes to see Darcy standing there, holding his hand over his nose. "That hurt." But his eyes were smiling as he looked at me. "Here I am, expecting to awake my beloved with a tender kiss and instead she bonks me on the nose."

"I'm sorry," I said. "How was I to know it was you?"

"You mean other men have been creeping in to kiss you lately?" he asked.

I was just coming to full consciousness and realization. The first thought was that I must look terrible, bleary-eyed, hair all out of place, and wearing an unromantic old cotton nightgown. But no sooner had that thought come to me when I remembered what I had seen at Ascot.

"It was nice of you to come to see me, finally," I said while I attempted to smooth down my hair, straighten my nightgown and put aside the thought that I was at a disadvantage sitting up in bed.

"Finally?" He looked puzzled. "My dear girl, I got off the boat train half an hour ago and took a taxi straight to you. I couldn't have come much more swiftly if I'd flown."

"The boat train from Paris?" I asked. I was trying to be cool and sophisticated and not let him see that he had upset me.

"Paris? No, from Dublin. I was with my father."

"Really?"

He stepped back, frowning. "Georgie, what is this about? Have you been hearing gossip?"

"It's not gossip. I saw you with my own eyes, Darcy. And I don't know if I can marry a man who lies to me."

"Lies to you? What are you talking about? I don't think I've ever lied to you." He was glaring at me now.

I was still trying to be brave, looking him straight in the eye. "I saw you, Darcy. I was at Ascot earlier this week and I saw you, not an hour away from here."

His eyes lit up then. "You were at Ascot? I had no idea. Why on earth didn't you come and say hello?"

"Because you were with another woman," I said. "And you were acting awfully chummy with her."

"Oh," he said. "Awfully chummy, eh? Well, you're right, there. I was actually making a proposal of a sexual nature to her, and I am rather happy to say she accepted."

I didn't know what to respond to this. I could feel my cheeks burning with anger and embarrassment. He looked at me, then burst out laughing. "Your face, Georgie. You were giving a really good imitation of your great-grandmother. 'We are not amused!'"

"It's not funny, Darcy. I don't want to marry a man who is unfaithful to me. I don't care what is accepted among our sort. I want to know that I can trust my husband."

He sat down beside me and stroked my hair back from my cheek. "You are sweet, but you leap to the silliest of conclusions sometimes," he said. "I came over to Ascot from Ireland on a mission from my father. He is trying to improve the quality of the stock at his racing stable—Zou Zou's idea, naturally. So he has bought two first-class mares he wants to breed. And the woman you saw me talking to owns a famous stallion who is about to be put to stud. My father wanted me to make sure we would be the first to get the goods, so to speak. So I had to turn on the charm a little."

"Oh," I said.

"And after we'd reached an agreement I got on the train and headed straight back to Dublin."

He paused, looking at me. "So you see, if you'd only come over to me at Ascot, instead of acting huffy and slighted, I could have introduced you to Mrs. Callendar and her famous stallion, King's Ransom, and all would have been well."

I still couldn't think of anything to say. I hated it when he was right.

"I can't have you thinking the worst of me every time you see me with a woman," he said. He stood up and walked across the room, turning away from me and staring out of the window. "You'll just make us both miserable."

"You're right." I got out of bed and came over to him. I put a tentative hand on his shoulder. "I'm sorry. I must be horribly insecure. Sometimes I still can't believe that you chose me."

"Well, it certainly wasn't for your money," he said, turning back to me and ruffling my hair. "I love you, you dope. Can't you ever get that into your head? We are going to be married and live happily ever after."

"Yes, we are." I smiled up at him. "Now could you please go downstairs until I've washed and dressed and look presentable? I feel at a frightful disadvantage here."

"Well, I suppose it was improper of me to creep into your bedroom before we are married," he said with a chuckle. "Is Zou Zou not home?"

"She went to Paris to do some shopping," I said.

"She flew there in her plane, I suppose? Didn't take the Golden Arrow like normal people."

"That's right," I said.

"That woman likes to live on the edge too much," he said. "I hope she doesn't come a cropper one day. And I wish she'd go and visit my father again. He's quite grumpy and clearly missing her, but he won't say anything, the old fool."

"You think he should propose marriage to her?"

"At least tell her how he feels about her."

"He thinks he has nothing to offer her," I pointed out.

"Well, he doesn't, does he? She's rich and has a huge circle of friends and a London house and he has a drafty old castle in Ireland. Hardly a lure for most women."

"Falling in love is not always rational," I said. "We don't always choose the most suitable man."

"I know. You could have been a princess."

"Prince Siegfried, you mean? Don't remind me. Odious man. Do you know he told me that once I produced an heir he'd never bother me again."

"Well, of course I'm going to be the same way," Darcy said.

"Careful, I might hold you to that," I said.

He laughed and caught my wrists. "Not you. I think you are looking forward to a good roll in the hay as much as I am."

He pulled me toward him, his eyes now holding mine. I shook him off. "Not now, Darcy. I must look a wreck."

"You look just fine to me," he said. "But I must admit it's a trifle too tempting to find you in your nightgown with the top buttons undone. . . ." One hand moved toward my neck. I pushed the hand away. He chuckled, gave me a quick peck on the cheek and left me alone.

When I had washed and dressed I came downstairs to find that Darcy was standing at the bar in Zou Zou's drawing room, helping himself to a gin and tonic. Clotilde was hovering in the doorway. "Is zere somsing I can bring for you, my lady?" she asked. She gave me a look that said that she was going to pretend she hadn't seen a man creeping into my bedroom.

"Drink?" Darcy asked as I came over to take one of the armchairs around the fireplace.

"It's a bit early for me," I replied. "Oh, and I have to go up and change soon. I'm afraid I've agreed to have dinner with my mother at Claridge's."

"Oh, so Mummy is in town, is she?"

"Yes. We're going trousseau shopping together."

"Her wedding must be coming up."

"In two weeks," I said. "I hope she buys me something suitable to wear as maid of honor. I imagine it will be horribly fashionable."

"Judging by the way Germany is going these days, you'll either have to wear a dirndl or a military uniform," he said. He looked up, suddenly serious. "It's getting bad, Georgie, and it's going to be worse. Your mother should think very seriously about whether she wants to live there."

"She likes Max and his money," I said. "I'm sure she doesn't think that politics will touch her."

"It will touch everybody," he said. "I don't believe anyone will be safe if they express an opinion that goes against Hitler and his crooked ideology."

"Mummy is a survivor," I said. "She knows how to charm men. She'll have Hitler eating out of her hand."

"Possibly," he said. "He is susceptible to beautiful women, especially blondes."

"Then it's lucky she's made an appointment to have her color touched up," I said wickedly.

"Make sure you stay well clear of Hitler and his cronies when you are there," Darcy said. "You look like their ideal of a true Aryan woman."

"Don't worry. I'm going over for the wedding and then coming straight home again. Besides, I don't speak German so we won't get very far in conversation."

"And speaking of weddings," he said. "What still needs to be done for ours? We've agreed on a time and place, haven't we?"

"Not exactly," I said. "It's getting complicated. Queen Mary seems to want to invite the crowned heads of Europe and hold it at Westminster Cathedral or the Brompton Oratory. And Fig would have a fit if she had to entertain the crowned heads of Europe afterward."

"That's not what you want, is it?"

"No, you know it's not. I want a small wedding with just friends and family. But the queen has indicated she wants to be invited, so that makes it rather more formal whatever we do."

"Good God," he said. "I hadn't counted on a royal wedding, but then I suppose they are your relatives so I should have expected it. This will take some thinking about. I'm surprised they didn't insist on Westminster Abbey with a Catholic priest allowed in at the end to give his blessing."

"They did, actually." I laughed. "I had to point out that it wouldn't be considered a sacrament for you if you weren't married in a Catholic ceremony."

"Well done! You are getting the terminology."

I sighed. "I rather wish we had managed to elope when we tried to."

"Me too," he said. "Then we'd be an old happily married couple by now and you'd be bringing me my slippers and pipe and slaving away in the kitchen to cook my favorite meals. . . ."

I leaned across and slapped him. "It's not too late to call it off, you know!"

He grinned. "But we should be doing something about finding a place to live. I know you don't want to spend the whole year at the castle in Ireland and I don't blame you. My father is hardly the most cheerful of individuals at the best of times and I'll be away quite a bit. We need a pied-à-terre in London so that I can come home and see you when I'm passing through."

"You make yourself sound like a migratory swallow," I said. "I hope you plan to do more than pass through my life occasionally."

"Of course. But I do need to earn money if I'm to support a wife and family, and I seem to be picking up more and more assignments from certain quarters."

He could be so infuriating. He had never actually told me what he did, but from people he associated with and what I had gleaned it was all rather hush-hush. "Darcy," I said. "When we're married will you tell me where you are going and what you are doing?"

"Sometimes," he said and gave me that oh-so-charming grin. "When I can."

"So are you a spy?"

"Whatever gave you that idea?" he asked. "I am a fact gatherer. I find facts for people who want them." The grin faded. "Now, about this flat in London. I'm afraid it won't be Belgravia or Mayfair. Not what you are used to."

"That's all right," I said. "I wouldn't want anything too big or grand for just the two of us. I'm sure there are plenty of charming little places like that one you stayed at in Chelsea once."

"I'll take a look at some advertisements and arrange to go and see some likely properties with you, shall I?"

"That would be good," I said. "I'm really looking forward to a home of my own. It seems as if I've been unwanted baggage in someone else's house for as long as I can remember."

He looked concerned. "Oh, I'm sure Zou Zou doesn't think of you as unwanted baggage. She's quite happy to have you staying here until the wedding, and me too, when I'm in town."

"I know. She's more than kind, but it's not the same, is it?"

"No, it's not," he agreed. "Here's to a home of our own." He raised his glass to me.

Chapter 6

I've been putting off the dreaded moment when I have to meet a priest
to give me instruction about marrying a Catholic. I have to make
sure he understands I don't want to convert—just know what I'm
letting myself in for.

But I'm so glad that Darcy is back in London and we're actually going
to be choosing our new home. How exciting!

At three o'clock I set out, wearing what I hoped was a suitably subdued
outfit—a cotton skirt and white blouse with a small black bow at the
neck—determined to find a priest to set up instruction. The closest
Catholic church was the Brompton Oratory. When I went up the steps
and into that vast and grand interior with its marble pillars and loads
of statues and side altars I decided instantly that I did not want to walk
up this aisle. It felt cold, like a mausoleum. I thought fondly of village
churches I had visited—simple affairs with sunlight streaming in

through tall leaded panes and vases of flowers on the windowsills. That was where I had always dreamed my wedding would be. . . . I sighed.

I looked up as I heard feet coming toward me. The priest was tall and thin, with a hollow face and hooked nose, his black robe flapping out around him as he hurried in my direction. He looked like a vulture descending upon me and I almost fled on the spot.

I was about to speak to him when he called, "Ah, there you are, you naughty girl. So what do you have to say for yourself about missing your catechism class?"

I froze in horror until I realized he wasn't speaking to me. He swept past to a young girl who was looking about as terrified as I was. That was enough for me. I'd wait until Darcy could come with me! I tiptoed out again and fled back to Eaton Square.

As I entered the front hall I nearly tripped over an enormous pile of boxes and was delighted when Zou Zou herself came out of the drawing room. She was looking as glamorous as ever in wide black trousers and a black-and-white-striped jacket. Her dark hair was today in an impeccable chignon, even though she must have recently been flying her little aeroplane.

"Let's take these boxes to the spare bedroom, Clotilde," she called out, then noticed me. "Georgie, my dear one, how are you? I can't wait to show you what I've brought you back from Paris. Come, let us help Clotilde with these." She picked up a ridiculously small box and went up the stairs. I followed carrying as many as I could without dropping them. For all I knew they contained Lalique crystal! Zou Zou placed her box on the dressing table in the bedroom. "Just put those on the bed, darling. They are all clothes," she said. "I've been so naughty, but how can one resist when they make such lovely, lovely things in Paris. You should have seen me trying to take off with my little plane stuffed with all of this!" She laughed merrily.

Clotilde arrived, her arms piled with the remainder of the boxes. "Where shall I put, Your 'ighness?" she asked.

"Oh, just anywhere for now. I want to show Lady Georgiana what

I have bought," Zou Zou said. She started untying the ribbons on one cardboard box after another. "Is this the one? Oh no, that's the new black evening dress." She held it up for me. "I had to buy it because I heard that Mrs. Simpson bought one just like it and it does so enrage her if anyone wears the same dress as her."

I laughed. "Zou Zou, you are naughty."

"I know, but isn't it fun? And somebody should annoy her. She spends enough time annoying everyone else."

She was untying more packages as she spoke. "Oh yes. Look at this, Georgie. I saw it and immediately thought of you." She held up the most gorgeous royal blue silk pajamas with a halter top. I had admired such items so much on other women. I assumed she had bought it for herself until she said, "Go on, try it on. It's about time you stopped looking like an innocent schoolgirl." She frowned as she observed what I was wearing. "Particularly right now. Why on earth do you look as if you are training to be a nun?"

"Because I've just come from church," I said. "I'm supposed to go for instruction before they'll let me marry Darcy." I looked up at her. "But I saw a terrifying priest and lost my nerve."

"Where did you go?"

"The Oratory."

"Well," she said, as if indicating what could I expect if I went there? She patted my cheek. "Don't worry, my sweet. I know a dear little Polish priest who adores me and will do anything for me. I'll arrange for him to come to the house."

"Really? You are an angel," I said.

"Anything for you and my darling Darcy," she said. "How is the dear boy?"

"Well. Out looking for a flat for us at this moment."

"Exciting," she said, "although I shall miss having two lively young people about the house."

"You make it sound as if you are ancient," I said.

"Sometimes I feel ancient," she said, brushing back an imaginery strand of black hair with a dramatic gesture worthy of my mother. "Come on. Don't keep me in suspense any longer. Try it on."

I was still a little hesitant to take off my clothes in front of another woman, especially one like Zou Zou, who probably had Parisian underwear on. I unbuttoned the blouse and stepped out of the skirt and petticoat. I was right. She took one look at my brassiere. "Darling, it's a wonder you've managed to lure any man with underwear like that. Or does Darcy rip it off so quickly that he doesn't notice?"

"I'm in dire financial straits, Zou Zou. I've had no allowance since I came out. Occasionally Mummy treats me to something, but . . ."

"Then you must let me completely kit you out for your future life," she said as she helped me step into the pajamas and hooked up the halter behind my neck.

"Zou Zou, I couldn't possibly let you . . ." I stammered. "I can't even accept this gorgeous creation. It far too sophisticated and haute couture for me."

"Silly girl." She gave my bottom a playful slap. "I love spoiling people. Take a look at yourself."

She spun me around to face the mirror in the wardrobe.

"Golly," I muttered. I looked quite different—svelte and, dare I say it, sexy.

"I knew it would be perfect," she said, beaming at me. "And wait until you see what else." She was rummaging among the other packages. "Ah." She held up the most gorgeous thing I had ever seen. It was a long evening gown, ice blue, and it shimmered. "I decided we really needed to update your evening attire. That burgundy velvet has seen many better days."

She unhooked my pajamas, almost as fast as an impatient lover, and then slipped the ice blue creation over my head. I think I gasped. It draped perfectly, giving me just enough curves, but the overall effect was long and lithe.

"Oh good show," she said, clapping her hands. "I told Elsa that it would be right for you."

"Elsa?" I asked.

"Elsa Schiaparelli."

"Schiaparelli?" I squeaked. "This came from Schiaparelli?"

"Where else, darling?"

I turned to her. "Zou Zou, I don't know what to say. What a lovely, lovely wedding present."

"I'll have to have a special party before the nuptials so that you can dazzle everyone." She took my hand. "After all, we will be almost family."

"Darcy's father hasn't proposed or anything, has he?"

"Of course not. Stupid man," she said. "I may have to drag him to the altar one day."

"Do you really want to marry him?"

"Well, I do adore him," she said. "And I love popping over to Ireland to see him and my racehorses, but I have to confess I like my freedom too. And this house. So it may just drag on as living in sin. But let's leave that for now. This is all about you. And my first task must be to find Father Dominik and bring him here." She walked to the door. "I'll call Clotilde to help you out of that dress and I'm off to hunt him down."

Zou Zou must have been partly magic because within an hour she had returned with a fat and panting little priest whom she had clearly made run all the way to Eaton Square. She had to sit him down with a glass of lemonade before he could even talk. Then he turned to me. "Her Highness, she says you wish to marry a Catholic boy," he said in heavily accented English. "You need the blessing of a priest. Is that right?"

"I'm supposed to have instruction," I said.

"You belong to the Church of England?" he asked.

"Yes, I do."

"You go to church?"

"Sometimes." I couldn't lie to him.

"You are confirmed?"

"I am."

"Well, Church of England." He gave a wonderfully expressive gesture. "That's close enough. Only difference—no pope. So I see no problem. You know about Father, Son and Holy Ghost? And you let your husband teach children to be good Catholics, no?"

"Oh yes," I said.

He spread his hands. "Well, good. That's all we need. I give my blessing." He stood up, giving the sign of the cross over me. "May your marriage be long and fruitful," he said. He turned to Zou Zou and said something in Polish. She laughed and escorted him to the door. When she returned she was still smiling.

"What did he say?" I asked.

"He said he hopes to be repaid with a good dinner at my house!" She came over and put a hand on my shoulder. "You see, my darling, it is all very simple if you know the right people."

"Zou Zou, you are a miracle worker," I said.

She smiled modestly. "I do my little best."

Chapter 7

I feel so much better now that the Catholic instruction business is all
taken care of. Zou Zou is a marvel. And now I'm about to go
and see flats with Darcy. So exciting. I can't wait for a home of
our own.

"Well, I think I might have found something at last," Darcy said. "It
wasn't easy. I had no idea how expensive London is these days. But I've
a list of a few possibilities. Are you ready?"

"Of course I'm ready," I said. "And it doesn't have to be too posh,
you know. I love my grandfather's dear little house and it's on a very
ordinary street."

He took my hand. "Let's go, then. The first one is in Bayswater."

"Oh, that's nice," I said. "Close to Hyde Park. I wonder if we'll be
able to see the park from our windows."

I had been told once that I was a supreme optimist. This proved
to be true. The flat was nowhere near the park. It was almost in Not-

ting Hill. But the tall brick Victorian didn't look too bad from the outside. Darcy rang the bell and a blowsy woman with a hard, foxy face answered it.

"Yes?" she said.

"We've come about the flat."

"Oh right." She looked from Darcy to me. "You two are married, I take it. I don't allow no hanky-panky in my place."

"We will be married when we move in. We're marrying in about six weeks," Darcy said.

"You don't want it for six weeks? I can't hold it for you. Going like hotcakes, property around here."

"If we like it, we'll take it now. We need time to furnish it," Darcy said.

"Right-oh. Come on, then, this way." Instead of letting us in she came out of the front door and then down the steps behind the railings to a level below the street. She opened the front door and the smell hit us. Drains and unwashed bodies. The door opened straight into a living room with dark brown wallpaper. To one side was a kitchen with a small square window looking out onto a brick wall and at the back a bedroom that looked out onto a yard with dustbins. The ensemble was completed by a horror of a bathroom with a stained and rusted bathtub. I swallowed hard. Darcy glanced at me, then said, "I think it's a little dark for us. We need more light."

"Suit yourselves," she said. "Someone's going to snap it up."

We waited until we were safely far away before I said, "Darcy, it was awful, wasn't it?"

"It was pretty grim," he agreed.

"Pretty grim? There wasn't one redeeming feature."

"No, there wasn't." He sighed. "I suppose you pay extra for the neighborhood."

"The neighborhood? Darcy, it was on a mean little backstreet with dog poo on the pavement. And that woman—can you imagine? She'd be snooping in on us all the time."

He put an arm around my shoulders. "Don't worry. There will be something better than this. I just thought we'd start with it because it was closer in. But I've an address to see in Chelsea."

"Chelsea's nice," I said. "Remember that time you were looking after a friend's house there? Such a pretty little place and right on the river."

We headed for Chelsea and found that a closer description might have been Fulham. This one was on the top floor, up four flights of stairs, with a stained ceiling where the roof leaked and mold on the walls. Everything we touched felt damp. And the view was not of the river but of a gasometer.

"Oh golly," I said, taking Darcy's hand. "Is this really all we can afford? I think I'd rather spend my time at the castle in Ireland than a place like this."

Darcy looked as crestfallen as I did. I could tell he was feeling badly about not being able to provide something better for his bride.

"We could stretch our budget a little, I suppose. I did see an advertisement for a place in St. John's Wood that sounded possible."

"Oh yes," I said. "Let's try St. John's Wood."

We took the tube to Swiss Cottage and walked up a pleasant tree-lined street. My spirits began to perk up, especially when we stopped outside a big white block of flats. This was more like it. We were met by a very superior type of young man and he escorted us up in the lift.

"It's a trifle bijou, but I'm sure we will meet your needs," he said. "Our flat dwellers are all most satisfied. We even had a titled lady here once. Lady Lockstone, is the name familiar to you? It was in all the society pages."

Darcy glanced at me and winked. "What happened to Lady Lockstone?" he asked.

"Unfortunately she passed away. She was ninety-three after all."

We disembarked on the tenth floor. "I'm afraid the lift does not go up to the eleventh," he said and led us up a narrow stair. "As I mentioned these apartments are a trifle bijou but for a young couple like yourselves who probably won't have too much furniture . . ." He turned the key. It was essentially a room. Quite a decent-sized room, but it was an attic. The ceiling sloped down on one side so that we would have to be careful not to bang our heads when we got up from the sofa. Over in one corner there was a curtain around a sink and tiny stove. "The kitchen," the superior young man said, pulling back the curtain like a magician revealing a rabbit. "So well designed and compact."

There was a dining area, a sofa and a bathroom so tiny that we could just squeeze between the sink and the bath to reach the loo. And . . . "Where is the bedroom?" I asked.

"Ah." He waved his hand like a magic wand and tugged at a string on a piece of paneled wall. This lowered into a bed. "Such a space-saving device," he added. "Everything you need right at your fingertips."

"You'll be able to reach out of bed and put on the tea and toast," Darcy said with a straight face.

"Will madam be bringing her maid?" he asked. "There are maids' rooms on the floor above this one, for an extra fee, of course. And sir's valet?"

I looked at Darcy. Would I be bringing my maid? I had left Queenie in Ireland and wasn't sure it would be fair to recall her, even if I wanted to. But could I exist entirely without a maid? I had tried at one stage but there were so many times when a maid was not only useful but essential—like when I needed someone to do up buttons down the back of dresses.

"Will you want your maid?" Darcy asked. "As for me, I've learned to survive perfectly well without a valet, but my wife . . ."

"I'm not sure," I said.

"It's of no consequence," the superior young man said. "You can add a maid to the lease at any time. Or a valet for that matter, should sir decide he needs one."

We descended again in the lift. I was feeling close to tears. I wanted to live with Darcy in our own dear little place, but not as little as this. And not damp and moldy and not in a dark basement. I wondered if I could ask Mummy to spring for a year's rent as a wedding gift.

"We'll let you know," Darcy said. We shook hands and departed.

"Do you really think we could survive in a place that small?" I asked Darcy.

"We'd probably murder each other within a few weeks," he said. "Bijou indeed! The fellow had a nerve. No, there's got to be something better out there, Georgie. I don't want us to start married life in a place that would make you miserable."

"Neither do I," I agreed. "But what are we going to do if this is all we can afford?"

"Something will turn up," he said. "I suppose your brother and sister-in-law wouldn't consider letting us pay rent to use the London house when they are in Scotland?"

"Don't even think of it," I said. "Fig wouldn't even let me live there when I had nowhere else to go. And besides, I'd hate that. She'd count the spoons every time she came down to London."

"That's too bad. It sits empty most of the year."

"I imagine a lot of houses do."

"I could ask around my friends—maybe one of them would consider subletting while they are away."

"Darcy, I don't want someone's charity or never knowing when they might want to come home and we'd have to get out."

"I agree it's not ideal." An idea came to him. "Perhaps your royal relatives have a grace-and-favor apartment to spare?" He grinned.

"Not any longer," I said. "I wouldn't even dream of asking. Remember I'm not royal anymore."

We headed back to Eaton Square. By the time we turned the corner I was sunk into gloom. I hadn't expected anything like Rannoch House or Eaton Square, but I had never imagined I'd actually be living in squalor. Eaton Square had never looked more desirable. A garden with flowering shrubs and tall shade trees in the center, sleek black motorcars with chauffeurs standing beside them. I swallowed back a tear, determined to put on a brave face for Zou Zou.

"Better luck tomorrow, maybe?" Darcy said. Then he saw my face. "Cheer up, old thing. It's not the end of the world."

"But they were all awful, Darcy." My voice quavered. "I don't expect to be living in a place like this. But at least I thought clean and bright and . . . happy." Then, to my embarrassment, a tear trickled down my cheek.

Darcy smiled and wiped the tear away. "Don't worry. Something will show up. I promise. It's not as if we'll be on the streets. We do have a castle in Ireland, remember. That's a lot better than most people who have to live in grimy backstreets all their lives."

"I know," I said. "I'm being silly. It's just . . ."

"Weddings are emotional events, I understand." He took me into his arms, right there in Eaton Square. "You and I are going to have a wonderful life together, even if it means living in a shoe box, all right?"

"All right," I said, sniffing back another tear that threatened.

He kissed the tip of my nose. "You're adorable when you cry."

"No, I'm not. My face goes blotchy," I said.

"I think you're adorable." Then he kissed me properly.

"Darcy, not here! What will people think?" I exclaimed, breaking away with some difficulty.

"They'll think what a charming young couple in love," he said. "See that nursemaid over there? She's smiling. Come on. Let's go and tell Zou Zou about our horrors and make her laugh!"

He took my hand and dragged me forward at a rapid pace.

As we entered Zou Zou called out from the drawing room, "Is that you, my darlings? Tea is just about to be served. Come in and tell me all about it. Oh, and there's a letter for you, Georgie."

I picked up the envelope from the salver on the hall table. It bore a lot of foreign stamps. Not Italian. Not German. I opened it, curious now. I didn't recognize the handwriting and turned over the page to see the signature.

Your affectionate godfather, Hubert Anstruther.

"It's from Sir Hubert," I called out to Darcy. "He must have heard about our wedding and is wishing me well."

It was headed from a place I had never heard of in Chile. I started to read.

My dear Georgiana,

I understand that congratulations are in order. I have just seen the announcement of your engagement in a copy of the Times *that someone brought out from London. Well done. I remember O'Mara's father when we were at Oxford together. He rowed well. I am currently in Chile, where we have been attempting a couple of unclimbed peaks, so it looks almost impossible that I shall be able to make it back to Britain in time for your wedding.*

However, I do want to offer you an early wedding present.

My spirits started to rise; Sir Hubert was known to be generous.

As you know you are now my sole heir and one day will inherit Eynsleigh. I remember how happy you were as a little girl when you lived there and wondered if you'd like to recall those happy days. It pains me that the house is left unoccupied for much of the time. It should be lived in and enjoyed by a family, which I hope you will soon have. I want to picture small children running naked through the fountain like you used to do!

I'm not sure if you have a place in mind to live or plan to settle over in Ireland, but I'd like to propose that you move into Eynsleigh right away and have time to arrange the place to your liking before your wedding day. Naturally I shall be home from time to time, more frequently as I get older, I suspect, but I'd like you to feel the place is yours. I'll merely keep a suite of rooms in one wing: a bedroom, sitting room and study will be ample.

It may be that you are planning a place in town but I have to point out there is a first-class train service from Haywards Heath station on the Brighton Line. You can be in town in half an hour. And of course the Bentley is at your disposal. So what do you say? I'll notify the servants of your arrival and do so much hope that I'll find you well ensconced there by the time I manage to return home.

"Golly," I said. I was tempted to say "bloody hell" but a lady never swears within the hearing of others.

"What is it?" Darcy asked. "You've gone quite pink."

I held out the letter to him. "It's Sir Hubert Anstruther. I'm his heir and he wants us to move into his house in Sussex right away. He says he's hardly ever there and it should have a family in it."

"Well, I call that splendid," Zou Zou said. "All your problems solved."

"Just a minute, Georgie," Darcy said, looking up from the letter and frowning. "How does he think we can afford to run a big place like that?"

"Oh crikey." The bubble was pricked suddenly.

Then he laughed and said, "It's all right. There's a postscript. Listen: *There should be sufficient funds coming into the household account every month to enable you to run the place to your liking.*"

Darcy opened his arms and hugged me, swinging me around like a small child.

"You're going to be mistress of Eynsleigh!" he crowed.

"It sounds frightfully Jane Austen," Zou Zou said, "but I couldn't be more happy for you."

"Neither could I," I said. "It's a lovely place. I was very happy when I was there. I can't wait to show it to you, Darcy. Sir Hubert has the nicest old butler and housekeeper, and a cook who used to let me lick the spoons when she was making a cake."

Darcy observed my face, now flushed with excitement. "We'll go down as soon as we've sorted out final details here."

"I'll miss you, my children," Zou Zou said. "And of course you are welcome to stay here at any time. But I really should be getting back to Ireland. I miss my racehorses too."

Darcy raised an eyebrow and I grinned.

As I was folding up the letter again I noticed the second postscript:

Frankly I should be happy to know that you are keeping an eye on the place. I get the feeling that all might not be as it should be at Eynsleigh.

Chapter 8

Final days at Eaton Square
June 22 and 23

I am so excited. Mistress of my own house! Imagine that. And close
enough to London that I can pop up on the train and see my
grandfather—strike that—my grandfather can come and see me. I
don't think I can stomach Mrs. Huggins ruling the roost at
Granddad's house. And wanting me to call her Granny or Nanny!
Golly.

Now that I was moving to the country, there were so many things to
do before I went. I made a list: See Belinda about wedding dress. See
Mummy about shopping. See Fig about reception. Visit church and
finalize wedding. On Sunday morning I went to mass with Darcy at
the church on Farm Street in Mayfair. I had expected it to be gloomy,
as other Catholic churches seemed to be, but this one was gorgeous.
Larger than I had expected and with a beautiful high altar and deco-
ration. Afterward we met a priest who invited us into the rectory for

coffee. He was charming and witty and didn't seem at all overawed that Their Majesties planned to attend the ceremony.

"If I preach a good sermon we might even convert them," he said with a wicked smile.

I came away happy that we had a place and a date. We went into Hyde Park, sat on a bench in leafy shade and mapped out a guest list. Mine was rather small, apart from the entire royal family and the crowned heads of Europe. I knew Darcy had a large group of friends, many of whom seemed to be female. We trimmed it down to fifty (not counting the crowned heads of Europe or the royal family).

"We don't really want sundry royals, do we?" Darcy asked.

"I don't. The queen thinks I should invite them. I have to invite the great-aunts—you know, Queen Victoria's last surviving daughters who live at Kensington Palace. They were jolly nice to me. And the immediate family. I suppose I should invite Nicholas of Bulgaria and his wife. We were involved in their wedding, weren't we?"

"Oh yes. I like good old Nicholas. And his brother too."

"I remember that Belinda liked his brother a little too much. I don't want to start anything there again. . . ."

"All right. No brother. And I take it you don't want Siegfried of Romania?" He laughed at my face.

"Absolutely bloody not," I said firmly.

"Then invite Nicholas and Maria and the Windsors. That's enough royalty for anyone's wedding."

"I don't know about my cousin David," I said thoughtfully. "I do like him and I see quite a lot of him, one way or another, but he'll bring *her* and that will make the king and queen furious."

"Then limit it to just the king and queen," he said.

"But the princesses want to be bridesmaids. So I'll have to invite the Yorks. And I was a bridesmaid at the Kents' wedding so I'll have to invite them. Then David will feel odd being left out." I looked up at Darcy. "Golly, this is getting so complicated, isn't it? I do wish we'd managed to elope."

Darcy took my face in his hands. "Invite who you want, my darling. It's your day. I want you to enjoy it."

Then he kissed me, right there in Hyde Park with nannies pushing prams past us and children running ahead. What's more, I didn't stop him this time. It felt wonderful. This is all that matters, I thought. Darcy and me.

※

ON MONDAY MORNING Darcy had business to attend to while I went to Belinda.

She was most put out when she found I was leaving London. "What about fittings?" she asked. "And you haven't even approved a final sketch, and we need to choose fabrics together."

"I can come up to town, Belinda. It's not as if I'm going to darkest Africa. And you could come down to stay and we could have fittings and tea on the lawn and play tennis and generally have fun."

"That does sound enticing." She smiled. "I'm so glad things are working out for you, Georgie. Working out for both of us, actually. Come and see the mock-up for the dresses I've designed for the princesses."

They were so charming, so perfect. Just right for two royal little girls, with simple lines and puffed sleeves. "Oh yes," I said. "They'll love them. I'll ask how you should go about fittings. I bet you'll have every mother in London wanting their daughters to wear your dresses after this."

"That would be lovely," she said, "but with my grandmother's money I won't have to worry anyway. I'm going to keep this little mews cottage because I like it, but I'm renting a workshop next to Bond Street and I'm getting together an autumn collection. You wouldn't like to be one of my models, would you?"

"Golly no," I said. "I remember my one modeling experience with you. Total disaster. I'm not about to repeat that."

Belinda laughed. "I'd forgotten about that. And it was with Mrs. Simpson, wasn't it?"

We went over her sketches of my dress and we agreed on details. So much better than the original drainpipe / boa constrictor design, I thought but did not say out loud. It was going to be beautiful. I was going to be beautiful. I sailed out with a silly grin on my face and went to track down Mummy. The day had really heated up now and I dabbed at beads of sweat on my forehead. Sweating is something a lady never does! Mummy was tucking into a large portion of Dover sole in the dining room at Claridge's. She invited me to join her and I ordered the same. She also pouted when she heard I was leaving London. "I thought we were going to have lots of time to do girly things together. I am still looking for the perfect going-away outfit after the ceremony and I can't find it anywhere. Nothing in Paris. Nothing here. I may actually have to buy it in a shop, like a housewife."

"Mummy, I love the way you forget that there was a time when you couldn't even afford to shop in places like Harrods or Barkers. Now they are beneath you."

"One doesn't want to look like everyone else," she said, patting her immaculate curls. "If I had the same clothes as a bank manager's wife I'd shoot myself."

I had a sudden brain wave. "Belinda might design something for you. She's starting her own design business again. She's frightfully avant-garde."

"Now, that's a thought," she said. "You must take me to see her. But when are you and I going to have time to shop?"

"I'm free today," I said.

"Oh, not today, darling. I have to go for a massage and after it one is so tired. Such a big, strong young man and he works over all my muscles as if he's kneading bread." She shuddered with pleasure.

"Then tomorrow? I want to go down to Eynsleigh as soon as possible because I want Darcy to see it."

"Tomorrow? Darling, tomorrow is busy-busy. I have to see my

little shoemaker in the Mile End Road. He's an Italian refugee and he makes the most divine shoes for me. Soft as gloves. And then afterward we'll go to the little Chinese lady who makes my undies. One can never have too many pairs of knickers, I think. I certainly can't. Max loves to rip them off me in moments of passion." She looked up at me. "I expect Darcy does the same."

"Er . . . not exactly," I said.

"Max is so passionate." She gave a cat-with-the-cream smile. "Anyway, Madame Chow fled from Shanghai bringing this most amazingly fine silk. Of course I bought up the lot from her and when I need more undies she makes them for me. You shall have some too. So fine it's like wearing gossamer."

And so it seemed that people like Mummy did not just go to a department store and come out with ready-made items. I left Mummy and had to face my last tasks of the day: Fig and Granddad. When I thought of the latter I wasn't sure I could face it. It was now baking hot in the city and the thought of a crowded tube train out to Essex with all those unwashed bodies and Mrs. Huggins at the end of it was almost beyond my endurance.

I was tempted to write a note with my new address on it and invite him to come and stay as soon as I was settled. I wouldn't mention anything about Mrs. Huggins coming to stay. And last but not least there was Fig. I had to see her to discuss wedding breakfast details. Darcy wanted to come too but I told him I'd spare him Fig in full fury.

I decided to get her over with first. So with trepidation I knocked on the front door of Rannoch House. It was opened by Hamilton, our aged butler. He beamed when he saw me. "Why, Lady Georgiana, what a treat. We were just discussing you belowstairs and wondered how your wedding was coming along."

"Splendidly, thank you, Hamilton. Is Her Grace at home?"

"They both are, my lady. His Grace is still recuperating from his surgery, in the drawing room." He led me through although I knew the way. "Lady Georgiana," he said and stood back to let me enter.

Binky was sitting on the sofa with his foot encased in a large bandage. Fig was perched on the edge of an uncomfortable chair, reading the *Tatler*. She looked up. "Oh, it's you, Georgie. I was telling Binky about your wedding plans."

Binky's eyes lit up. "Why, it's Georgie! How jolly splendid to see you, old thing."

I went over and kissed his forehead. "Hello, Binky. How's the invalid?"

"All the better for seeing you," he replied. "As you can see, a bit under the weather."

"That's a large bandage," I said. "Did they remove a couple of toes?"

"No, just a bit of toenail from my flesh, but dashed painful," he said. "Do take a seat, old bean. How about a drink? Gin and tonic?"

"I'd prefer a cup of tea, please," I said. "I've been rushing around, trying to schedule fittings and shopping with my mother. All quite exhausting and it's beastly hot out."

"I know. Quite unpleasant. One remembers why one doesn't stay in London during the summer months," Fig said. "I keep telling Binky to jolly well hurry up and heal so we can go home. Or at least to my sister's place in Cheshire."

"The quack said I should stay put," Binky said. "Too much risk of infection, you know." He looked across at Fig. "Well, order tea for Georgie, then, Fig. You have the bell near you."

I was impressed. Was he finally learning to stand up to his wife? If so, that would be a miracle. Fig shot him a look as she leaned across to pull on the bell. I hoped he wouldn't pay for his bravery later. Soon a tea tray appeared, complete with slices of Mrs. McPherson's delicious cake. "Cook said to make sure you got some of your favorite cake, my lady," Hamilton said, putting down the tray.

"I must apologize for having the butler bring in the tea tray," Fig said as Hamilton retreated, "but we only brought a skeleton staff with us. Which reminds me—your wedding. Have you finalized the place and date yet? If the reception is to be held here we'll need a full complement down from Scotland."

"Yes, this morning," I said. "July 27. Two o'clock. At the Church of the Immaculate Conception, Farm Street."

"Are you going to put that on the invitation?" Fig asked, wincing as if in pain.

"Why, yes. Why not?"

"It sounds so horribly strange and Roman," she said. "Couldn't you have chosen a St. Mary's or a St. Michael's?"

"Not within easy distance of Rannoch House."

"I expect there will be incense and things," Binky said, looking worried. "And if I give you away, will I have to chant in Latin?"

I laughed. "It will be a normal wedding ceremony. You'll recognize the words."

"Phew, that's a relief," he said. "I've been worrying about it. I failed Latin at school, you know."

"You failed most things," Fig said.

"Well, yes, that's true. I wasn't the best student, but then I hated school and was horribly bullied there. We are certainly not sending Podge to a school like that."

"We probably won't be able to afford it anyway," Fig said.

"Are the children here with you?" I asked, being exceptionally fond of my niece and nephew.

"Good God, no," Fig said, rather too emphatically. Then she added, "Nanny thinks it's not wise to interrupt their routine, particularly as Adelaide is proving very stubborn in potty training. I mean, she's over a year old and still has accidents. I believe it's deliberate. I hope that child isn't going to be a handful."

"You will be able to bring them when you come down for my wedding, won't you?" I said. "I do want Podge to be a page boy."

"He'd love that," Binky said. "Dashed fond of you, old bean. Well, we all are. And we've missed you, haven't we, Fig?"

"What?" She reacted with a start.

"I was saying we haven't seen enough of Georgie lately and we've missed having her around."

"Well, she does have her own life to lead, Binky," Fig replied without answering the question.

"Will you at least come up to Scotland for a while before your wedding? Last-chance-to-be-at-home sort of thing," he said.

"That's kind of you, Binky," I replied, "but I'm afraid I'm going to be busy settling in to my new home."

"You are moving in before marriage?" Fig looked shocked. "Not with that O'Mara person, I hope. Word would get out."

"No, Darcy will stay on in London until the wedding."

"So where is this place?" she asked. "Will you not live in the family seat in Ireland?"

"Part of the year, I expect, but Sir Hubert Anstruther wants me to live at his house in Sussex."

"Sir Hubert?" Fig looked puzzled. "Wasn't he one of your mother's men?"

"She was married to him, Fig. And he was very fond of me. He wanted to adopt me. So I received a letter from him inviting me to start married life at Eynsleigh. He's hardly ever there and he wants me to enjoy it."

"Without paying rent?" Fig said.

"Well, I am his heir," I said. "I'd inherit it one day, and as he says, it is a pity to have a fully staffed house and nobody in it."

"A big house, is it?" Binky asked. "I don't recall ever visiting it."

"It's lovely, Binky," I said. "Tudor. Glorious grounds. A fountain in the forecourt. You must come and stay when we're married."

"How kind. Look forward to it, eh, Fig?"

Fig's eyes were blinking rapidly, something she did when she wanted to shut out painful information. I'm ashamed to say that I wanted to get up and do a little dance.

Chapter 9

Off to become mistress of Eynsleigh. I still can't believe it! Of course I'm a trifle apprehensive. I mean, running a large house with a flock of servants . . . Golly. But Rogers, the butler, and the housekeeper will make sure everything goes smoothly for me, I'm sure. And Darcy looks like the sort of person who expects to be obeyed.

Two hectic days followed. Buying clothes with Mummy. Planning menus with the cook at Rannoch House and wondering if she could make a presentable-looking wedding cake. Zou Zou announced that she was going away again, flying over to Ireland to see her horses run, she said. I wondered if she was really flying over to be with Darcy's father. I hoped she was.

I was almost ready to depart myself, but there was one thing left to do. I took a deep breath and caught the District Line to Upminster Bridge to see my grandfather. I thought he was looking rather tired and frail, but Mrs. Huggins was very much in evidence, strutting around the place.

"So you've got a date for your wedding now, have you, ducks?" she asked. She had given up calling me "your ladyship" now we were going to be related.

"Yes, we have. We just mailed out the invitations today. You should be getting one."

"We couldn't send you an invite to ours because we didn't know where you was staying," she said. "Go and get her one now, Albert. They are on the dining table in the front room."

My grandfather got up and left.

"He's looking a bit seedy, ain't he?" she whispered. "That week's honeymoon down at Clacton will do him the world of good. Nice sea air. And I'm going to build him up too. He's nothing but a bag of bones—" She broke off as Granddad came back and handed me the invitation.

"I hope you can come, my love," he said.

"I wouldn't miss it for the world," I replied and got a big smile from him.

"Now, about your wedding," Mrs. Huggins said. "I was thinking about young Jewel. You know, my son Stan's girl. She's eleven now. Just the right age to be a bridesmaid. You are going to have bridesmaids, I take it. I told her she can be a bridesmaid at ours, along with Queenie, but I know she'd be tickled pink to be one at a posh wedding like yours."

I tried not to look too horrified. My bridesmaids: two princesses and young Jewel, whom I remembered from photographs was a podgy child, like a small version of Queenie. How on earth could I say no tactfully? I left promising to let them know our plans and whether Mrs. Huggins should make her a dress. She'd seen a length of pink satin down the market that would do a treat. Make a smashing dress. And maybe a little crown, seeing as I was almost royal. I gave a wan smile, not finding the words to answer her. Oh golly.

On Wednesday morning I took the train to Sussex. My heart was beating so loudly I was sure other people in the compartment could hear it as we pulled out of Victoria Station. The only disappointment was that Darcy was not with me. The evening before he had received a telephone call and came to me with a worried frown on his face. "Something's come up and I've been called away," he said. "I'm so sorry but I won't be able to come with you tomorrow, in fact I'm not at all sure when I'll be back. . . ."

"Before the wedding, I hope," I said, hiding my anger in a joke.

"Definitely well before the wedding. I've made that clear," he said.

"What is it? Another lady with a racehorse?" I was still fighting back anger.

"No, rather more serious, I'm afraid. I can't tell you more, but it's not good."

Then, of course, I was worried. "Do be careful," I said. "And write if you can. Just a postcard saying 'I'm all right.' That's all I need."

He took me in his arms. "This is beastly for you, I know," he said. "But if I don't accept assignments when they come my way . . . well."

"I know." I sighed and looked up at him. "I do worry when you are away."

"I can take care of myself, I promise," he said. "And you take care of yourself. Have a lovely time arranging things to your liking in our new home so that it's just perfect by the time I come back!"

"I will."

He kissed me then, a kiss that was full of longing and frustration. And in the morning he left early, catching a boat train to heaven knows where while my train chugged more modestly out of London. We were soon in leafy Surrey and my spirits perked up as they always do in the countryside. Mistress of Eynsleigh, mistress of Eynsleigh, I chanted to myself to the *clickety-clack* of the rails.

I alighted at Haywards Heath Station, about five miles from Eynsleigh. I was bringing just a small suitcase with me. Zou Zou's maid was going to have my big trunks sent on in a few days. At the station

I found an ancient taxicab. "Eynsleigh?" he said. "There isn't nobody living there at the moment. Sir Hubert's away on one of his jaunts."

"Well, I'm going to be living there," I said. "I'm Sir Hubert's heir and it's going to be my home."

"Well, I never," he said. "God bless you, miss."

I was going to say it wasn't "miss," it was "my lady," but decided against it.

Word would get around soon enough, I was sure. We drove along lanes shaded with spreading oak and horse chestnut trees. Cows looked up as we passed by lush green fields. We drove through small villages with whitewashed cottages. Fifteen minutes later we turned in between tall stone gateposts, each topped with a statue of a lion resting a paw on a marble ball, and there ahead of us was the house at the end of a long straight drive, shaded by sycamore trees. Its red Tudor brick almost glowed in the sunlight. It was built in the shape of an E, with two wings and a central forecourt, with a fountain in the center. I peered out of the taxi window, trying to catch a glimpse of the fountain I had loved so much, but I couldn't see it.

The tires scrunched on the gravel as we turned into the forecourt. I saw then that the stone fountain base was still there, only it wasn't playing at the moment. Of course, I thought. How silly of me. There was no need for a fountain when the owner of the house wasn't at home. I'd soon have it turned on and working again. I paid the taxicab driver, took a deep breath and picked up my suitcase to ascend the broad flight of steps to the front door. As I picked up the suitcase I realized that I would not be making the best impression, carrying my own bag and not bringing my maid with me.

Still, it didn't matter. I had nobody to impress.

I rang the bell and waited for a long time. I was about to go around to the back of the house and the servants' entrance to see what was the matter when the door opened. A head peered around it. He was a man probably in his forties with a rather podgy face and dark hair, parted in the middle. He looked me up and down.

"Well, you've got a nerve," he said in a voice betraying a slight Cockney accent. "Coming to the front door and ringing the bell, indeed. You should know better than that."

"I beg your pardon?" I demanded. "Who exactly are you?"

"Plunkett," he said.

He said it very quickly and for a second I thought he'd said something very rude. "What?"

"I'm Plunkett," he said. "And I presume you've come about the maid's position."

In times of extreme annoyance I tend to channel my great-grandmother Queen Victoria. "I most certainly am not the new maid," I said. "I am Lady Georgiana Rannoch and I assume that you are expecting me."

"Expecting you?" He was still standing at the door, essentially barring me from entering. "We weren't expecting anyone. The owner is away at the moment."

"I am quite aware of that," I said. "Now, if you'd move to one side so that I may enter."

"But the house isn't ready for guests," he said, grudgingly stepping aside as I moved into the foyer. "We weren't told—"

"You've not heard from Sir Hubert?" I asked. "Concerning my arrival?"

"No, miss."

I did correct this one. "I am not 'miss'; I am 'my lady' or 'your ladyship,' which I'm sure you should know." I turned to face him. I was quite pleased to notice that we were about the same height. "Now, to get this straight right away. I am Lady Georgiana. I am Sir Hubert's heir and he has invited me to come and live here while I prepare for my upcoming wedding, and then to make this my permanent home with my husband."

Plunkett looked quite ill. "You're coming here to live?" he asked. "When?"

"Right now. My trunks will arrive in a few days. In the meantime you can show me around the house so that I can arrange things to my liking."

I saw his face twitch. "Nothing is set up, my lady," he said. "We've only kept on a skeleton staff while Sir Hubert is away."

"I presume you are a footman here," I said. "Now, if you will just notify Mr. Rogers that I have arrived I'm sure he'll take care of everything splendidly."

"Mr. Rogers isn't the butler here anymore," he said. "He retired and I was hired in his place."

"You're the butler now?"

"That's right." He now looked almost smug. The smirk said, What are you going to do about it?

"And Mrs. Holbrook, wasn't it? Is she no longer housekeeper?"

"She retired too," he said. "We don't keep a housekeeper anymore. Sir Hubert is never here."

I sighed. "Then I see I'll have some hiring to do. You will let the entire staff know that I will meet with them after I've had a tour of the house. Oh, and I'd like you to find a local maid for me. Maybe there is a suitable girl in the village who can be trained. My maid has been left in Ireland for the moment at my future husband's family seat."

"Why were we not informed of any of this?" he said, reverting to his former belligerence.

I realized that Sir Hubert might not have informed the staff, waiting to hear whether I accepted his offer. But I didn't want Plunkett to know that. "One must presume that Sir Hubert's letter got lost on the way from South America," I said. "But as to that, it is not always necessary to inform servants." I was managing to keep up my Queen Victoria imitation and feeling quite proud of myself, although I could feel my knees shaking under my dress.

"It's just that—how am I to know that you are really who you say you are and that it is really Sir Hubert's wish that you stay here?"

"You are questioning my veracity?"

"Just being ultracautious on behalf of my employer," he said. "I wouldn't want to do nothing he wouldn't approve of."

I was going to correct his grammar, then decided against it. "Very well," I said. "It goes against my better judgment, but I will show you the letter from your employer. But I have to warn you that if your attitude doesn't improve you may be looking for another position soon."

I opened my handbag and held out the letter. He read it, his face twitching again. "I'm sorry, my lady," he said, handing it back to me, "but you have to understand that you could be just anybody coming here, knowing that the owner was gone, and then living at this house for free."

"I don't think that happens very often, does it?" I said. "Now, shall we take our tour of the house?"

"Should I perhaps first inform the other servants that you want to meet them when we're done?"

"Yes, good idea," I said. "And you should also let Cook know that I will want luncheon at one o'clock. I will understand today that it might be a simple affair because you did not know I was coming."

"Yes, my lady. I'll tell him," he muttered.

I stood in the front hallway, looking around me, while he went through the baize door into the servants' quarters. I thought I heard raised voices and scurrying. I suspected that things had become rather lax under Plunkett's leadership and there would be some rapid cleaning and tidying. I crossed the foyer and opened the door on my right. Everything was shrouded under dust sheets. The heavy velvet curtains were drawn and it felt musty and gloomy and damp. I shivered. I was trying to remember if I had ever been in here and what it had looked like. The chandelier was bundled up and hung like a great wasps' nest above my head. A shroud covered something that might be either a statue or a tall lamp. It was rather unnerving, like a ghost standing beside me. I felt I had to know what was beneath that shroud. I gave a small tug and to my horror it fell off, revealing a suit of armor. I was enveloped in a great cloud of dust and retreated coughing.

"Oh, my lady," said a relieved voice behind me. "I wondered where you'd got to."

I was conscious that I was now covered in dust. My dark blue jacket was liberally speckled and I could feel dust sitting on my face and hair. I fought back the desire to sneeze. I wasn't going to let him see I was at a disadvantage. "A suit of armor in need of a good cleaning," I said in my most sprightly voice as I brushed off my shoulders and blew dust off my nose. "Just trying to remember the lay of the land. I don't think I ever came into this room much when I lived here before."

"You lived in this house?" He sounded surprised.

"Yes, when I was a small girl. My mother was married to Sir Hubert in those days and I spent three happy years here. I remember it as very grand."

"I expect it would seem that way to a little girl after what you were used to," he said. "Where did you live before?"

"Castle Rannoch, in Scotland," I said. "My father was Duke of Rannoch. My grandmother was Queen Victoria's daughter."

He swallowed hard. I watched his Adam's apple go up and down and tried not to grin at scoring this small point of victory.

"And I returned to the family seat when my mother and Sir Hubert separated." I didn't actually say that my mother did another of her famous bolts. The Monte Carlo racing driver, I believe she had said. "Now, shall we begin the tour? Lead on." I was feeling so proud of myself, acting like the mistress of Eynsleigh already.

"Very well," he said. He escorted me out of the drawing room, through a long gallery with a great fireplace at its center; its walls were hung with paintings but each was shrouded, making it feel quite eerie. On the other side was a large dining room.

"I will need this cleaned and made ready as soon as possible," I said. "Although I will understand if my luncheon today is served on a tray in one of the rooms that is vaguely habitable."

From the dining room we moved on to a music room with a grand piano—at least I presumed it was a grand piano—under its own dust sheet. The room was at the back of the house and had a splendid view over the grounds. My spirits bucked up again. When it was all spruced up it would be wonderful to live here. Next to the music room was a room with a large bay window.

"Oh yes," I said. "Now, I do remember this."

"The morning room, I believe," Plunkett said. "Perhaps you will take your luncheon in here."

"Good idea." At least we agreed on something.

We then walked through a library and another sitting room and came to a grand staircase. Plunkett was about to go up when I said, "What about that side of the house? We haven't seen it yet."

"I was given to understand that the west wing was to be kept for Sir Hubert's personal use," he said.

"Oh, quite right," I answered. "He told me in his letter that he'd like to keep a suite of rooms for his own use."

He had actually said only a bedroom, sitting room and study, but I wasn't going to press the point at this moment. I'd have plenty of time to explore later. So I followed Plunkett up the stairs. There were several rooms that seemed quite devoid of furniture, some rooms absolutely piled with mounds of what had to be assorted furniture under dust sheets, then a couple of bedrooms with enormous four-poster beds and giant wardrobes that I found impossibly depressing, and at last a corner bedroom at the back of the house with windows on two sides and an adjoining bathroom. I recognized this too. My mother's old room. I had climbed onto that window seat and watched the deer in the park beyond the lawns.

"I think this will do quite nicely as my bedroom for now," I said. "Have one of the maids make up this room before tonight. Oh, and please make sure the hot water is working in the bathroom."

"We'll do our best, my lady," he said. "You have to understand that Sir Hubert has been gone for several years."

"And the staff has become slack," I added. "I understand. But when I visited the house last time, when Rogers was still butler, Sir Hubert was away but the house was in immaculate condition. I think Sir Hubert would like to think he could return home at any time and find his house as he left it, don't you?"

"Yes, my lady," he muttered grudgingly.

Clearly there was a lot of work to be done. No wonder Sir Hubert had sensed that not all was right with Eynsleigh.

Chapter 10

Well, I have arrived as mistress of Eynsleigh but not exactly what I had
expected. Sir Hubert was right to be worried that his house was
not running as smoothly as he would have liked. So far I'm rather
proud of myself, the way I have managed to act like the lady of the
manor. But gosh, I'm not sure how long I can keep this up!

After I had concluded my tour of the house, or at least those parts
of the house that Plunkett had deigned to show me, I retreated to
the bedroom I had chosen and hastily brushed the layer of dust
from my jacket and washed my face before going downstairs to face
my staff. I knew the protocol when a person of importance arrived at
a great house. The staff were lined up outside in order of seniority. I
think I had half expected this, although to be fair, they did not know
I would be arriving. But I was now escorted by Plunkett into the dining room to meet my motley crew. I expected that staff numbers would
be reduced while the owner was away, but I was shocked to see only

four individuals standing in front of me, shuffling nervously as I came in.

"This is the staff, my lady," Plunkett said.

"All of them?" I asked.

"Well, there are two gardeners, but I didn't have time to call them in," he said. He went over to the first man in line, a broad-shouldered chap with flaming red hair. "This is McShea, the footman."

McShea gave a little bob of a bow and avoided eye contact.

"How do you do, McShea?" I said.

"Not so bad, thank you," he said in broad Irish tones.

"Oh, so you are from Ireland," I said. "What part?"

"Near Cork, your ladyship."

"My future husband's family comes from near Kildare," I said. "Lord Kilhenny. You have heard of him?"

"Horses, my lady. Racehorses."

"Quite right." I smiled and got the ghost of a smile in return. I thought I might have an ally there, now he knew I was marrying an Irishman.

"And this is Joanie, the housemaid." She had a sharp little face and the look she gave me was challenging, to say the least. Clearly she didn't welcome my presence, as I suspected she knew it meant lots of work for her.

"Only one housemaid?" I asked. "How does she cope with a house this size?"

"Most of it is under dust covers and has been shut off, my lady," Plunkett said. "And we have two women from the village come in once a week to help."

"I see." I turned to a little scrap of a girl who looked positively terrified. "And you are also a maid?"

"Scullery maid, your ladyship," Plunkett said for her. "Her name is Molly. Also from Ireland."

"Molly." I gave her a nod and a smile, then looked around for the cook.

"Is Cook still in the kitchen?" I asked.

"This is our cook," Plunkett said. "Fernando. He comes from Spain."

Fernando had black slicked-down hair and dark flashing eyes. They now flashed at me. "Your 'ighness, you like e-Spanish food?" he asked. "I make-a good e-Spanish food."

"I'm not sure. I've never been to Spain," I said. "But I hope you can cook good English food too."

"The English—they do not know good food," he said, tossing his head. "They tell Fernando no garlic. No spices."

"Yes, well, I'm not too fond of garlic or spices myself," I said. "When I've settled in we'll go over menus together. I can tell you what I like and find out which dishes you can cook and which you'll have to learn. Well-cooked English food, Fernando."

"Yes, lady, okay," he said. I believe I noticed a little shrug.

I took a deep breath and addressed them all. "So Plunkett will have told you that I am Lady Georgiana Rannoch and I am now coming to live here. Sir Hubert has invited me, as his heir, to make this my home when I marry and I am now here to see that everything in the house is to my liking and ready for us when we return from a honeymoon."

"And how soon will that be, my lady?" Plunkett asked.

"Our wedding is the twenty-seventh of July," I said, "and I presume we will be away on honeymoon after that. But I shall be gone at the beginning of July to my mother's wedding in Germany, so we don't have that much time to spruce up the place."

"Will Sir Hubert himself be coming for your wedding?" Plunkett asked.

"I fear not," I said. "He is currently in South America and thought it might take too long to reach Buenos Aires and then find a ship that can bring him back to England in time."

Did I see a visible relaxing of his features?

"As you can see, my lady," Plunkett said, sounding more confident, "the house has been shut up for a long time. May I suggest you go back to London for a few days and then I will write to let you know when everything is clean and ready?"

I had to admit that sounded like a good idea. It was sorely tempting, but I wasn't about to be defeated or presented with a fait accompli. "That won't be necessary, Plunkett," I said. "I shall want to supervise the cleaning and reorganization of the rooms and it will save you work in the long run if you do not have to move furniture around twice."

"As you wish," he said flatly. "I only thought it might not be pleasant to be breathing in dust."

"I'll survive," I said. "Oh, and before we do anything else, I would like the fountain working again. You will please let the gardeners know."

"I don't think it does work right now," Plunkett said. "A broken pipe or something."

"Then fix it, Plunkett," I said sweetly. "So the first order of things will be to have the morning room, this dining room and my bedroom made ready for me." Seeing the clear hostility in their faces, I couldn't resist adding, "And I will take my luncheon in the dining room after all, Plunkett. Please have a place laid for me."

I gave them a gracious little smile. "That will be all."

I turned and walked from the room, allowing myself a little grin of triumph. See, I could be lady of the manor if I tried. I wasn't at all sure about Fernando and I hadn't taken to Joanie the maid, but I should give them both a chance before I made any rash decisions. For all I knew Sir Hubert had hired Fernando himself and loved to eat Spanish food.

While I waited for luncheon to be served I went out onto the forecourt and examined the fountain. It had been turned off for some time and had collected leaves and debris in the base. I was determined to get it going again. I wandered farther into the grounds. The lawns had been mown but the flower beds needed weeding and the ornamental topiary I remembered had been allowed to go wild. Clearly more gardeners were needed and I realized I needed to see the household accounts to know how much money I had to budget for extra staff. I remembered the place when I had lived here, although I was only a small child. There had been upstairs maids and downstairs maids and footmen in black-and-gold livery and a lovely old cook who made me welcome in her kitchen. It was my task to bring the house back to those standards!

As I walked around the house I heard voices, men's voices, raised. "It's just not going to work, is it?" one of them said. Was it Plunkett? In which case, whom was he talking to?

"We'll have to make it work," came a low reply. I had them rattled.

I came back into the house to find the dining room more or less dusted and the table set for one.

"Luncheon is ready, my lady," Plunkett said.

Soup was brought in. I recognized it as soon as I tasted it. A tin of tomato soup. I had subsisted on such things when I attempted to live in London alone with no money. The cook had opened a tin of soup for me! So much for Spanish cooking.

The footman whisked away my plate, and the next course was a couple of sorry-looking lettuce leaves with some anchovies on top of them and a cold potato. I said nothing but ate because I was hungry. There was no pudding but a plate with a slice of old cheddar cheese and some crackers.

That was enough for me. I got up, leaving McShea to clear away the plates, and went straight through the baize door and down the steps to the kitchen. Fernando was sitting at the table reading the newspaper and smoking.

He jumped up, looking guilty, as he heard me enter.

"I don't know where you have been employed before," I said, "and I don't know whether you think I am only a young woman and therefore will accept anything, but I will not accept another meal like that again."

"Sorry, lady," he said. "You have to understand we not expecting you. No good food in house."

"Then what do the servants eat?" I asked.

"I make them a stew, or a rice dish. Peasant food."

"Well, peasant food would be better than this," I said. "Tinned soup? And that lettuce was wilted."

"Sorry. I'll have the shop send up some good vegetables for you."

"Is there no longer a kitchen garden here?" I asked. "I remember a beautiful big garden with all kinds of fruit and vegetables."

"I don't know what they grow. Not much. No people to feed. And I no go to pick vegetables. Most time come from shop."

"Then send someone to the shop today if you must, but I expect a better standard of food tonight," I said and stormed out again.

At the top of the stairs I paused to catch my breath. I found I was shaking. I wasn't used to this and I hated it.

Chapter 11

Being mistress of Eynsleigh is tiring. I'm tempted to get rid of the entire staff and start afresh, but I can't really do that without Sir Hubert's permission. Fernando might cook well for him! It's that they see me as an interloper and clearly resent having me here.

By the end of the day my bedroom had been cleaned and dusted and the bed made. I met with Plunkett and told him to bring in the women from the village as much as he needed to make the house habitable. He looked worried. "It all costs money, my lady," he said, "and we've been living on quite a tight budget."

"Sir Hubert assured me there were funds in the bank to run the place," I said.

"Maybe he's been gone longer than he expected and planned for," Plunkett said. "Perhaps you should write to him and ask him for more."

I could see that this might be true. Explorers scaling mountains across the world probably aren't the most practical people and lose track of time.

"Then do your best for now," I said. "What is the name of the bank? I shall visit the bank manager."

"That wouldn't do any good," Plunkett said. "There is a standing order for a specific amount to be paid in every month. Only Sir Hubert can change that."

"But I do still need a maid," I said. "I can pay for her out of my own pocket until we sort things out with Sir Hubert."

"Then I suggest you contact one of the agencies in London, my lady," he said stiffly.

"I don't wish to pay their prices. I'd prefer a local girl who is willing to learn. I'm sure you can ask around."

"We don't have much contact with the local people," he said. "You can ask the women when they come in. They'll know."

I wasn't sure whether he was being deliberately unhelpful or not.

"Maybe you can send up Joanie to help me, until you find someone," I suggested.

"Joanie has enough to do with cleaning a house this size." He was now only a small step away from insolence.

"I'll only need her for a few minutes to dress and undress me."

"I'll ask her. See if she's willing," he said.

There was a pause during which I tried to formulate many conflicting thoughts. "How long have you been here, Plunkett?" I asked.

"Just under a year, my lady."

"And before that?"

"I was with the old Lady Malmsbury. Do you know her, by chance?"

"No, I'm not acquainted with her."

"A grand old lady. One of the old school," he said.

"I hope she expected a higher standard than you've achieved in this house," I said.

"Of course. But standards do slip when there is only a skeleton staff and nobody in residence. If Sir Hubert had told us he was coming home, everything would have been shipshape by the time he arrived."

"Then let me see what you are capable of so that I can write to Lady Malmsbury and tell her."

"That wouldn't do no good," he said hastily, reverting to his Cockney background for a second. "She died. That's why I had to look for another position."

Clearly we weren't making progress.

"Will that be all, my lady?" he asked.

"For now. I shall wish to examine the household accounts."

"Now?" He did sound startled this time. "May I suggest tomorrow morning when I can have them ready for you?"

I should have insisted on right that minute, but I didn't think he'd have time to create a fake accounts book by the morning. Anyway, I'd easily be able to verify with the bank how much was coming in each month.

"Very well, tomorrow morning," I said in a voice that indicated I was displeased. "And I'd like to meet with the gardeners later today." I paused. "On second thought, I'll take a stroll through the grounds and find them myself."

"They could be anywhere," he said.

"They had better be on the grounds and working," I added.

I thought about Plunkett as I walked away. I couldn't picture anyone of my class, especially an older countess, hiring a butler like Plunkett. Perhaps he had taken great pains to act the perfect butler, subservient and refined, to his former mistress but was simply not bothering with me. I had never come across a butler who didn't have impeccable manners and speech. In fact most of them behaved as if they were at least ten rungs above us on the social scale.

I put on stout shoes and went out for a walk. No sign of gardeners in the formal part of the grounds. I went around the house, past the tennis court, and headed for the kitchen garden. To my surprise I found fruit trees with plenty of fruit on them, a bed of strawberries, runner beans and peas almost ready to be picked. So why had Fernando claimed there was no produce coming from the kitchen garden? Unless, of course, there was something going on behind my back. Was the produce being sold by the gardeners, or even by Fernando, for a nice profit?

When the cat's away, I said to myself. It was possible that Sir Hubert had even given them permission to sell excess produce. I'd have to tread carefully. I came around a potting shed and found two young men, sitting on upturned barrels, smoking. They leaped to their feet, startled.

"Yes, miss?" they asked. "Was you wanting something?" They were skinny specimens who would have looked more at home loitering on a street corner than digging in a garden bed.

"Yes, I was wanting my gardeners to be doing some work," I said.

"You've taken over this place?" one asked. "We didn't hear nothing about that."

"Anything," I corrected. "We didn't hear anything. And apparently you didn't hear about my arrival because Sir Hubert's letter went astray. I am Lady Georgiana, so you will refer to me in future as 'my lady.' I am Sir Hubert's heir and am going to be living here in future with my husband. I have arrived before my wedding to make sure the house and grounds are in good shape."

I saw the gardeners shoot each other a quick glance.

"I must congratulate you," I said. "The kitchen garden is looking splendid. The Spanish cook doesn't seem to have much idea about English food, so please make sure that good fresh vegetables are delivered to the kitchen each morning. The runner beans look almost ready to be picked. And those plums and strawberries are wonderful."

"Yes, melady," one of them muttered. I realized then that I might be right in my assumption that produce was being shipped out to be sold.

"And I notice that the fountain is not working. I was very fond of that fountain in my childhood. Please make sure it is working as soon as possible."

"That's not really our job," one of them said. "There might be broken pipes and things."

"Are you the only outdoor staff these days?"

"Yes, your ladyship," the other one said. "Plunkett said we didn't need more than two gardeners."

"Then I suggest you take a look at the fountain and if you can't fix it yourselves we will call in a plumber from the nearest town." I stood looking at them until neither one could meet my gaze. "What are your names?"

"Bill, your ladyship," one muttered. "Bill Bagley."

"And you?"

"Ted Hoskins." He didn't meet my gaze.

"And you are local men?"

"No. I'm from Croydon. He's from Hastings."

"And what happened to the former gardeners? I remember some older men."

"I don't know, your ladyship. We were both hired recently."

"I see. Well, I shall be inspecting the grounds and making a note of areas that need work. Those herbaceous borders, for example. There are more weeds than flowers. Get working on those right away."

"Yes, my lady," came the muttered reply.

I sensed them still staring at me as I left. Now I was feeling really worried. Why had the entire staff been replaced? None of these people seemed overly suited to their jobs or like the sort of servant I was used to. I realized our servants at home were Scottish and maybe servants in the south of England were not as likely to be humble and polite. But I had stayed in great houses nearby. I had actually stayed at Farlows, not more than a mile away, and that house had certainly run smoothly: smoothly enough to hold a house party with the Prince of Wales as a guest!

I put it all down to Plunkett. I surmised he had been hired to replace the retiring Rogers and had brought in his own sort of people, servants who would be likely to get along with him. Oh dear. I sighed. I hated conflict. I was almost feeling ready to go back to London, to write to Sir Hubert thanking him for his kind offer but telling him I'd rather live in a basement flat with a nosy landlady or a bijou room on a top floor! I wondered if I should call Zou Zou. If anyone could sort people out, it would be she. But then that would be admitting my own failure. I'd have to be mistress of my own house someday, and the sooner I learned the skills, the better.

Thus resolved, I went back into the house. Plunkett was hovering. I rather suspected he had been spying on me from the window. I decided to telephone Belinda. Perhaps she could bring my dress down for a fitting and cheer me up.

I looked around the front hall for a telephone.

"Where is the telephone, Plunkett?" I asked.

"The only equipment is in Sir Hubert's study and he keeps that locked when he's not here," he said. That smug look had returned. "Besides, the line is disconnected when the master goes away."

"Then we will have to have a new connection made and the telephone in the front hall hooked up again," I said. "I shall need to speak with people to coordinate my wedding plans."

"You're not planning to be married from here, are you?"

I was so tempted to say yes, I was. And what's more, the king and queen would be in attendance. But I'm too honest by upbringing, having had a nanny who once washed out my mouth with soap for a lie. "No, I'm being married from my family's London home."

"And you don't want to stay with them now, while all the arrangements are being made? So much more convenient."

"Anyone would think you were trying to get rid of me, Plunkett," I said sweetly.

He had the grace to blush then. "Oh no, my lady. Just thinking that this is harder on you, being so far from London."

"That's very thoughtful of you," I replied. "But I am determined to surprise my future husband with a perfect home when he returns from abroad."

"He travels a lot, your future husband, does he?" I could see him weighing up how often he'd have to deal with an assertive male around the place.

"He does."

"What sort of line of work is he in?"

"It's terribly hush-hush," I said. "He goes around the world apprehending criminals."

The wary look had definitely returned. I've rarely seen a man whose face betrayed his emotions more clearly.

"So to get back to basics: those gardeners do not seem to be working hard. You will make sure they understand that their jobs depend on their willingness to work."

"I'll tell them," he said.

"What happened to the older gardeners?" I asked. "When new young men are hired there is usually an older retainer who can teach them their duties."

"The old gardeners either died or wanted to retire," he said. "Sir Hubert hadn't changed his staff for years, so they all got old at the same time. And these two came highly recommended. One of them had worked for the parks in Hastings and the other had worked at a big nursery."

"But not in a large estate like this," I said. "And I presume that both of them had a supervisor who told them what to do. Not the same as taking initiative, is it? Anyway, the gardeners have been told to examine the fountain. If they can't get it to work, then a plumber will have to be called from Haywards Heath."

"That could be expensive," Plunkett said quickly.

"Then we will have to examine the books and see where we can save a little. Maybe the staff wages are too high, given the amount of work they are doing."

I made a grand exit, worthy of my mother, going up that sweeping curved staircase. It was only marred by my catching my toe on one of the stair rods and pitching forward. Luckily I was able to save myself and I don't think Plunkett saw. I opened one door after another along the bedroom floor. So strange, I thought. A couple of bedrooms completely devoid of furniture, and others clearly piled with items under dust covers. Why not leave all the rooms as they had been with beds ready for guests? I went up one more floor. This staircase was not so grand, but I found myself in familiar territory. I had run along this corridor as a small child! And at the end was my nursery. I opened the door and there it was, just as it had been. The big rocking horse in the window. The low bookcase with a couple of rag dolls sitting on it looking forlorn, the small bed with the embroidered quilt. It was like stepping back in time. And a wonderful thought came to me—one day my child would be sleeping in that little bed and I'd tiptoe up to kiss him or her good night.

I came down again in a much better frame of mind. It was just a question of making this new staff toe the line. I expected it was the same for any new mistress of a great estate, trying to mold the staff into her way of thought. I was now determined to stay on and to bring Eynsleigh back to its former glory!

$\mathcal{C}$hapter 12

I went to sit in the morning room, which is not normally done in the afternoon! But the more formal rooms had not yet had the dust sheets removed. I rang for tea and had a cup of pale liquid brought to me, with a biscuit in the saucer. Oh dear. Fernando made tea in the continental fashion. I drank it and sat there, making lists of things that would have to be done before the wedding as well as things that needed doing to the house.

> *Find a maid for me.*
> *Bring women in to clean.*
> *Mend fountain. Plumber if necessary.*
> *Hook telephone up again.*
> *Go through accounts. See where we can cut.*

It all seemed quite daunting and I felt terribly alone and vulnerable. I had had such high hopes. I remembered Eynsleigh as a warm and friendly place. When had it all started to go wrong? I wondered if Mr. Rogers was still living nearby or if he had retired to his own part of the country. Perhaps he or Mrs. Holbrook could shed some light on how someone like Plunkett was hired.

I went up to find writing paper and wrote to Belinda. I tried to make it sound cheerful, but I finished with *I shall try to come up to town in the next few days, but I need to get Eynsleigh back to working order first. A lot to be done. You wouldn't like to come down and work on my dress here, would you?*

I addressed the envelope, put a stamp on it and rang for Plunkett. "Can you see that this goes out when the postman comes tomorrow?" I held it out for him.

"The postman doesn't come here," he said. "All of Sir Hubert's mail goes straight to his solicitor."

Oh golly, I thought with a sigh. We really were well and truly cut off from the world. I would have to go into town and see if the postman could put me on his route again.

At six o'clock I went upstairs to change for dinner. I knew it was only me, but I wanted the staff to know that standards would be kept. I had brought one evening dress, leaving the lovely new creations for my trousseau. I tried to get into it single-handedly, but in the end I had to give up. Whoever made evening clothes expected their wearers to have a maid, or at least a willing husband. I went over and rang the bell. After a few minutes Joanie appeared. "You rang, my lady?" she asked.

"Yes, Joanie. I need help getting dressed. These evening gowns all have hooks down the back. Impossible to put on alone."

"Right-oh," she said. At least it wasn't "Bob's yer uncle," which was what Queenie always said. I thought of her quite fondly at this moment. At least she was willing and cheerful. This one looked as if she could curdle milk. She yanked the dress over my head and swore to herself as she wrestled with the hooks. "You can do your own hair, can't you?" she asked. "Because I've got ever so much work to do, what with cleaning all these rooms."

"Yes, I can do my own hair, thank you, Joanie. And I have told Plunkett that we are to employ the women from the village until the house is back in working order. When I have examined the books I shall see if we can take on a second maid."

"Can I go now, my lady?" she asked.

"Yes. But I shall need you to help me out of this dress after dinner. I realize I need to employ a lady's maid as soon as possible."

"Didn't you have no maid where you came from?" she asked.

"I was staying with a Polish princess and I borrowed her maid," I said. "My own maid wanted to stay near her mother in Ireland, I'm afraid."

"A princess," she said for a moment, looking almost like an impressionable young girl. "Fancy that! What was she like, this princess?"

"Very glamorous but very generous."

"Did you ever meet our princesses? Elizabeth and Margaret, I mean."

"They are going to be bridesmaids at my wedding," I said.

"Go on!" She smirked as if she didn't believe me.

"No, really. I'm their cousin."

"Blimey," she said. "Mr. Plunkett never told us. So might royalty be coming down here?"

"Quite possibly," I said. I grinned to my reflection in the mirror as she departed. That news would certainly shake them up. Maybe I'd get better service in future.

As I came down to dinner I smelled quite an appetizing smell coming from the kitchen. Frying onions, I believe. Perhaps Fernando was working hard to make up for my dismal luncheon. I had a glass of sherry in the morning room before Plunkett came to announce that dinner was ready. I felt quite hopeful as I went through to the dining room. A candelabra had been lit on the dining table, making it look quite festive. I sat and McShea brought in a dish hidden under a cover. The cover was removed and what was placed before me was about the least appetizing thing I had ever seen: a piece of boiled cod, so over-cooked that it was dry, a solitary boiled potato and cabbage that had been boiled to the point of turning gray.

This was the final straw. I jumped up.

"Is something wrong, my lady?" McShea asked.

"There certainly is," I replied. "Bring Fernando to me immediately."

I waited, heard voices rising in an exchange, and soon Fernando appeared with Plunkett hovering in the doorway.

"What do you call this, Fernando?" I demanded, pointing at my plate.

"Is fish," he said.

"Yes, I know it's fish. Was it a piece you had ready for the cat?"

"No. Is good fish."

"I never had a meal this bad even when I was at school," I said. "Look at it. The fish is positively dry. There is no sauce. And the cabbage . . ."

"You say you like your food well-done," he said. "So I make it well-done."

"No, I didn't say that," I snapped. "At least I didn't mean you to interpret it that way. I believe I said I wanted my food cooked well. Well prepared. Prepared properly. Not overcooked."

"And you say no garlic and spices," he went on belligerently. "So how I make the sauce?"

"I'm sure there are plenty of sauces that don't have to be spicy. Use your cookbook." I pointed at the table. "And you can take this away."

"You don't want?"

"What are you having for dinner tonight in the servant's hall, Fernando?" I asked.

"We have the fish stew."

"Then I'll have some of that."

"Has garlic in it," he replied, his chin stuck out defiantly.

"I'll risk it. Have a bowl sent up to me. Oh, and some of that good wine I saw on the kitchen table. Châteauneuf-du-Pape. My, but the servants drink well. Either Sir Hubert is generous or he'll be counting the bottles when he returns."

Fernando glared at me. As he turned to go I added, "One more chance, Fernando. If you can't prove to me that you are a good cook, then I'm afraid I'll have to let you go."

"You can't do that," he said, still looking defiant. "Sir Hubert, he my boss. He hire me. He the only one who can sack me. I no leave until he tell me to go."

"We'll see about that," I said. I resumed my place at the dining table and waited until a bowl of stew was brought up to me with a glass of wine. I took a large gulp of the wine to steady my nerves. Golly, what a day! The fish stew was delicious, and after it McShea brought up a plate of strawberries and cream. I decided that I'd meet with Fernando in the morning and plan out menus for a week. That way there should be no more horrible surprises.

By the time I'd had a second glass of wine I was feeling exhausted. I announced that I was going up to my bedroom to read and that Joanie should come up to undress me. She appeared soon after and asked me about the little princesses as she hung up my clothes. It seemed I might have one ally among the staff after all. I sat in the small armchair reading for a while. There was an unpleasant odor in the room, sulfuric. I wondered if a dead mouse lay undetected under the wardrobe. And I realized that my windows weren't open. I had been raised at Castle Rannoch, where windows were religiously kept open, even in the most howling gale. I went over and opened the windows. Night sounds drifted toward me: the gentle sigh of the wind through the trees, the hoot of a distant owl. In every direction no sign of a light. It felt like being lost at sea.

Then I heard voices, male voices, kept quite low. I leaned out of the window and they seemed to be coming from the far wing, where Sir Hubert had his rooms. I bet that telephone was not turned off, I thought. One of them is using the phone. Tomorrow I'd go and investigate. The voice or voices were too far away for me to make out what they were saying. I was too tired to go on reading, and the light was not good. In fact my eyes were feeling heavy and my head was beginning to throb a little. Too much wine, I thought. I wasn't used to drinking much and the wine was very rich. So I gave up, turned out the light and went to bed.

As I lay there I was conscious of complete stillness. It seemed that the breeze had dropped. Nothing stirred outside. But then my acute hearing picked up the smallest sound. A slight hissing noise. It was the sort of noise the gaslights used to make in houses that didn't have electricity. I got up, turned on the light again and examined the room. I hadn't noticed before but a gas fire had been installed in the fireplace and . . . and the gas tap was partly on. I turned it off hurriedly and stood staring down at it, my heart thumping. Someone had made sure the windows were closed and turned the gas on. Not full on, or I might have been dead by now if I hadn't smelled it. But if I'd fallen asleep in a closed room with that small amount of gas escaping, would I have woken up in the morning? Did someone want to kill me or just scare me off?

I got up and did what Darcy had shown me when we were in Stresa together. I took the upright chair and placed it beneath the door handle. Now nobody could enter my room without the chair clattering over. But I couldn't fall asleep. They were trying to scare me off, I thought. They had been enjoying an easy life doing very little work and now they would have to buck up and spend the housekeeping allowance on me instead of themselves. Well, I wasn't going to be intimidated! But as I lay there, watching the curtains stirring in the breeze, which had picked up again, I felt very alone. If only Darcy hadn't had to go away. If only I were back with Zou Zou.

I was almost drifting off to sleep when I heard a noise. Surely that was the crunch of motorcar tires on gravel? I got up, removed the chair from under my door handle and crept out onto the landing. I made my way down the hall to one of the rooms that faced the front of the house. The only one with a good view of the forecourt was piled with furniture under dust sheets. I attempted to squeeze past and in my haste I caught my foot in one of the dust sheets and stumbled, putting my hand out to save myself. My hand touched the sheet, and then I was pitching forward into nothing. I tried to stay calm as I attempted to get up. It was dark in the room, the only light coming in from the anemic bulb farther down the hallway. I pulled the sheet away and saw to my utter surprise that there was nothing beneath it. I removed the other cloths. There were three bed frames in the room, that was all, and the cloths were draped between them like the tents one made as a child. But why? I could have sworn I saw shapes beneath the cloth when I was taken on my tour of the house. How could they have just vanished?

I draped the cloths back into place. Nobody should know that I had been here. Then I remembered my original purpose: the sound of car tires on gravel. I pulled back the heavy curtains and peered out. The forecourt below lay in complete darkness. No headlights, no sign of a motor that I could see. And no sound. Maybe noises carried easily on the night breeze and the motorcar I had heard was driving onto a nearby property. Still feeling uneasy, I went back to bed.

Chapter 13

THURSDAY, JUNE 27
EYNSLEIGH, SUSSEX

Had a bad night's sleep. That gas tap gave me a nasty scare, so perhaps
    I was imagining the other things that happened. But I'm not going
    to let Plunkett and his motley crew defeat me. This is going to be
    my home, whether they like it or not!

I was awoken at first light by a deafening dawn chorus. One forgets,
living in town, how incredibly loud birds can be. My little traveling
clock said almost five. I got up and went over to the window. The first
rays of sun were slanting over dewy grass. Sweet smells of roses and
newly mown grass wafted in through the window. It was the sort of
morning when I'd love to go out for an early ride. Horses, I thought.
When I was settled here maybe I could have a horse again.

So I was in a better mood until I remembered last night's incident
with the gas tap. Should I just say nothing or should I confront them?
I tried to decide which might be more effective. Keeping cool and

saying nothing? But this was more than a scare. Was one of them expecting to find my dead body this morning? I decided that I'd use the element of surprise and watch their reactions. I washed and dressed, without help from Joanie, and was on my way downstairs when I remembered that room I had been in the night before. I went back to examine it and sure enough there were only old bedsteads with cloths draped over them. Most odd. I didn't think I'd get the right answer if I asked the question so decided to ignore it.

I went into the morning room and rang the bell. Plunkett appeared after a long pause, still buttoning his jacket.

"You rang, my lady?"

"Yes, I did. Good morning, Plunkett. It seems the household is rather late to rise here. Please assemble the entire staff immediately. There is a matter of great urgency that I need to speak to them about."

"Now?" He was so surprised he forgot to say "my lady."

"Yes, right away. In here."

He went. I heard voices, grumbling voices. Then they shuffled in, Joanie still arranging her cap, Fernando with his chef's jacket buttoned hastily. I sat looking from one face to the next. "Something very troubling happened last night," I said. "When I went to bed I heard a hissing noise and I found that the gas tap in my room had been turned on. I am not sure what to believe at this moment: I would like to think it was an accident. I sincerely hope it was not a gesture of ill will from any of you and that this is not a matter for the police."

Fernando was not meeting my gaze. Plunkett was looking shocked, or at least pretending to look shocked. McShea was shuffling nervously from one foot to the other, and Joanie, she was looking down at her feet. "I presume you were the one who cleaned my room, Joanie," I said. "And you were also up there helping me to undress. So I'm afraid that suspicion has to fall to you . . . and if it were ever hinted that you tried to do harm to your mistress, I'm afraid you would never get another job."

Joanie looked up. Her lip trembled. "I'm awful sorry, my lady. I really am."

I waited for the confession to go on. "I must have hit against the gas tap when I was sweeping. It won't happen again, I promise."

"It had better not," I said. I was trying to think whether it was plausible that gas had been seeping into my room since it was cleaned. Surely I would have been aware of the odor earlier. No, whoever did this came up while I was at dinner, or Joanie herself did it when she was undressing me.

"You do all realize that you have not made the best first impression," I said. "I may have to write to Sir Hubert immediately telling him that I have had to replace the entire staff. So I suggest you all are on your best behavior from now on. If necessary I shall go to see Sir Hubert's solicitor and obtain his permission to dismiss all of you without a reference."

"Hang on, your ladyship," Plunkett said hastily. "Joanie has said she was sorry for the accident. She'll make sure it won't happen again."

"Then let's start anew today, shall we? Fernando, I would like a proper breakfast this morning: eggs, bacon, sausage, tomatoes. I expect it in half an hour and I would like some coffee brought to me immediately. And as soon as breakfast is over you are to come to the morning room to discuss menus for the coming week."

"Yes, my lady," he muttered. "I be there."

"And after breakfast you and I will go through the books, Plunkett," I went on.

"Very good, my lady," he said in a suitably humble voice.

Had I just won that round?

Breakfast appeared, not badly cooked, except that the fried egg was a little greasy.

And after breakfast Plunkett appeared with the household accounts book. I stared at the columns of figures, trying to give the impression that I knew all about household accounts and how much it would take to run a great house like Eynsleigh. Actually I didn't have any idea. I knew that Fig always complained they had no money, but I didn't know what no money meant to them. I ran my finger down one page, then the next. I had to admit the amount coming in did not appear to be overly generous—and very much balanced the amount going out. It was just possible that Sir Hubert had been out of England for so long that he had underestimated how much everything cost.

"This all seems to be in order, Plunkett," I said. "And I agree that there does not seem to be a lot left over to hire extra staff. I think I will have to talk to Sir Hubert's solicitor to see if more money can be made available. In the meantime I find that the only amount that is a little too generous is your salary, Plunkett."

"But, my lady, the butler should be paid considerably more than the rest of the staff, surely?" he protested.

"In a large house with a full complement of servants I would agree," I said. "But when you are only supervising four other people, it does seem rather a lot."

"It was the salary agreed upon when I took this job," he said, giving me that defiant look again.

"Well, I won't be too hasty," I said, "but when my fiancé returns we may have to give this more thought."

He stood up, almost snatching the accounts book from me. "Will that be all, my lady?"

"There is one more thing. I wish to go into the nearest town. Haywards Heath, isn't it? I presume there is no chauffeur at the moment?"

"No, my lady. He was let go when Sir Hubert last went abroad."

"Then I shall have to drive myself. Please have the Bentley driven around to the front of the house at ten o'clock."

"I doubt there's any petrol in it," he said. "It's hardly been used for years now. It might not even start."

"Plunkett, do you take great delight in being difficult?" I could hear my voice rising now. "If there is no petrol in the motor, then someone must walk to the nearest service station and ask the mechanic to come here with a can of petrol and to make sure the Bentley is in good running order."

"It's a long walk, my lady."

"Then use a bicycle, Plunkett." I gave him a sweet smile. "I expect the motorcar to be ready by ten."

Then I made a grand exit. I was feeling jolly proud of myself. "Mistress of Eynsleigh," I muttered again.

I tried to maintain that air of authority and poise when I discussed menus with Fernando. He remained sulky and unresponsive when I suggested kidneys for breakfast. He didn't even know what kedgeree was!

"What must I catch?" he asked. "I do not know what a ree is."

I sighed. I told him I did not expect the standard that I was used to in great houses, no quails in aspic or seven-course meals. But I wanted simple food, well cooked: soups that did not come from a tin, grilled chops, meat pies, steamed fish with parsley sauce or grilled fillets of plaice. Maybe scones and crumpets for tea. He didn't understand that last word.

"A pet? This is a small animal, no? A crumb I understand."

"Go and look it up in the cookery books that I'm sure are on a shelf in the kitchen," I said.

I came away feeling that I wasn't about to get any of the above, and again I wondered why Sir Hubert had hired him. Perhaps he had relied on an agency and had no idea what he was getting. Of course when I had lived here before I had eaten only nursery food and had no idea what the cuisine was like downstairs. But Sir Hubert had never struck me as the sort of man who wanted paella and olives at every meal. Surely my mother would have mentioned it.

"One of the reasons I bolted was the food, darling. All that oil and garlic."

But she had never said that. And now the big question: how was I going to get rid of him?

THE MOTORCAR APPEARED miraculously outside the front door by ten o'clock. It seemed to be in perfect working order and not a cobweb in sight, making me suspect that Plunkett or his minions might have used it for personal errands when no one was watching. I drove into Haywards Heath and went first to the telephone exchange. There I was told that the line to Eynsleigh was hooked up and active. Aha. So the telephone in Sir Hubert's study was being used. I just had to make sure the equipment in the front hall was also hooked up!

Feeling rather triumphant at my small victories, I returned to the nearest village, called Linfield, where I went into the post office at the back of the village shop. I was now living at Eynsleigh, I said. Could any post with my name on it be held for me at the post office?

"We can deliver, my lady. No trouble at all," said the jolly postmistress. "Jones has one of them motorbikes now for his rural route."

Two successes in one morning. As I passed the greengrocer's something caught my eye. A basket of strawberries with the title *Locally grown*. Locally grown, all right, I thought. I had seen that basket sitting next to the potting shed at Eynsleigh. So my hunch was right and the gardeners were making extra income. We'd have to have a little talk about that!

"Can I help you, miss?" The greengrocer came out of his shop as I stood there.

"I am Lady Georgiana Rannoch and I've just moved into Eynsleigh," I said. "I think those strawberries came from our garden."

The shopkeeper beamed. "They did indeed, my lady. Your gardeners grow the finest strawberries hereabouts."

"So we've been supplying the shop for some time, have we?" I asked.

"Oh yes. Sir Hubert has always let us buy any produce he couldn't use. Can't get any fresher than that, can you?"

"And you pay the gardeners, do you?"

"Oh no, my lady. We settle up with the household accounts once a month."

"Thank you," I said. One item that hadn't appeared on the household books I'd seen that morning. I wondered what else might be missing. I was heading back to the Bentley when I passed an old man sitting on a bench under a big beech tree.

"I know you," he said, wagging a finger at me. "You're her little ladyship. I remember when you were a little girl."

I looked at him, trying to remember his face. Vaguely familiar, I thought, but then he looked like a lot of countrymen. "You used to work at Eynsleigh?" I asked.

"I did. Over forty years there, man and boy," he said. "I were assistant head gardener."

"Of course." I smiled and sat on the bench beside him. "Have you been retired long?"

"Not retired," he said. "Not willingly. Let go. But I still had a lot of life in these old limbs. But that new bloke, he wanted new blood. Someone with more modern ideas about things, he said."

"I see." I paused, digesting this. "What was your name again?"

"Old Ben. That's what I was always known as. Ben Wayland."

"Ben." I smiled at him. "I'm sorry to hear that. I've just come to live at Eynsleigh and I find that everything has changed."

"It has indeed," he said. "And not for the better. Nothing were the same after Mr. Rogers . . ." He paused and sighed.

"Did Mr. Rogers retire near here? I'd like to visit him if he's in the area still."

"Oh no, my lady," he said. "He died. Didn't you hear that? He was planning on retiring, but then he took a fall down the back stairs at Eynsleigh and broke his neck. Awful tragic, that was. Never got to enjoy his retirement."

"Yes, awful tragic," I echoed.

"And that new bloke. Plunker or whatever he was called. He came in and got rid of the lot of us. Even Mrs. Holbrook, who had been housekeeper since Sir Hubert was a young man. Out we all went."

"And what happened to Mrs. Holbrook?"

"Oh, she's still around here," he said. "Bought herself a nice little cottage out Haywards Heath way."

"I'm glad to hear it," I said. "Maybe I'll pay a call on her."

"You do that," he said. "She'd like that."

"And, Ben," I said, "I wonder if you'd come back to Eynsleigh and get those two young gardeners in line. There are so many things that need doing and I don't think they have much idea. The fountain's not working for one thing. They said I'd have to get a plumber."

"Get a plumber?" Old Ben gave a chuckle that turned into a cough. "I reckon it's just turned off. We always turned it off when the master went away. No sense in wasting water. There's a tap round the other side of the yew hedge. Have them try that first. But I'd certainly like to come back, couple of days a week, and show them young'uns how things are done properly. If you think that's all right, I mean?" He looked worried, almost scared. "I wouldn't want to get on the wrong side of that Plunkett bloke."

"Ben, I am mistress of Eynsleigh now."

"You are? What about the old lady? What does she say?"

"Old lady?"

He suddenly looked confused, almost embarrassed. "Oh, I don't suppose I should have said anything. Opened my big mouth again. Never mind, forget what I said."

"What old lady?" I repeated, but he got up. "I should be getting back. The missus will have my dinner on the table and I'll be in big trouble." He started to walk away. "But I'll come by the house and see how things are in a few days. All right?"

I watched him go, wondering if his mind was still all there. Old lady? Did he think there was a new housekeeper who had replaced Mrs. Holbrook? But he had seemed upset, almost afraid. I was in a pensive mood as I drove back to the house. All the staff let go, and poor Rogers, the butler I remembered, had died in a horrible fall down the back stairs. I would have taken it for granted that this was nothing more than an accident—failing eyesight, unsteadiness and steep uncarpeted stairs—except for the gas-tap incident last night. It came to me that I would have to be extra vigilant until I got to the bottom of what was going on at Eynsleigh.

Chapter 14

I'm not sure what to think or exactly what to do next. I thought I was
   dealing with annoyances, with someone dipping into the
   household accounts, maybe, and a staff no longer willing to work.
   But the news of Rogers's death has really shaken me up. Now I'm
   inclined to believe that the gas tap was no accident and someone
   wants me out of the house, or even dead. Not a comforting
   thought. I wish Darcy would come back. He'd know how to deal
   with these people. I think that Princess Zou Zou would too, but I
   don't want to seem like a helpless person and run to her for help on
   the second day! Oh golly. And I so looked forward to this!

I mulled over what to do as I drove back to Eynsleigh. I could confront
Plunkett about the produce and ask why it wasn't part of the accounts.
I could ask him about Rogers's death, but then from what Old Ben
had said, Plunkett wasn't even part of the household then. Rogers was

only thinking of retiring and Plunkett was hired to replace him. So someone else on the staff at that time—someone who helped Plunkett get the job? But who would that be? McShea didn't seem like the sort to push an old man down the stairs. And Joanie . . . well, she had admitted she might have accidentally turned on my gas tap. I should find out when she arrived and try to see if she had any connection to Plunkett.

But I had to tread very carefully, I reminded myself.

And the old lady Ben had mentioned. Maybe his mind was going and that was just senile rambling. There certainly wasn't an old lady on the staff that I had seen. There could, of course, be a perfectly reasonable explanation. A housekeeper had been hired to replace Mrs. Holbrook while Ben was still there. But she had been too domineering, clashed with Plunkett and was let go. Yes, that might well have been it. I gave a sigh as I pulled up in the forecourt and went up the steps. As I came in I saw that the dust sheets had now been taken off the big drawing room to my left. The red velvet curtains were now drawn back and the room was ready for use. Little by little, I thought.

I stepped into the room and stood looking around, trying to bring back memories. Yes, I had been in this room before and it had always seemed to me to be very grand. Now it seemed rather ordinary—a large room to be sure, but in no way ornate. A couple of faded red brocade sofas. Some Queen Anne chairs around a large marble fireplace. Some pictures on the walls. But a rather tired room. I sighed and went out again.

On the way back I had come to another decision—or rather two more decisions. I was going to take a look at the forbidden wing. And I was going to write to the current Earl or Countess of Malmsbury, asking about Plunkett. I could also ask Belinda—or rather my mother—to find out about agencies in London that supplied top-level servants. Mummy must have used one before now. And I could ask for a copy of Plunkett's letter of recommendation. If he came from an agency, they were usually most particular in their screening process. In fact, trying to hire a servant from one was slightly harder than choosing a new pope.

As I emerged from the drawing room, Plunkett appeared with that uncanny feeling that all butlers seem to possess of knowing when one has come home.

"Welcome, my lady. I trust the motorcar ran smoothly?"

"Perfectly, thank you, Plunkett."

"Fernando has luncheon prepared whenever you are ready."

"Tell him I'll eat in fifteen minutes. Oh, and Plunkett: I went to the telephone exchange. I was told that the line to Eynsleigh was in perfect working order. So please make sure that the receiver is reconnected in the entrance hall. It is not needed in Sir Hubert's study while he is not in residence. "

I stared at him with my best Queen Victoria look.

"Very well, my lady," he said. "I will see if one of us can reconnect it. We don't exactly have a handyman on the staff any longer."

"So I believe, since the gardeners didn't realize that all that was needed to make the fountain play again was to turn on the tap." I decided I was doing well and risked forging ahead. "And speaking of gardeners, I am gravely concerned that they have been stealing from the estate. I was at the village shop just now and saw a basket full of strawberries that the shopkeeper admitted had come from the estate. Did you know about this?"

To my delight he turned red. "My lady, Sir Hubert has always instructed the staff that excess produce not go to waste and can be sold at the village shop."

"I've nothing against that. But the produce belongs to Sir Hubert, not the gardeners. The money should come into the household accounts, especially since you have shown me how short we are." I paused, then added, "Since the gardeners might not have been told otherwise, I will not dismiss them this time, but from now on I expect the correct amount to be appearing in the weekly books."

"As you wish, my lady," he said.

Another small victory, I thought, as I went up the stairs to my room. I decided to change out of the frock I had been wearing into a cotton skirt and blouse, as the day had become quite muggy. I opened my drawer and stood staring at it. I remembered folding my long petticoat on top of my underwear. Somebody had been through my things. I wasn't sure what that person expected to achieve by this. I had only brought one suitcase of clothes, none of my books or personal papers. Maybe it was the curiosity of a young girl about what the undergarments of the aristocracy might look like. But it left me feeling even more uneasy, as if I could not let my guard down for one moment in this place.

I changed my clothes, then went down for luncheon. This time I was served ham and salad. At least the lettuce, spring onions and radishes were fresh this time and the ham was tasty, but it was the sort of meal one would expect for high tea, not luncheon, and it required no effort on the part of the cook. It was followed by more strawberries and cream. I even had to request that coffee be brought to me in the morning room afterward. Could I dismiss Fernando? I wondered. What if he wouldn't go? I couldn't have him thrown out. And he was probably right in stating that if Sir Hubert had hired him, only Sir Hubert could sack him. Darcy would know what to do. Golly, I hoped he would return in a hurry, because I needed an ally.

Then a brilliant idea came to me: Queenie! She had now become a passable cook and she could double as my lady's maid when I needed help dressing or undressing. I knew Darcy's aunt Oona and uncle Dooley would miss her, but they could survive without her for the time being. And I needed her. I wrote her a letter telling her how much I needed her help before the wedding, especially her newfound cooking skills.

The Bentley was still sitting outside the front door. I was going to drive into the village, but first I went to seek out the gardeners. They were working half-heartedly on one of the herbaceous borders.

"Come with me," I said.

They followed, reluctantly. I led them around the yew hedge and found what I was looking for.

"What do you see there?" I asked.

"That looks like a tap, my lady," one of them said.

"Please try to turn it on."

One gardener shot the other a look that indicated I was clearly not quite right in the head. He bent down and wrestled with the tap. It had not been turned for some time and it was hard work, but finally he moved it. There was a hissing, splattering sound from beyond the hedge. I went to a gap and peeked through.

"Well, what a surprise!" I said. "The fountain is actually working again."

I turned back to the gardeners, both of whom were looking rather crestfallen at this moment.

"And neither of you had figured that out?" I said. "Now it just needs the leaves and debris cleaned from it. I expect it to look sparkling clean, is that understood? Oh, and just to warn you, I am bringing back Old Ben to help you get the gardens back in shape. And to teach you what you need to know if you continue to work here. But if any more produce goes out of this garden without my permission, then I'm afraid you may be looking for other jobs."

"It wasn't us, my lady," one of them—Ted Hoskins—said, glancing at the other to see if he was saying the right thing. "Mr. Plunkett told us it was all right and the boss always let the surplus fruit and veg be sold."

"I understand," I said. "But the word is 'surplus.' You will let me know each morning what is ripe and ready to eat and I will tell you which items I do not need. And there is bottling and preserving for the winter to consider. Since Fernando doesn't have much cooking to do at the moment, he can put up fruit for the winter. I'll speak to him about it later."

I gave them a big smile. "That will be all," I said.

I drove into the village, posted my letter and asked if the postmistress knew where Mrs. Holbrook might have gone.

"I do, your ladyship," she said. "Because I have a forwarding address for her letters." She wrote it out for me. I asked and it was about five miles away. I decided that since I already had the motorcar out, I'd pay her a call. I drove through pretty leafy lanes until I came to a small cottage. It was whitewashed, with roses climbing up the front porch, and quite charming.

Mrs. Holbrook frowned when she saw me standing at the front door; then recognition dawned and her face broke into a big smile. "Well, I never," she said. "Come in, your ladyship. What a lovely surprise to see you."

She led me into a spotless living room and rushed into the kitchen to make me a cup of tea. She reappeared soon afterward with a tray of shortbread and gingerbread and a blue-and-white-striped tea set. She sat opposite me and plied me with questions about my upcoming wedding. When she heard that Sir Hubert had invited me to live at Eynsleigh, she looked surprised and delighted. "Well, that is good news," she said. "You'll soon get the place back to the way it should be." She leaned closer. "I told the master it wasn't wise to leave the place unoccupied for so long. I mean, while me and Mr. Rogers were there we saw that standards were kept up. But that new person—well, I expect you've found out for yourself."

"I have, Mrs. Holbrook, and frankly I'm surprised that Sir Hubert ever hired him in the first place."

"Well, he came with good credentials, your ladyship. The highest recommendation from a titled lady. And of course Sir Hubert wasn't here in person. He had to rely on his solicitor and an agency in London. It was all rather rushed through on account of poor Mr. Rogers. You heard about that, of course. Falling down the back stairs. He was getting a trifle doddery, I have to say. He knew he should think of retiring, which was why he had the solicitor contact the agency in London." She stopped, blinking back tears. "All the same, it was a terrible shock.

We'd worked together in that house for thirty years and I was ever so fond of him. Well, everyone was, weren't they? He was a lovely kind man." She managed a weak smile. "You should have seen the funeral. The church was packed. Ever so popular around here, Mr. Rogers was."

"And you decided to leave after his death, did you?"

"Well, my lady"—an embarrassed look came over her face—"I was made such a generous offer to retire that I couldn't turn it down. I mean, I wouldn't have been able to buy a cottage like this without that sort of money. I'm comfortable for life now, I am, and ever so grateful. I expect the master was behind it. He always was such a kind man."

We chatted some more and I promised to visit again. I was half tempted to invite her to come back for a while, but she clearly had no love for Mr. Plunkett. "A common individual, if you ask me," she said.

As she accompanied me to the front door I asked her if she knew the name of the solicitor.

"Well, of course I do. Eaton and Harris in Haywards Heath, my lady. Been the family solicitor for generations."

Now I felt I was getting somewhere. I had the name of the solicitor. I would find out the truth about a lot of things. But who had given Mrs. Holbrook the money to buy a cottage? Certainly not Plunkett. Butlers do not make that sort of money. Was it perhaps a bequest from Sir Hubert himself, left with his solicitor for when she decided to retire? Yes, that seemed the most logical. I'd ask Eaton and Harris about it when I visited them.

Chapter 15

This is all getting more and more confusing. The former butler met his
death when he fell down the stairs. Someone had been through my
drawers. And someone had given Mrs. Holbrook a handsome sum
to retire—enough to buy a cottage. What on earth is going on
here? I have to confess I'm a little uneasy now.

It was lovely to return to Eynsleigh and see the fountain playing merrily in the forecourt. Sunlight sparkled on water droplets and I stood
for a long while just watching the dance of the water. Several spar-
rows were perched on the rim, enjoying the spray. For a moment I
wished that I had taken a room at the front of the house and could
watch the fountain from my windows. But I had to admit that the
room I had chosen was the nicest and the view from the back windows
over the parkland was stunning. I was glad that I had had a good tea
with Mrs. Holbrook because I rather feared that tea at Eynsleigh would
have been another biscuit from a packet beside a pale beige cup of

liquid. But I could hold out until Queenie arrived, I thought. And I'd wait until tomorrow to confront Fernando about using the fresh produce from the estate. I doubted he'd have any idea about bottling and canning, but it would be satisfying to catch him out! Maybe one of the ladies from the village would be available. In my experience all country ladies knew about preserving fruit and vegetables.

The house was quiet. I decided this might be a perfect time to examine Sir Hubert's wing. I wanted to see for myself exactly how many rooms there were and what they were used for. I found myself tiptoeing through the long hallway that connected the two wings, which was silly because I was mistress of Eynsleigh now. I reached the other wing without being seen and stood in a dark hallway. No light came because all the doors were shut. I tried the first and it was locked. So was the second. Now I was rather annoyed. I went back to the drawing room and rang for Plunkett.

From the state of his hair I'd say he had been having an afternoon nap.

"Plunkett, I wanted to visit the rooms in the other wing and they all seem to be locked," I said.

"That is correct, your ladyship. Sir Hubert's instructions were that these rooms not be disturbed."

I swallowed back my anger.

"And yet you have obviously been in them to use the telephone."

"I have been in on occasion just to make sure everything is dusted and ready should the master return."

"Well, I should like to see them now, as new mistress of Eynsleigh," I said.

"I'm sorry, my lady, but my instructions come from Sir Hubert, and if he said I was to keep those doors locked, then I'm not unlocking them until he tells me."

My anger was rising now. "You do realize that you will be looking for a new position shortly, Plunkett. The moment Sir Hubert returns and hears how obstructive you have been."

He was still looking at me with a smug expression on his face. "We don't know when he will return, do we? It may be a while. He's been off on climbing expeditions for years before. You know yourself that he had a fall and was ages recuperating in a Swiss clinic." He allowed himself a little smirk. I fought back the desire to smack his face. "And when he eventually does return," he continued, "he may be impressed that I obeyed his orders against all comers. And if you ask me, I don't know why you are so intent on seeing the master's study and his little sitting room. You have enough rooms at your disposal, don't you?"

"That's not the point. The point is that I asked you to do something and you refused. In any household where I have lived, a defiant servant would be packing his bags the next day."

"When Sir Hubert tells me that he is no longer the master of Eynsleigh, I shall be happy to obey anything your ladyship wishes," he said. "But in the meantime . . ." And with that he left me.

Crikey, I thought. I don't know what to do about this. If I sack him, he simply won't go. I retreated to the drawing room and wrote a letter to Mummy, asking her to inquire among the domestic agencies in Mayfair to see who might have recommended Plunkett. I wasn't about to go out again to post the letter, and I certainly didn't trust one of the staff to do so.

I was doubly glad that I had had a good tea with Mrs. Holbrook because dinner was another dismal affair. This time it was a rice dish with various bits of unidentifiable meat and sausage in it. This was followed by a custard such as would have been served in the nursery. I had to request that cheese and biscuits be brought to me. I summoned Fernando again.

He appeared, wiping his hands on his apron and scowling.

"Fernando, I thought I made clear what I wanted you to cook for me. I don't recall saying rice and leftover meat."

"Is Spanish dish. Paella. Everyone like."

"I didn't like. And I don't recall the word 'paella' on the list of dishes I would like to eat for dinner." I took a deep breath. "I'm afraid I may have to let you go, Fernando. You are simply not up to snuff."

"Snuff?" he demanded. "This is taken for sneezing, no? You wish to have food that makes you sneeze?"

"It is an English expression, Fernando. It means you are not up to the standard required in this house."

"Me, I don't go until English lord return and tells me to go."

"We'll see about that," I said, but I was feeling sick and scared. What if none of them would leave and Sir Hubert did not return for a year or more? Then I told myself his solicitor might know how to contact him. And his solicitor might also know whether I was legally able to remove defiant servants. Tomorrow, I thought. I would go to the solicitor tomorrow.

I didn't even bother to ask for a cup of coffee after dinner. The way things were going it would probably have poison in it. Or Ex-Lax at the very least. I went up to my room and managed to undress myself, rather than summon Joanie again and risk more open gas taps. Soon Queenie will be here, I thought excitedly. She wasn't that bad, was she? And at least she was loyal.

I opened all the windows again and stood at one of them. A rising moon was painting shadows across the park. I heard the distant hoot of an owl. The bark of a fox. The night creatures were abroad. Then I heard a noise I couldn't identify. It sounded like a maniacal laugh. It was quite chilling and my heart did a little flip. A peacock? There had once been peacocks in the park, but I hadn't seen any when I walked to see the gardeners. Besides, peacocks slept at night. And then I noticed light coming from the other wing. It was on the far side, so I couldn't see which room was involved, but in the absolute darkness I could make out a glow. Either someone was outside that wing with a torch or a light had been turned on in one of the forbidden rooms.

I put on my dressing gown and tiptoed out of my room and along the upper hallway to the stairs that led down to the other wing. I crept down, one by one, holding on to the rail. I stood on the bottom step and took a deep breath before tiptoeing forward. The bottom hall was still in complete darkness, but there might be a sliver of light coming out from under one of the doors at the far end. I was about to go ahead and listen at each of the doors when I heard the sound of feet approaching. I retreated and flattened myself against the wall of the staircase. The footsteps came closer and then a figure emerged right in front of me, turning into the forbidden hallway. I put my hand to my mouth so that I didn't cry out. The figure was dressed in a flowing skirt with some kind of shawl over the head. It was swallowed into the darkness of that hallway. I waited to see if a door opened and closed but heard and saw nothing. Then from the darkness that awful maniacal laugh.

I'm afraid my fear got the better of me. I retreated up the stairs and into my room, putting that chair under the door handle again.

Chapter 16

Thursday, June 27, and Friday, June 28

Rude and unhelpful servants, gas taps, a fall down the stairs and now a
    ghost. Goodness, what more can there possibly be?

I lay in bed, my heart still thumping, wondering if what I had seen
was indeed a ghost. The flowing skirt and the shawl over the head
signified a bygone age and way of dress and didn't belong to anyone
on the staff. Joanie and Molly were the only two females, and they
were both slight little things. This woman was taller and straighter,
but certainly not as big as Plunkett, Fernando, or McShea. Besides,
why would any of them be creeping around at night wearing women's
clothes? And what about that laugh? It didn't even sound human. My
mind wandered over demons and vampires . . . subjects I would have
laughed about in the daylight.

I tried to examine what I had seen logically. Having grown up in
a Scottish castle and stayed at various old houses, I was well acquainted
with ghosts. I had seen them for myself at Kensington Palace. But did

ghosts make a sound? I had been alerted by the approaching footsteps. The ghosts I had seen just wafted, moved without effort. And they were accompanied by a sort of chill in the air, an uneasiness that made one shiver.

So I had to conclude that this had to be a real person. But what was she doing at Eynsleigh and whom had she come to visit? I remembered Ben asking about the old woman and then becoming embarrassed and shutting up quickly. Well, I wasn't about to go downstairs again in the darkness. I'd wait until daylight and then I'd quiz Plunkett.

I lay in bed, my mind still in turmoil. So many things that didn't feel quite right about this house and now this. Sir Hubert had sensed something was wrong from far away. Then why the devil didn't he come home and put everything right, I thought angrily. I didn't want to be here alone. I couldn't cope with it alone. I wanted an ally. Most of all I wanted Darcy's arms around me. Not long now, I told myself, and I'd have him lying in bed beside me, his arms around me, and then . . . I stopped myself from going into more detail about the next bit.

Morning dawned bright and sunny. Looking out onto the dewy grass, it was hard to believe how unnerved I had been last night. Now I was determined to get at the truth. I washed, dressed and went down to breakfast. There was no sign of kidneys or kedgeree on the sideboard, but there were scrambled egg and toast. Clearly I was to live on nursery rations, whatever I said to Fernando. Hurry up, Queenie, I thought. At least if she was cooking I wouldn't go hungry. That girl loved to eat! Then, of course, I worried that she was having such a good time with Darcy's relatives that she wouldn't want to rejoin me. I remembered all the times I had wanted to get rid of her, wished she'd go away, and now I was actually pining for her. How strange life is.

After breakfast I summoned Plunkett.

"You rang, my lady?"

My nerves were already frayed. I almost snapped back, "Who else do you think pulled the bell rope? The ghost?" But I took a deep breath. "Plunkett, last night I saw a person walking down the lower hallway of the other wing. A female person, Plunkett."

His face twitched nervously. "Maybe it was Joanie going to check on something."

"Check on what?" I asked. "You told me yourself that the rooms were to be kept locked. Besides, this person was bigger than Joanie and wore strange clothing . . . a big shawl over her head and flowing skirts."

He was shifting anxiously from foot to foot, something I had noticed he did when nervous. "You must have been mistaken, my lady. Of course it is possible that the house is haunted, although I have never seen a ghost myself. But these old houses . . . well, they are bound to have at least one ghost in residence, aren't they?"

"It wasn't a ghost, Plunkett. I heard footsteps. Ghosts make no sound—at least, I suppose they might moan, but their feet don't tap on the floor. Now, clearly you know something about this, so I'm going to have to ask you to give me the key to those rooms so that I can take a look for myself and find out the truth."

"I told you, my lady. I can't give you the key," he said, but he was rattled now.

"Then I shall have to take measures on my own. I will report to the police that I saw an intruder last night and we need to know if anything was taken. They will do a thorough investigation, I expect, and want you to open every door."

He blinked a couple of times; then he said, "Very well, my lady. We were trying to keep it from you. If we'd had time to prepare and had known you were coming we could have handled things differently."

"What are you trying to say, Plunkett?"

He couldn't meet my gaze. He was staring down at his boots. "The master's mother."

"Sir Hubert's mother? She's here? Why wasn't I told?"

"She didn't want anyone to know," he said. "She didn't want her son to know." He shifted uneasily from foot to foot. "She was going . . .

well, a bit senile, you know. Acting unpredictably. Roaming out at night. So before he went away last time he put her into one of these homes where they take care of elderly gentlefolk. For her own safety, you understand. Well, she didn't like it. She's not the sort of person who likes being bossed around or restrained in her room. So she escaped and came back here a few months ago. And made us promise not to tell anyone she is here, because she won't be sent back."

"Then I must go and meet her. Does she know that I am in the house? She will think me rude that I haven't done so."

"Maybe not, my lady," he said. "She is . . . well, she's not quite all there now. Lives in her own little world. Sleeps most of the day and tries to wander around at night."

"Do you think it right that she remains here? Wouldn't she be receiving better care at the home she escaped from?"

"She's being well looked after here," he said. "We've hired a woman to be with her day and night. She still enjoys her food and wine, that's for sure. I would have written to Sir Hubert but the only address we have for him is the British consul in Buenos Aires. It could be months before he gets the letter and in the meantime it's not up to us to make decisions for her ladyship."

"I suppose not," I said. "Nevertheless I would like to meet her once. Maybe she will welcome a chat with one of her own kind. It may bring her back to the real world for a while."

"You never know, my lady. Sometimes she can seem almost normal; then other times she's off with the fairies."

"When would you suggest a good time, then, Plunkett?"

"Maybe after dark, my lady. Like I say, she sleeps for most of the day and then wanders around all night. Like a ruddy bat . . . Sorry for the language, my lady."

I actually laughed. "Then you shall take me to see her when it gets dark," I said.

"Very well, my lady. I'll inform Mrs. Pritchard, who looks after her."

After he had gone I felt a lot better. Now so many things were explained: the light and noises from the far wing. The bottle of good wine in the kitchen. Maybe even the fact that we were eating so poorly, since the good stuff was going to the Dowager Lady Anstruther. Maybe she even had a taste for Spanish food, which was why Fernando had been hired. And then another idea came to me. Maybe she was the one who had turned on the gas tap and been through my things. I'd have to see about getting a lock for my door.

After breakfast I went into the library to look for *Burke's Peerage.* It's a volume that every family like ours has on hand. The library was one of the rooms that had not been opened up and dusted yet, and the big table in the center was still covered in a dust sheet. Sunlight came in through leaded panes and dust motes danced in the air. The walls were lined with ancient leather tomes and a spiral staircase led up to a gallery above. It was a splendid room, even shrouded and dusty as it was now, and I stood there, looking around with satisfaction, wondering how many generations had read these same books and realizing with awe that this was now effectively mine. Golly. I pulled the dust sheet off the table and chairs, creating a cloud that made me cough. Then I starting searching the shelves. Eventually I found what I was looking for. I sat at the leather-topped table as the sunbeams fell onto me. It was all very tranquil and timeless and for the first time I was able to appreciate that this lovely house was my home. Oh, there were annoyances at the moment, but soon all would be smoothed over and Darcy and I would have a wonderful life here.

I found the entry for Cecil Peregrin, Eighth Earl of Malmsbury, Kilton Castle, Cumberland. This must be the son of the old lady who'd employed Plunkett. So far away, I thought. What had made Plunkett take a position there? By his speech he was clearly a Londoner. I found writing paper in the drawer and wrote a letter to the current earl. I asked him whether the family had been satisfied with Plunkett and whether he had been given a good letter of recommendation. Then I had the Bentley brought around again. I wanted to post my letter to Mummy and also to go into Haywards Heath to visit the solicitor.

"If you just have letters to post, one of us can bicycle into the village, my lady," Plunkett said, sounding quite pleasant for once. I suspected he was relieved that I now knew the secret of Lady Anstruther.

"Kind of you, but I have some errands to run in Haywards Heath as well," I said. "Oh, and about the telephone . . ."

"It will be hooked up this morning, my lady."

I was feeling quite pleased with myself as I drove between the high hedges and was brought back to the realities of life only when a tractor emerged from a field right in front of me and I had to slam on the brakes, missing by inches the cart of manure he was towing. After that I drove with more caution. The letters were posted. I exchanged pleasantries with the postmistress about how fine the weather was and how one could never expect it to last but she hoped it would last until the village fete on Sunday.

"If we'd known you were going to be living at Eynsleigh I'm sure the vicar would have asked you to open it," she said. "As it is they've got some girl who was runner-up for Miss Sussex Dairy Queen. She'll show a lot of bosom and leg if you ask me."

I was about to leave when she added, "There was a letter came for you this morning." Hope leaped in me that it was from Queenie, answering me that she was on her way. But then I remembered I had only written to her yesterday and even though the post office was incredibly speedy I couldn't expect a reply from Ireland for a few more days. Then the postmistress went on, "Awful grand, it were. With a crest on it and all."

"Thank you," I said. "May I have it?"

"I sent it out with Jones on his morning round, my lady. It will have been delivered at Eynsleigh by now."

Then the worry returned. Had Plunkett got his hands on my letter and was maybe reading it before he delivered it to me? Or had he even destroyed it? I couldn't see any reason to do so, other than sheer spite, but it certainly had not been on the salver in the front hall when I had left.

I drove on into the small town of Haywards Heath and found the offices of Eaton and Harris, solicitors. When I introduced myself there were whispered conversations and I was whisked through immediately to the inner sanctum, where Old Mr. Eaton resided.

He rose from his seat and extended a hand to me. "My dear Lady Georgiana. Welcome. What a pleasure to see you here. Please, take a seat."

He had a shock of white hair and would have made an excellent Father Christmas. I pulled up a comfortable leather chair. "Mr. Eaton, I wonder if you have been told that Sir Hubert has invited me to make Eynsleigh my home after my wedding?"

He nodded, still smiling. "He did discuss the matter with me. I told him it was an excellent idea. When do you intend to move in?"

"I am actually staying there at the moment. Sir Hubert suggested I have everything to my liking before I take up residence with my husband."

"Splendid." He rubbed his hands together. "And you find the place to your liking?"

"The house is as lovely as I remember it," I said, "but to be truthful I'm having a little problem with the staff. They don't seem to be of the level of Sir Hubert's former servants."

"No? I am surprised." He was staring at me with raised eyebrows. Since his eyebrows were like two large prawns this was quite startling. "Of course we were sorry to lose such a wonderful old retainer as Rogers, but I thought that we had managed to find a suitable replacement. So Plunkett is not what you expected?"

"He is not," I said. "And I don't think he'd be what Sir Hubert wanted either."

Mr. Eaton shook his head. "Dear me. He came with the highest of references. His former employer seemed most satisfied with his work."

"That's what I find puzzling," I said. "Maybe he sees me as a young thing of no consequence and therefore is not bothering too much, but his manner is not that of a good butler."

"This is most distressing," Mr. Eaton said.

"Did you interview him personally?" I asked.

"No, I did not, but I put the matter in the hands of a good agency in London and they wrote to say that they had found a suitable replacement for Rogers and sent me a copy of his reference."

"Do you still have that copy?" I asked.

"Yes, I'm sure we do." He rang a little bell and a middle-aged woman in a navy two-piece suit appeared. She was the sort of woman who has every hair in place. "Miss Tompkins. Would you bring me Sir Hubert's file? We need the reference for the latest butler."

"Certainly, Mr. Eaton," she replied and left the room only to return remarkably quickly with a large file box. This she opened; then she handed Mr. Eaton an envelope. He opened it and passed it to me.

I read:

It is with great pleasure that I recommend my former butler, Charles Plunkett. He has been exemplary in his duties, most solicitous to his employers and scrupulously honest at all times. His knowledge of wines, of silver and of protocol is unsurpassed and I believe he would be comfortable running even the largest of homes smoothly.

I looked up. "Golly," I said. "I don't know what to think. He has been most slapdash in his behavior toward me."

"That's shocking, my lady. I too do not understand this. Would you like me to give him a talking-to on your behalf?"

"Very kind of you, Mr. Eaton, but I think I shall have to learn to handle my own staff and I had better start now."

"That's the spirit." He clapped those big meaty hands. "Sometimes servants need to be put in their place."

"Let me ask you—if I wanted to dismiss any of the servants, would I be allowed to?"

His face clouded. "Oh, I'm not sure about that one. I mean, if Sir Hubert saw fit to employ someone, one could hardly go against his wishes, at least not without putting the matter to him."

"No, I see that. It's just that the cook, Fernando, is not what I would wish."

"The cook was hired recently, through an agency I believe, after the old cook wished to retire. I think you would be quite within your rights to dismiss him if he didn't prove to be suitable."

"He says he won't leave until Sir Hubert tells him to go."

Now he looked worried. "And do you wish to dismiss him immediately? Can you not give him some time to learn your wishes and your ways?"

"I suppose I could," I said slowly.

"That's the ticket." He beamed. "Now, was there anything else I could do for you?"

"About the money for the household accounts," I said.

"The bank handles it," he said. "The Westminster, here in Haywards Heath. Is there a problem?"

"Well, no." I hesitated, not wanting to hint that Sir Hubert was being stingy with us. "It's just that the amount was adequate when there were just household staff, but if my husband and I want to entertain . . ."

"Then I suppose you would have to do so out of your own funds, if you do not find the amount adequate, my lady." I was being told off. Clearly he thought Sir Hubert had done the right thing and I was somehow being ungrateful. Perhaps I was. After all, I was being given free accommodation and a staff to run it. So Mr. Eaton was quite right. I should be supplementing the amount from my own purse. . . . If I had a purse, that was. Oh dear, it looks as if it will be rice and custard for the rest of my days here.

After a few more pleasantries I thanked him and left. I realized, as I drove away, that I had not asked him about Mrs. Holbrook's bequest and whether it came from Sir Hubert. Actually I was glad I had not done so. He might have seen it as none of my business what Sir Hubert did with his money. The one thing I had learned was that Plunkett had been an exemplary employee with Lady Malmsbury—unless he had forged his reference? That was not unknown. I'd have to wait to see what the current earl said about him.

Chapter 17

This evening I am to meet the Dowager Lady Anstruther. A little
nervous about this. I'm not sure I'm good with batty old
women. Also I'm of two minds whether to write to Sir Hubert
about her. I mean, if he had put her in a home for her safety,
wouldn't he want to know that she had escaped? I'm not bound
by Plunkett's promise to her. The problem is I have no idea
where to reach him, other than the British consulate in Buenos
Aires. He wrote to me from a hotel in Chile, but he'd be long
gone from there. How utterly frustrating! I wish I knew what
the right thing is to do in this circumstance. I suppose she is safe
here and can be looked after until he returns. And it's not my
problem.

As I drove up the drive to the house I was again struck by the great
beauty. The red brick glowing. The leaded, paned windows sparkling
in the sunlight. The strange, curly Elizabethan chimneys, the great oak

and beech trees providing a backdrop and the fountain now playing merrily. Perfect, I muttered. I pictured myself showing it to Darcy for the first time. When was he going to come home? I wondered. Why didn't he ever write? Of course I knew the answer to that: because he couldn't let anyone know where he was. Wretched man!

I left the Bentley and went up the front steps. Plunkett met me as I was crossing the foyer.

"A nice drive, my lady?"

"Yes, thank you, Plunkett. Has the post been delivered yet?"

"Why, yes, my lady. There are letters for you waiting in the morning room. Shall I bring coffee?"

"Yes, please do."

I went through feeling very pleased. All was now sorted out. Plunkett's behavior to me could be put down to his nervousness at having to conceal a batty relative and to worry about her behavior. Now I finally had a butler.

I saw the two letters lying on a silver salver, placed on a low table by the window. I noticed, with trepidation, that one indeed bore the royal coat of arms. I looked at the other in the vain hope that by some miracle it could be from Queenie. Then I recognized Belinda's handwriting and smiled.

I opened the royal one first. One does. It was in Her Majesty's own hand, not written by her secretary. So a personal note. I read:

My dear Georgiana,

We have received your invitation and gladly accept. I trust your preparations for the upcoming wedding are going well. Elizabeth and Margaret are excited to be bridesmaids. Margaret especially—she loves dancing around in frilly frocks. Elizabeth would be quite happy to wear her riding britches all the time! I gather the dressmaker will have the dresses ready for a first fitting soon. I am anxious to hear details.

As to the guest list: I wonder if we should not include the Bavarian princess you never did manage to host (the real one, I mean). Who else are you planning to invite from among our European relatives? If there are any monarchs involved I feel that the king and I should offer them hospitality at the palace.

Regarding your honeymoon: the king and I would like to offer you the use of Balmoral before we all descend on the place for the usual shoot in August. As you know it is so quiet and peaceful and the staff will take care of your needs.

I looked up and stared out of the window. Then I sighed. Balmoral wasn't exactly what I had in mind for a honeymoon. After all, I had grown up in a similar Scottish castle a few miles away. They tend to be cold, drafty and bleak. What's more, it had tartan carpets and tartan wallpaper, and there isn't anything much more depressing than that. Darcy had said he would come up with somewhere to go, but I had pictured a romantic setting like Lake Maggiore, where we had just stayed, or even Nice, where Mummy had a charming little villa. One could hardly enjoy a honeymoon with oodles of servants shadowing one's every move. Maids would barge in with morning tea, thus stifling any bouts of early ardor. But could I say "No, thank you" to her? And had Darcy planned anything better?

I went on to the second letter, from Belinda. She told me how hard she was working and how satisfied she was with her progress. I'd be thrilled with the dress, she was sure. And as for those bridesmaids gowns . . . she thought they were exactly what little princesses should wear to a wedding. She had been requested to bring the designs to their residence so that the duke and duchess could see them, and she wondered if I'd come up to London on that day so that I could see my dress and accompany her to 145 Piccadilly. She added that she was surprised to find they weren't living in a palace. She was a bit nervous about showing her designs to royalty and I knew them well. She went on.

How are you enjoying being lady of the manor?

I must pop down and see you when you've settled in. Rather a change from when you first came to London and camped out in your family home eating baked beans because they were the only things you knew how to cook. And speaking of cooking . . . my new maid, Huddlestone, will have to go, I'm afraid. She can't, or won't, cook. She says she was trained to be a lady's maid, not a general dogsbody. Since I can't or won't cook either I've been living on hampers from Harrods and Fortnum's. Rather an expensive way to eat, don't you think? So I regret that Huddlestone must go. She was a sour-faced old puss, anyway. No sense of humor and very prudish. If I ever did invite a gentleman home (which I won't, of course, having renounced men for the rest of my days), she'd be so disapproving that the poor chap would flee in dismay!

I smiled as I folded the letter. Poor Belinda. She and I were both having servant problems, but I thought that hers were more easily solved. I glanced down again at the queen's letter. One should respond to the queen immediately, but I did not want to accept Balmoral. In the end I thanked her and said that I did not know what plans my future husband had for our honeymoon as he was away at the moment, but I would let her know as soon as he returned. Then I stamped the letter and went to put it on the hall table. That was when I noticed a telephone sitting there. A small miracle! I decided to try it out immediately and call Belinda. Then I decided to telephone Mummy first. She might need chivvying along to check on the agency that had sent Plunkett.

"Operator, would you connect me with Claridge's, please?" I said. I waited and then the Claridge's operator came on the line.

"You have the former duchess of Rannoch staying with you, I believe," I said. (Mummy was eager to bolt from the realities of being a duchess but more reluctant to give up the title, which she used whenever she was in London.)

"We do, madam. But I'm not sure—"

"This is Lady Georgiana, her daughter," I cut in.

"Of course, my lady. One moment please." And I was connected.

"Hello?" I heard Mummy's voice, a trifle breathless. Then: "Thank God, Georgie. I've been trying and trying to reach you. I called and called what I thought was the right number, but nobody answered. I was desperate. I didn't know what to do."

"What's wrong, Mummy?" She sounded distraught.

"Everything. Everything is wrong. Oh, Georgie, my life is in ruins."

"Max has found out about some secret of your past?"

"Worse than that. Far worse than that." And she gave a great gulping sob.

Personally I couldn't think of what might be far worse than Max finding out that she had been sleeping with other men, but she gave a second sob before she said, "His father has died."

"I'm so sorry," I said because that is what is expected of one on such occasions. Not that I had met Max's father, and I didn't have much warm feeling about Nazis.

"You're sorry? Not nearly as sorry as I am." Another sob. "Georgie. Max telephoned me to say that the wedding is off. He will have to take over the running of his father's business interests, which are many. That I can understand. But he says that his mother is distraught and he will have to stay with her and comfort her."

"Well, I can understand that too," I said. "He's being a dutiful son. And it only means postponing the wedding, doesn't it?"

"No. It doesn't." She sounded quite hysterical now. "I always knew that his mother was strictly Lutheran and quite prudish and didn't approve of me. So Max says that in her current state of distress he wouldn't feel right going ahead with the marriage. In fact in the circumstances I should stay in London."

As all of this gushed out I couldn't help wondering how Max managed to convey this over the telephone. His command of the English language had always been minimal and Mummy's German was non-existent. But I had to be sympathetic.

"Give him time, Mummy. Let him sort things out with his mother and then he'll come back to you."

"He won't. I know it. I'll never see him again. The man I loved. The man I worshipped." (You can tell why she was a famous actress, can't you?) "I'm doomed, Georgie. Doomed to a life of loneliness and despair. And how am I going to live?"

"I'm sure Max won't be callous enough to cut you off without a penny," I said. "And you do have that villa on Lake Lugano he bought you."

"He bought it for us," she said. "How do I know if I'm even welcome there any longer? I don't think he put it in my name. I should have insisted. I should have been more demanding. But I've always been so naïve. So trusting . . ."

Actually she had done rather well from most of her various liaisons. "You do have that little villa in Nice. That's all yours," I reminded her.

"Yes, but one can only go to Nice in the winter. Nobody goes there in the off-season. What will I do then? Where will I go? I have nowhere to spend the summer and I certainly can't afford to stay at Claridge's for months and months. I may become a pauper. A beggar on the streets."

"Mummy, calm down," I said. "You are always welcome to come here. It's pretty basic at the moment but it is a roof over your head and you can stay here until you hear from Max again and decide about your future."

"You are such a dear, kind girl," she said. "I was hoping you'd say that. I know you and Darcy will be living there as newlyweds and I certainly wouldn't want to be in the way."

"That's still over a month away. Come down now. You always loved this house. You'll feel so much better and be able to look at things in perspective."

"Yes," she said. "Yes. You're right. That's what I'll do. And I'll give Max time to miss me and realize he can't live without me and that he'd rather have me than his boring old mother!"

You couldn't keep Mummy's fighting spirit down for long!

Chapter 18

**Now Mummy is complicating things by coming down to Eynsleigh.
And I still have to meet the old woman tonight. Crikey. Feeling
rather apprehensive, actually.**

The news that the former duchess of Rannoch was coming to join me
was not met with great joy by the staff at Eynsleigh. I informed Plunkett that I would need one of the best bedrooms cleaned and aired,
and that Fernando should be informed that from now on meals of the
right standard should be prepared.

"I will inform him, my lady, but I rather think he does his best
with limited resources."

"I saw a bottle of Châteauneuf-du-Pape on the kitchen table when
I went down there," I said. "If I had not requested it for dinner, I
wonder who would have drunk it. Lady Anstruther or the staff? That
does not sound to me like limited resources. I've already made it clear
that I expect the best produce from the estate to be delivered to the

kitchen each morning. And the money from the sale of excess produce can now go toward ordering decent food for myself and my mother. If absolutely necessary I shall select the produce myself and collect the income from the shop."

He swallowed hard. I watched his Adam's apple dance up and down above his stiff collar. "That will not be necessary, my lady. I shall ensure, personally, that food is up to your standard."

"Thank you, Plunkett. That will be all."

I watched him walk away. Mummy was used to getting her own way. I wondered if she'd have more success with him than I had had so far.

Two women from the village appeared with lots of clanking of buckets and mops, and the bedrooms in my wing were given a good cleaning. I selected the one overlooking the forecourt and drive for my mother and inspected as they made up a big brass bed for her. She wouldn't be arriving until the next morning, as there were things she still had to do in London, including collecting shoes from her little Italian shoemaker. I wondered about all the wedding and trousseau outfits she had ordered. Poor Mummy. I think she was looking forward to the security of being married to a very rich man, even if he was German and in league with Nazis.

THAT AFTERNOON I went into the gardens to pick flowers for Mummy's room. I had Joanie put them into vases and carry them up; then I stood looking around, making sure it was suitable for a former duchess and a very picky lady. While I was up there I heard footsteps on the gravel. I looked out of the window and saw a rather distinguished-looking elderly man walking up toward the house. The day was now a warm one. The sky was clear and in spite of this he was carrying an umbrella. He was wearing a dark three-piece suit and a bowler hat. Halfway up the drive he paused to take out a handkerchief, remove the hat and pat that bald head before disappearing from my view as he approached the front door. I heard the doorbell ring. I waited, trying to suppress my curiosity, but Plunkett didn't appear to summon me. I plumped pillows on Mummy's bed and made sure there were no spiderwebs at the back of her wardrobe, all the time wondering who the man was and why I was not being called. Of course I realized that the caller was probably not for me. Only a few people knew I was living here now. But should I not be at least greeting any visitor to the house?

When I finally went downstairs Joanie was hovering in the front hall, dusting statues. "Oh, there you are, my lady," she said. "Would you like to take your tea out on the lawn today? Mr. Plunkett thought it might be a nice idea. We've put out a table and deck chair. Under the big beech tree."

"Thank you. That would lovely," I said. "But where is Mr. Plunkett? And where is the visitor who arrived recently?"

"I didn't see any visitor, my lady," she said.

"A man came to the house. The front doorbell rang."

"I'm sorry. I was at the back of the house, cleaning the rooms we hadn't touched yet. Mr. Plunkett said that the duchess would want everything just so."

I went through to the drawing room, but it was unoccupied. I tried the morning room and the library. Finally in frustration I rang the bell. After a long wait Plunkett appeared. "You rang, my lady?"

"I did, Plunkett. I wanted to know about the visitor. Where is he?"

"The gentleman came for Lady Anstruther, my lady. Apparently wanting to appraise her jewelry or something. I told him she wasn't up to seeing visitors. He was a bit put out, having come all this way. She must have written to him in one of her more lucid moments."

"So where is he now?"

"He left again in a huff," Plunkett said. "I offered him a cup of tea but he wouldn't stay. Said he had more important calls to make in the neighborhood."

"So why was he not taken to Lady Anstruther?" I said. "Surely it was not up to you to decide whether she was up to receiving visitors or not."

"You haven't met her yet, my lady," he said. "The gentleman would have been shocked. And she doesn't like men, which is why I try to stay well away from her room. She can be . . . well, you'll probably see for yourself."

"At the very least you should have notified me if we had a visitor to the house, Plunkett," I said. "As current mistress of the place it would only be right that I should greet him."

"He didn't stay long enough for that. When he heard he couldn't see the old lady he didn't even want to come in and sit down. He said he had important calls to make while he was in this part of the world."

Joanie appeared then to tell me that my tea was ready under the beech tree. This time there was a decent pot of tea and cucumber sandwiches. We were improving.

∗

It was close to nine o'clock that evening when Plunkett came to announce that Lady Anstruther was now expecting a visit from me.

"She seems quite calm at the moment, her nurse tells me," he said, "but she can be volatile. Be prepared to duck. She throws things."

Golly.

I took a deep breath as I followed Plunkett through the great gallery between the wings and turned toward the room she was occupying.

"I forgot to ask you." Plunkett stopped short in the dark hallway. "How are you with birds?"

"With birds?" It came out as a squeak.

"Lady Plunkett keeps birds," he said. "Parrots. That sort of thing. Very fond of birds, she is."

"Oh, I don't mind birds," I said. "I like all sorts of animals."

"That's good. Then you won't be alarmed." He went ahead of me and tapped on the door at the far end of the hall. It was opened by a woman dressed in a nurse's gray uniform. "Come on in," she said. The door was shut behind me. I noticed Plunkett had not followed me into the room.

The drapes were shut and the room was lit only by a couple of standard lamps in corners so that there were areas of deep shadow. There was an unpleasant smell that I couldn't quite identify. I felt a shiver of alarm as a figure rose from a high-backed chair and came toward me. She was all in black with a black shawl, trimmed with jet beads, over her head. Her face, in the deep shadow of the room, looked like a skeleton. She was wearing too much makeup, her mouth a bright red gash, not applied with much skill, and her cheeks white with powder.

"Who is this?" she asked, tilting her head to one side, like a bird herself. "What's she doing here?"

"This is Lady Georgiana," the nurse said in a gentle voice. "She used to live here when she was a small girl. You might remember her."

"I don't remember her. She's an interloper," the old woman said. She spoke in a hoarse whisper. Then she sighed. "I don't remember anything. It's all a fog."

Then suddenly there was a flapping sound and a bird came flying across the room. A large bird. In the half-darkness it looked like the size of an eagle. Without warning it landed on my head.

"Oh, Charlie likes you," the old lady said, chuckling now. "He doesn't take to everybody."

I could feel the claws digging into my scalp.

"Who's a pretty boy now?" said a voice on my head. "Give Charlie a treat."

"Stand very still," the old lady said. "Any sudden move might frighten him."

Might frighten him? I thought. I'm standing here with a large bird on my head. I wondered how I could tactfully ask her to call him off, then realized it was probably a test of whether she liked me or not.

"Well, girl?" she said, peering at me now. "Cat got your tongue?"

"How do you do, Lady Anstruther," I said. "I'm Georgiana. I trust you are well?"

"Of course I'm not well, stupid girl," she said. "I'm eighty-five years old and I have rheumatism, my digestion is terrible and I have a constant headache."

I wasn't surprised, if large birds constantly landed on her head!

There was another sound of fluttering and a small yellow bird, a parakeet, I believe, flew around the room a few times; then the old lady stretched out a hand, bedecked with multiple rings, and the bird landed on it.

"Hello, my precious. Were you feeling left out?" she whispered to the bird, then brought it up to her mouth to give it a kiss.

Charlie, still on my head, danced up and down and gave a piercing laugh/shriek that nearly made my heart stop. "Give Charlie a kiss. Give Charlie a kiss!" he shrieked.

"So jealous." She chuckled again. "He can't stand it when I make a fuss of Rani." She held out her arm and the bird ran up to her shoulder. "I call her Rani after my time in India. I was Empress of India once, you know. There was a mutiny and they deposed me. I barely escaped with my life."

"You were never Empress of India. Your husband was in the army in India once; that's why you were there, remember?" the nurse said.

"Don't contradict me!" the old woman snapped. "I know who I was. I do remember some things. But I don't remember that girl. What is she doing here? She's come from the institution, hasn't she? Come to take me back?"

"No, Lady Anstruther," I said. "I haven't come from the home."

"Because I won't go back, you know. I won't. I'll throw myself from the battlements first." She reached out a hand to the nurse, who stood ready to aid her. "It was terrible," she said. "Everyone there was insane. My son put me there, with crazy people. And I'm not mad. I'm as sane as anyone."

"Yes, of course you are, Lady Anstruther," the nurse said. "Now, why don't you sit down and let's take Charlie off this poor lady's head."

"He likes her," she said. "He doesn't take to everyone. He pecked nearly all the inmates at the asylum. He can give a vicious peck when he's angry."

I had visions of my scalp being attacked. Strangely enough he wasn't that heavy, but his claws were certainly sharp.

The nurse eased the old lady back into the chair.

"So what's she doing here?" she asked, pointing a finger at me. "If you tell me she hasn't come from the asylum, what does she want?"

"I've come to live here, Lady Anstruther," I said. "Your son invited me to make this my home, as he is away so much. He was very fond of me when I was a little girl. He wanted to adopt me."

"Rubbish," she said. "Utter nonsense. My son didn't go around adopting orphans."

"I wasn't an orphan," I said. "My mother was married to your son at the time."

"Utter lies. I don't remember you!" She pointed a finger again. "I know what you want. You've come to steal my home, haven't you? Come to throw me out into the cold? Or to send me back there!"

She stood up again suddenly, making me take an involuntary step back and causing Charlie to dig his claws into my hair.

"No, really, Lady Anstruther. You are quite safe here, I promise," I said hastily, as I sensed she might advance on me.

She grabbed a silver-tipped cane and waved it in my direction. "Send her away, do you hear me? I don't want her in my house any longer. She's a scheming vixen, I can tell. Send her away!" And without warning she picked up an ashtray from the table and hurled it in my direction. Luckily her aim wasn't very good. It crashed onto the floor beside me and shattered into a thousand pieces. Charlie flapped and took off from my head, taking some of my hair with him. As she looked for another object to hurl, the nurse stepped between us. "I think you had better go, while the going is good, your ladyship," she said. "She gets quite violent when she's riled up."

I didn't need to be told twice. What with birds and hurling ashtrays I had had quite enough.

Chapter 19

Mummy comes today. Normally I am not thrilled to see her, but this
time I can't wait. Having someone else in the house will make all
the difference. Crikey, Sir Hubert's mother was rather frightening.
No wonder he wanted her put in a home. I think I should write to
the British consul in Buenos Aires and ask him to trace Sir Hubert.
I think he'd want to know about his mother. If she were confined
to her room, that would be one thing, but I've already caught her
wandering around once, and my gas tap was turned on . . .

I must have jinxed the fine weather by sitting out sunning myself on
the lawn yesterday, because I awoke to an absolute deluge. Poor
Mummy, I thought, having to travel in this weather. Everything seemed
to be going wrong in her life at the moment. I lingered on this thought.
What if she and Max did not reunite? What if she wanted to live with
us permanently? I knew it was a big house and she could have a suite
of rooms, but did I want her hovering during the first year of my mar-

riage? Then I told myself that my mother was not likely to stay unattached for long. She liked men too much. To be frank, she liked sex too much. She'd latch on to some poor, unsuspecting banker or American millionaire or South American polo player and she'd be off again, quite happy, Max quite forgotten. Thus reassured, I went down to breakfast. Again it was scrambled eggs. I rang for Fernando.

"My mother, the Duchess of Rannoch, is arriving today, Fernando. She is used to the highest standards. She has been staying at Claridge's. She has a villa in Nice, and another on Lake Lugano, and she has been living in Berlin. Nursery food will not be good enough for her. Do you understand?"

"If she live all over Europa, she like good Continental food, not boring English food," he said. "I make for her."

"That's just it," I said. "She likes good Continental food. Things like caviar. Now, I know we are on a budget, but I expect you to do your best. You would not want to see my mother when she is not happy."

I told him to make sure there were plenty of strawberries and raspberries and that he should buy cream and a decent piece of meat for dinner. He didn't look at all keen at having to ride into town on his bicycle, so I took pity and telephoned the local butcher to have them deliver meat.

"Pork chops would be acceptable," I said. "And maybe a leg of lamb."

"You don't want the usual rump steak then?" he asked.

"Oh yes. Definitely rump steak," I said. I put the receiver down thoughtfully. So Lady Anstruther, and/or the staff, was eating rump steak while I had bits of unidentifiable scraps in rice. This was coming to an end right now. If she was, as Plunkett put it so succinctly, off with the fairies, then she wasn't getting any more special treatment.

I waited for Mummy all morning, occasionally glancing out of the window as I sat in the drawing room. I spotted one of the gardeners, looking quite miserable as he pushed a wheelbarrow, making heavy weather of the mud. At least they were finally doing some work. That was good. Lunchtime came and I went through to the dining room. It was fish again, this time covered in a tomato sauce. It wasn't too bad, actually, and it was followed by strawberries. I realized then that the gardener had probably been coming up to the house to deliver produce and felt rather guilty about making him work in the rain.

I was halfway through my strawberries when I heard the doorbell. I wanted to jump up but protocol demanded that I stay put until my butler announced the visitor. I expected Mummy to sweep past him and burst into the room, shouting, "Darling, I'm here."

When this didn't happen I was curious. Another visitor for the old lady, perhaps? Then Plunkett appeared. "There is a person to see you, my lady."

I didn't think that anyone in his right mind could describe my mother as a person.

"What sort of person, Plunkett?"

"A rather common person, my lady. Looks like a drowned rat. I would have sent her away but she says you were expecting her. She says she came as quickly as she could."

I jumped up and forced myself not to run to the foyer. Queenie was standing there in a puddle of water, looking indeed like a drowned rat.

"Watcher, miss," she said. "Blimey, it ain't half wet."

"Queenie. You came." I beamed at her.

"Well, I thought it sounded like you needed me, and Lady Whyte said that my first duty was to you. So I said Bob's yer uncle and here I am."

"Did you walk all the way from the station?" She looked so pathetic standing there, water running down her face and dripping from her sodden clothes onto the floor.

"Oh no, miss. I hitched a ride with a baker's wagon. But he dropped me at the gate and it ain't half a long way up the drive."

"Yes, it is," I said. "We must get you into dry clothes and give you something warm to drink."

I turned to Plunkett. "This is my maid, Queenie," I said. "She's come all the way from Ireland to help out. Please find a bedroom for her where she can change her clothes and then take her down to the kitchen for a cup of tea."

"Very good, my lady." Plunkett looked at Queenie with distaste. "If you'll come this way. I'm Plunkett, the butler, and you'll be reporting to me. In future you will use the servants' entrance at the back of the house on the lower level, is that clear?"

"Bob's yer uncle, ducks," she said.

I watched her following him down the hall, leaving a trail of drips behind her. I don't think I've ever been happier to see anyone.

When Queenie had changed I took her to meet Fernando. "This young lady will be assisting you with the cooking from now on," I said. "She knows what I like to eat."

Then I retreated and left them to it. A little later I heard raised voices coming from the kitchen. I knew it would be the butler's job to go and see what was happening, but I'm afraid I couldn't resist.

"What the bloody hell do you call this?" Queenie was saying. "This ain't no cup of tea. This is bleedin' dishwater. And where are the cakes and biscuits? What have you been feeding my lady—mouse droppings?"

I stood, unnoticed, in the doorway.

"Go on, bugger off," she said, giving him a hefty shove. "I'm going to make a decent pot of tea. And then I'll want plenty of butter and flour and I'm going to whip up a batch of shortbread."

I retreated again. Fernando was looking rather scared. I would be too. Queenie was a large girl and quite alarming when riled. O'Shea came into the morning room a little later with a tray of tea and shortbread.

"Your girl just baked for you, my lady," he said. "Jesus, Mary and Joseph, but she's a good cook. She let me try a piece of that shortbread.

Fair melts in your mouth. Will she be taking over from Fernando?"
Clearly he did not appreciate Spanish food either.

"That we'll have to see, O'Shea. For now she's just going to help
him learn what I like to eat."

"My, but she's a fine, strapping girl, isn't she just?"

Wonders would never cease. O'Shea was attracted to Queenie! I
tried not to grin.

"How long have you been here, O'Shea?" I asked.

"Coming up for two years now. I've never actually seen the master
yet. Mr. Rogers hired me."

"Oh, so you were here before Plunkett?"

"I was, my lady."

"And Joanie?"

"She was hired just after me."

So two of them had been here when Rogers fell down the stairs.
Interesting. Although I couldn't see Joanie pushing a large man down
the stairs and McShea seemed just too nice. Perhaps it was an accident
after all.

I had just finished my second cup of good strong tea and probably
my fourth piece of shortbread when I heard the sound of a motorcar.
I looked up to see a taxi arriving. The driver jumped out and held up
a great umbrella as a small blond person got out. I hurried to the front
door.

Mummy was all in black, making her light complexion look ghostly
white. She wore a small pillbox hat with a black veil over her eyes and
she held out her hands when she saw me. "Georgie, darling. My angel.
My savior." And she flung herself into my arms.

Plunkett had arrived on the scene. Mummy, ever alert even in her
most dramatic moments, noticed him.

"And who is this delightful young man?"

Plunkett could not, in his best moments, be described as either
delightful or young. He went red.

"I'm Plunkett, Your Grace. The butler."

"What happened to Rogers? I used to adore him."

"He died, Mummy," I said.

"How sad. But he was quite old, wasn't he?"

I was going to say that he fell down the stairs and watch Plunkett's face but then I reminded myself that Plunkett wasn't even hired at the time that Rogers died. So if Rogers's death wasn't an accident, I couldn't blame it on Plunkett.

"Well, I'm glad to meet you, Plunkett," my mother said, turning on that charm that had made men across the globe go weak at the knees. "I know you're going to take care of me splendidly."

"I'll do my best, Your Grace," he said. "Do I take it you are in mourning? Her ladyship didn't mention it."

"I am, Plunkett. My fiancé's father died. So tragic. And my darling daughter invited me down here so that I wouldn't be alone in my sorrow."

"My condolences, Your Grace."

He looked up as the taxi driver staggered up the steps with a trunk. "One moment and I'll send for the footman."

McShea came to assist with two valises, a jewelry case, and a hatbox.

"I'll show you the room I've chosen for you, Mummy," I said. I led the way up the stairs. As we passed my room she stopped and put a hand on the doorknob. "Will I not be sleeping in here? This was always my room, I remember. Such an enchanting view."

"I'm sorry but I'd already chosen this room for Darcy and me."

"I see." She gave a huge dramatic sigh. "Still I'm sure what you've selected for me will be better than nothing."

She was good at getting her own way through guilt. But my new-found strength, forged during the last few days, was not going to bend to her will. "You'll be quite comfortable, Mummy, and it may not be for long. You'll probably get bored here and want to go to Nice or Lugano."

"No. I don't think I'll want to be seen in public," she said. "People will talk. One thing I can't stand is pity. This will do quite nicely as a base. When I have conquered the worst of my grief I shall go up to town to see dear Noël. Remember he wanted to write a play for us to star in together? Now I may have to start earning my own crust again and the sooner I start the better."

"Your own crust." I had to laugh. She gave me a haughty stare. I led her down the hall of the wing and opened the door to the room I had selected.

"Oh," she said. "Yes, I suppose this will do." She put on a falsely bright smile. "And it doesn't matter that these north-facing rooms are always so cold. I expect I've a good eiderdown on the bed."

"You have. And it's summer," I pointed out. "And if the room isn't right for you, then take a look around and select the one you like."

"There was quite a pretty one in the other wing, I seem to remember," she said. "The matching room to yours, but in the far corner."

"We're not using the other wing at the moment," I said. "Sir Hubert wanted those rooms kept for his personal use when he returns."

"Is he returning soon?" she asked with a tremble in her voice. "I don't know if I'd be strong enough to face him. I did behave so badly before, you know. I broke his heart. Just like mine has now been broken."

"He won't be back for a while, I don't think," I said. "He's somewhere in South America, climbing the Andes."

"Then he won't mind if I select one of his rooms, will he?"

"Sleep here for now. We'll talk about it later," I said, conscious that Plunkett was still hovering in the doorway, and the tramp of feet indicated that trunks were being carried up the stairs.

"What are you doing about a maid?" The idea suddenly struck me. I didn't think she'd do well with either Queenie or Joanie.

"Claudette will be coming down from London by train with the rest of my things," she said. "I hope there will be a suitable room for her available. She is rather particular."

"I'm sure we can arrange something," I said. I glanced back and saw Plunkett still loitering. "Her Grace's French maid will need a room,

Plunkett. Please select something suitable and have Joanie give it a thorough cleaning."

I took Mummy's arm. "Why don't you take off your hat and gloves and come and have some tea. Queenie's baked shortbread."

"Queenie? Oh God, Georgie, you haven't brought her here. She'll burn the place down."

"She's turned into a decent cook, Mummy. You wait until you taste the shortbread."

I led her down to the sitting room. She looked around, frowning. "I don't remember this room as being so drab," she said. "It certainly needs sprucing up. Wasn't there a lovely ormolu clock on the mantelpiece? And Chinese dogs? And a little cabinet with all kinds of silver knickknacks? I suppose Hubert locks everything up in the bank or in a strong room while he's away."

Another tea tray was brought and Mummy admitted grudgingly that the shortbread was quite edible. Things were going to be improving at Eynsleigh, I thought. I waited until I was sure no servant was hovering, then closed the door and drew her aside.

"There's something I have to tell you," I whispered.

"Oh God, Georgie, you're not pregnant?"

"No, nothing like that. It's Sir Hubert's mother. She's here. In the house."

"Is she? I remember her well. Feisty old thing, isn't she? Completely disapproved of me. But then most mothers do, I find. Pure jealousy, if you ask me. Will she be joining us for dinner?"

"That's just the point. She won't. She's gone quite gaga and is confined to the other wing with a nurse. I went to visit her last night and she has great birds that fly around the room and land on your head and she throws things."

"Good heavens. Why isn't she in some kind of institution, then?"

"She was. Sir Hubert left her in one but she escaped and came here and now she refuses to go back."

"How strange. How tiresome," she said. "So we won't be seeing her?"

"Not unless you want a bird on your head."

"Oh, how ghastly. I can't stand birds." She shuddered. "I don't remember her keeping birds when we visited her."

"Oh, and one more thing. She sleeps all day and wanders at night. I'd lock my door if I were you."

"Gracious, Georgie. It's like moving into a house of horrors. We must put her back in the home as soon as possible."

I chewed on my lip. "I wasn't sure whether it was my place to interfere or not. I planned to write to Sir Hubert, but who knows when he'll get the letter."

"Write to him? We must cable him and tell the embassy to find him immediately. The old bat could set fire to the place or kill us all in our beds."

"She does have a nurse, Mummy. I'll speak to Plunkett to make sure she doesn't get out again."

I sighed as I went to change for dinner. If I had known that running this house would prove so complicated, would I ever have accepted Sir Hubert's kind offer? I took out my evening dress and realized that Mummy would expect me to dress properly for dinner. I rang my bell and eventually Joanie appeared.

"Joanie, I'm not sure if Queenie has time to dress me if she's preparing dinner. Maybe you can do it until we work out a schedule."

"I'm not being paid to be a lady's maid," she said sullenly.

"That's because you don't have the skills yet," I said. "Wouldn't you like to learn and have experience so that you can become a lady's maid and earn more money?"

"Not me," she said. "I don't plan to stay in service longer than I have to. I'm off to America and going to make a fortune."

"There is nothing wrong with ambition, but right now I need someone to help me with doing up my dress."

She put it over my head. "It doesn't seem right, does it?" she said. "Your lot do nothing and us lot have to wait on you."

"No, I suppose it doesn't seem right," I said. "But at least you have a job and a roof over your head, which hasn't been true for a lot of people since the beginning of the Depression. My own father lost all his money and killed himself, so I've had to make do without much help."

The last buttons were being done up when the floor shook and in barged Queenie, red-faced and sweating.

"What's she doing up here?" she demanded. "I came as quick as I could to dress you for dinner, miss."

"I thought you'd be too busy cooking so I asked Joanie to help me."

"I'm your ruddy maid, not her. She ain't taking my place," Queenie said.

"Don't worry, you're welcome to it," Joanie said and stalked out.

"She's trouble, that one," Queenie said. "I'd watch her if I were you, miss."

"In what way?"

"She's too friendly with Fernando for one thing. And she looks sneaky." As she spoke she brushed my hair and fixed a diamanté comb to the curls on one side. "You can do your own face, can't you, or my pudding will burn."

Then she departed again, making the vases on the shelves start to jingle. I sat staring at myself in the dressing table mirror. Queenie might be annoying, but she wasn't stupid. The fact that she had picked up on Joanie as being sneaky . . . Maybe she was right.

MIRACULOUSLY A GOOD dinner appeared: a passable soup, grilled pork chops and meringues with strawberries and cream.

"Not bad," Mummy commented.

I decided it was time for positive reinforcement. I went down to the kitchen.

Two scowling red faces looked up at me.

"Her Grace was pleased with the dinner tonight, Fernando," I said. "Please keep it up."

"I no cook," he said, his face so red it looked as if he was about to explode. "This woman, she tell me to bugger off and she will cook for her mistress."

"Then you did very well, Queenie," I said. "The meringue was delicious."

"Thank you kindly, miss," she said. "But old sourpuss here didn't half make a fuss. We almost came to blows."

"I am cook here," Fernando said in dramatic fashion. "No woman going to come and take my place."

"No woman will take your place until Sir Hubert returns, Fernando," I said, "but since you apparently don't know what English aristocrats like to eat, then I'm putting Queenie in charge of my meals. You may continue to cook for the staff." I turned to Queenie. "You and I will discuss menus in the morning, Queenie."

"Bob's yer uncle, miss."

"Who is this Bob person?" Fernando demanded. "Is he also coming to this house?"

"Just an English expression, Fernando," I said.

"The English, they have ridiculous expressions," he said.

"If you don't like the way we do things, why don't you just bugger off and go home to wherever you came from," Queenie said, giving him a cold stare.

I thought this was a valid question. Why did he stay in England if he clearly couldn't or wouldn't cook English food? And why had anyone hired him?

Chapter 20

I'm feeling so much better now. Mummy is here and will soon whip Plunkett into shape and Queenie has actually become a good cook. Wonders will never cease.

Fortunately the rain had stopped by the next morning and a watery sun poked through an early morning haze. I breakfasted alone: eggs and bacon, marmalade and toast, cooked by Queenie. I was beginning to think of her as a treasure, her old disasters already fading from my mind. Mummy appeared much later, looking like the heroine of some tragic and romantic novel in a long black gown with a black headband tied around her forehead.

"I hardly slept a wink in that room. I kept thinking I heard things—people coming and going all night. We'll have to find another room for me. I suspect that one may be haunted."

"I'm sorry," I said. "But at least Queenie will cook you a good breakfast."

"Nothing too elaborate, please. You know I haven't been able to eat a thing since the terrible news. Just some smoked haddock, maybe, oh, and kidneys to go with the bacon, and the eggs poached . . ." She looked around, hands raised. "Where are the newspapers?"

"I'm sorry. I haven't got around to ordering any yet."

"But I must have the *Times* in the morning. I can't live without the *Times*. And the *Tatler*. I have to see if anyone is writing anything about me."

"I have to go into the village later. I'll pick you up a copy of the newspaper and order it to be delivered for you," I said. It had just struck me that Mummy's contribution to the household budget would at least ensure that we ate and drank well. I'd tell her about our meager allowance and suggest she chip in. After all, she wasn't destitute yet.

"Thank you. I suppose I can do without it for an hour or so. Is there any coffee?"

"I've been drinking tea," I said. "I'll order some for you."

It seemed that coffee was one thing Fernando could do well. Mummy was satisfied and cheered up.

"Why don't you come in to the village with me?" I asked. "It's the local church fete. It might be fun. I promised to attend."

"A fete? Oh, good God, no." She shuddered. "You know what it would be like. They'd want me to open it and give speeches and present the prizes for best jams and vegetable marrows and I look so awful at the moment that I simply couldn't do it."

"They've already got the runner-up to Miss Dairy Queen of Sussex to open it," I said, grinning. "But I do understand. I won't stay long and I'll be back with your newspaper."

I had the motor brought around and drove myself into the village. There was bunting strung across the street and a brass band was playing outside the church. The green was covered with booths, selling everything from homemade jams to white elephants. Children clustered around the games: hoopla and cakewalk and coconut shy. Apparently I had missed the grand-opening speech, as everything was in full swing.

And speaking of swings, there was a giant swing boat on one side and screams emanated as it went up and down. Such a jolly, innocent scene, and I stood watching wistfully, feeling like an outsider. A few people recognized me and smiled, murmuring, "Welcome, your ladyship. Good of you to come." I bumped into Old Ben, the gardener, and reminded him that I looked forward to seeing him back at Eynsleigh as soon as possible.

"I've been thinking it over. If you're sure that my presence would be wanted, your ladyship," he said, "I'd be more than willing."

"The current gardeners may well resent you," I said. "But I want you there and I am the lady of the manor at the moment. If you have any trouble with them, come to me."

"Very well, your ladyship. Let's give it a try, shall we? I don't like to think of those grounds going to rack and ruin after all those years I put into them."

"Thank you, Ben. I'd be most grateful," I said. As he was about to walk away, touching his cap to me, another thought struck me. "Ben, about the old lady. I've met her now. You seemed to know that she was back in residence."

He turned red. "I shouldn't have said nothing. I realized she'd want to keep it hush-hush."

"So how did you know she'd come back?"

"I've seen her, haven't I? First time must have been a few months ago now. She was sitting in the back of a big car and she looked out and she spotted me and gave me a little nod. Then I saw her again, only a week or so ago. Again she was in the back of that big car and this time she didn't see me, but I recognized that black shawl she wore around her head."

"Who was driving her?"

He shook his head. "I couldn't tell you that."

"Thank you, Ben," I said, ready to move away. He reached out and touched my arm lightly. "You won't give her away, will you? I was quite unsettled when I heard that the master had put her into one of those homes, and I knew she wouldn't like it."

"No, I won't give her away, but I feel I should write to Sir Hubert and let him know. It is his mother, after all."

As we parted company and were swept apart by the crowd I found myself rethinking this. She was being well cared for by her nurse. She was in her own home, and if she wandered around at night, then what was the harm in that? Maybe I should mind my own business until Sir Hubert came home.

I bought a few obligatory items at the various booths: a pot of rhubarb jam and a crocheted bookmark at the Women's Institute, a sweet little enamel brooch at the white elephant stall run by the church Mothers' Union. Then I tried my hand at the bran tub run by the Scouts, winning a hair ribbon and comb, which I promptly donated to a small girl standing nearby. This elicited jealousy among her friends, so I distributed a few sixpences for them to try their luck too.

I felt I'd done my duty and turned to leave. As I did so I heard someone calling my name and saw Lady Mountjoy. She lived at Farlows, that very grand estate only a mile from Eynsleigh, where I had attended the infamous house party with the Prince of Wales and a certain American woman (and almost been killed, but that's another matter I won't go into here).

"Georgiana! Good heavens," she said. She had two huge Irish setters on a leash and had to restrain them as they tried to jump up at me. "What are you doing in this neck of the woods?"

"I've come to live at Eynsleigh," I said. "Sir Hubert invited me."

"He's not back, is he?"

"No. He's still in South America. But I'm getting married and he wants us to make Eynsleigh our home."

"How splendid. And lovely to have you as a neighbor. Of course, we saw your announcement in the *Times*. You're engaged to Darcy O'Mara, aren't you? We've always adored the dear boy. So dashing. In fact we rather hoped he might do for Imogen . . . apart from the Catholic thing, you understand." She broke off, realizing she might not have been tactful. "You must come to dinner soon. And bring your intended."

"He's off in foreign parts somewhere at the moment," I said. "But we'd love to come when he returns."

"Splendid. Let us know what date might work." The dogs were now pulling her in the direction of a stall that was selling grilled sausages. "Heel, you brutes. Heel!" she yelled. At the last moment she turned back to me. "Oh, and I should warn you to take extra care, Georgie. There have been burglaries in the neighborhood. We were burgled ourselves. The good silver taken. And it wasn't some sort of amateur job either. There were no signs of forced entry. We've no idea how they got in, unless they propped a ladder to an upstairs window. But then how did they get a ladder of that length onto the estate when the gates are closed? My husband has kept an eye on the antique shops in the Lanes in Brighton hoping to spot some of our items, but so far nothing has shown up. Such a pity. Some have been in the family since the seventeen hundreds."

"I'll warn the servants to make sure they lock up at night," I said, "but frankly there isn't much worth stealing. I suspect Sir Hubert locks all the valuables in a strong room while he's away."

"Probably does. Such a sensible man, apart from this absurd desire to keep scaling impossible mountains. I don't know where he gets it from. His father was such a boring man. Never left home if he didn't have to." The dogs gave a final jerk and broke free. "I must run," she squealed. "We'll make a date. I promise." And she took off across the green yelling, "Come back here at once, you stupid brutes," while the two dogs paid no notice.

I drove back to Eynsleigh to find that Claudette, Mummy's maid, had arrived with trunks of various sizes, which were now being carried upstairs by McShea and Joanie. Mummy herself was nowhere to be seen, but I located her in the morning room.

"Did you know that Claudette has come with your things?"

"Yes, darling. Of course I did."

"Don't you want to supervise?"

"Don't be silly, darling. Claudette knows where to put things," she said. Then her eyes lit up. "You marvelous girl. You've brought the *Times*."

"And I've arranged for it to be delivered starting Monday morning," I said.

"Lovely. You're such a good daughter. Now, if I can just have some more of that delightful coffee and some of Queenie's shortbread I think I might last until luncheon." For a small person, in mourning, she had an impressive appetite.

Coffee was brought by McShea, who seemed as fascinated with my mother as he was with Queenie. He couldn't stop staring at her; then he blurted out, "I've seen your picture in all the papers."

"Of course you have, dear boy," she said, giving him that smile that turned his face bright red. "I expect I have a photograph somewhere that I could sign for you if you'd like."

He left, stammering his gratitude.

"How do you do it?" I asked.

"Do what?"

"Have this hold over men? They see you and instantly they are reduced to jabbering idiots. Even Plunkett blushed."

"It's a gift, I suppose," she said, idly turning the page of her newspaper. "You have to have been born with it and you, unfortunately, inherited too much from your father's side of the family, where the word 'sex' was never mentioned."

I heard only part of this because I was staring at the page of the newspaper that was now facing toward me. A small paragraph at the bottom of the page and a photograph of someone I thought I recognized.

"Just a minute, Mummy," I said. I knelt on the floor at her feet so that I could study the page she was holding up. "Keep it still. There's something I want to read."

The small headline read:

CITY FINANCIER GOES MISSING

I read on.

Arthur Broadbent, financial adviser for the City firm Harrison and Weekes, was reported missing by his wife, Annabel, when he failed to return home two days ago, on June 28th. He told his wife he was going to visit clients in Surrey and Sussex that day. Mr. Broadbent is an employee of a firm that recently made headlines in a scandal that rocked the financial world. They were part of a broad investigation into the manipulation of foreign currencies and the provision of tax havens for their richest clients. Although it must be pointed out that Mr. Broadbent's name was never mentioned in connection with the scandal.

"What is it?" Mummy asked, turning the page toward her.

"That man," I said, pointing at the photograph. "I'm pretty sure he was the one who came to the house a couple of days ago."

Chapter 21

Oh dear. Now I don't know what to think. A man disappears after
coming to visit. I wouldn't be suspicious except that so many
strange things have been happening here.

Mummy picked up the newspaper and held it closer. I suspected she
needed glasses but was too vain to wear them. "Such an ordinary-
looking little chap," she said. "Are you sure it's the same one?"

I got up and perched on the arm of the sofa beside her. "Pretty
sure," I said. "Of course I only saw him from above, looking down
from your window, and his face was rather red and sweaty."

"What did he want anyway?"

"That's just it. I don't really know. Plunkett never came to me to
tell me there was a visitor and I rebuked him for it afterward. And
when I asked him who the visitor had been he said the man had wanted
to see Lady Anstruther and Plunkett had had to tell him that she was

in no state to receive visitors. The man left in a huff, annoyed that he had come all this way on a hot day, and even refused a cup of tea."

"Perfectly reasonable explanation," Mummy said. She stared at the photograph again. In the newsprint it was grainy and I wondered if I might have made a mistake. Then I remembered that Plunkett had said that the visitor had come about appraising some antique jewelry. So either it was a different man or Plunkett was lying. I found it easy to believe the latter.

"It's always the inoffensive ones, isn't it?" Mummy said, rousing me from these thoughts.

"Who do what?"

"Well, it's obvious he's done a bunk with the cash, wouldn't you say? Lots of rich clients, entrusting money to his care. Too, too tempting. He's probably in Bermuda or heading for South America by now."

"Oh golly, I hope so," I said. Wild thoughts were still racing around my head. He came to the house but I never saw him leave. Of course, I wasn't exactly watching the driveway and he could have left without my seeing him, but . . . I wouldn't allow that train of thought to continue.

"Do you think we should telephone the police and let them know that he came here?" I asked.

"Darling, one never gets involved with the police unless absolutely necessary," she said. "If the man came and went, then there is really nothing to tell them. As I said, he's probably far away by now and the firm has probably noticed a large amount of cash or jewelry missing."

"Yes," I said. But at the back of my mind was a horrid thought. I kept picturing Lady Anstruther throwing that heavy cut-glass ashtray that just missed my head. Plunkett had said she didn't like men. What if the man had been taken to see Lady Anstruther? And what if she had thrown something at him and accidentally killed him? I wrenched my thoughts to more manageable topics. "Mummy, we should have a talk with Fernando and Queenie so that they can plan meals you'd

like. Then tomorrow we might have to go into Haywards Heath and
stock up on your sort of food."

"Anyone would think I was a racehorse with a delicate constitu-
tion," she said. "You know me, plain and simple food. Just a morsel
here and there. That's all."

"But we should have a talk with the cooks," I said. I rang the bell
for Plunkett. I wasn't sure whether to mention the man who was now
missing. I didn't think it was the right moment and it would be wise
to wait until we found out more. Mummy was right; inoffensive-
looking people disappeared every day: they ran off with a mistress or
with the cash. No doubt we'd read in a future newspaper article that
Mr. Broadbent was caught boarding a steamer at Tilbury Docks.

"You rang, my lady? Your Grace?" Plunkett asked.

"Yes, we would like a word with Fernando and Queenie."

"I will send them up immediately." He gave Mummy a little bow.
So he was impressed by having a former duchess in the house when he
hadn't been the least impressed by having the daughter of a duke. It
was more likely he was impressed with having a celebrity in the house.
And a beautiful woman!

Fernando and Queenie appeared. Fernando was glaring. "This girl!
I no can work with her. She is impossible! She ruin my dish."

"What happened, Queenie?"

"How was I to know them veggies on the counter were for the dish
he was making? I thought they was the old scraps and peelings nobody
wanted anymore."

"They were julienned. Ready to be sautéed. I slice tiny strips, very
thin. And this, this imbecile, she throws away. I cook the beef, I look
around . . . where are my vegetables? All gone. And then . . . then she
throws away my oil."

Queenie shrugged as if she thought he was being rather silly. "It
was just a pot of green-looking nasty-smelling stuff."

"I have the olive oil when I cook the garlic and onion. She throw
away. Where I find more olive oil in a place like this, huh?"

"I'm sorry, Fernando," I said, trying not to grin. "Queenie, please do not interfere with Fernando's cooking."

"Well, the kitchen is a right mess. Never cleaned up properly and I can't find things," she said. "That girl Molly is useless. Doesn't have a clue."

"Perhaps Fernando hasn't taught her. It's up to you to show her what you want done. Is that clear?" She nodded, grudgingly. Fernando glared.

"Now, about our meals." I listed some things my mother might want to eat. I made sure the menus included most things that I had spotted growing in the kitchen garden. "And tomorrow we are going into Haywards Heath to arrange for the grocer there to deliver food that Her Grace likes."

I dismissed them then. The rest of the day passed pleasantly enough and we actually had roast beef and Yorkshire pudding for Sunday dinner. I tried to brush the worry about the missing Mr. Broadbent from my mind when I went to bed. He was not my concern.

On Monday morning Mummy protested about going into Haywards Heath, in case she was recognized, and insisted on wearing the hat with the veil, which I thought made her rather more noticeable. There weren't many people in a small country town who wore Chanel and a veiled hat to go shopping. In spite of her claim that she only wanted simple things, the list was quite long and beyond the scope of a country store. She came out pouting. "I'll have to send to Fortnum's for the caviar and the quail and my favorite marmalade. . . ."

"Mummy," I said, not knowing quite how to broach the subject. "I have to point out that the household allowance Sir Hubert left is not very big. It certainly doesn't run to caviar. I'm not sure how you are situated financially, but you may have to cut back a bit and eat more simply."

"Don't be silly, darling. I'm not about to starve. I still have a bank account that Max set up for me and I don't think he'd be mean enough to close it. At least not yet. So let's eat, drink and drown our sorrows, shall we? And spend his money for as long as we can."

She then suggested we go into the bank and she'd withdraw enough money to boost the household accounts. It turned out to be the Westminster Bank. While she was at the counter I asked to speak to the bank manager. He was a jolly, portly sort of person with a gold watch chain slung across his waistcoat in the old-fashioned manner.

"Sit down, young lady. Sit down. Now, what can we do for you?" he asked.

I told him I had moved into Eynsleigh and I was finding the amount that Sir Hubert had arranged for the monthly household expenses to be not quite enough. Was there any possibility that he could release more funds?

He frowned at me then. "I thought the amount was quite ample," he said. "Unless you are planning large house parties every weekend."

"No, of course not," I said. "I plan to live quite simply."

"Well then. You should be able to manage on forty pounds a month."

"How much?" I asked.

"Isn't that the amount? I thought that's what we set up for Sir Hubert." He went to a filing cabinet and pulled out a folder. "Yes, that's right. Forty pounds to be made available on the first of the month."

I came out red-cheeked and furious. So Plunkett had made a false set of books to show me and was clearly pocketing the rest of the money. He must have thought me horribly naïve, which I suppose I was. I had no idea how much it took to run a large household. And now that I had proof that Plunkett was corrupt I began to wonder whether the man who disappeared had not come to see Lady Anstruther at all, but Plunkett himself. Perhaps they were both involved in some nefarious scheme. What made no sense to me was that he had come with such good references from a noble family. Had he swindled them in any way, I wondered? I hoped I'd receive a reply to my letter to the current earl soon.

I was determined to face up to Plunkett the moment we arrived home. This took longer than I expected because Mummy had apparently run out of her favorite French soap and we had to hunt through every chemist shop in Haywards Heath before she had to admit that local chemists did not stock soap that cost two shillings a bar. Then she had to select her favorite magazines in the newsagents—to take her mind off the tragedy, she said.

It was time for luncheon when he returned and Mummy declared herself to be starving, so we went straight through to the dining room. Mummy paused and looked around her. "This room is also impossibly dreary, isn't it? Really, Hubert has let the place go. I suppose that's what happens when a fellow lives alone with no woman to brighten up the place. We must go and see the gardeners after luncheon, Georgie. Let them know I require fresh flowers in the rooms every day."

Good luck with that, I thought but didn't say. But then knowing my mother, they'd both be growing orchids for her and fighting to present the best bouquets.

We had a simple but delicious luncheon of a gammon steak with parsley sauce and tiny new potatoes and peas from the garden. This was followed by a berry charlotte. Hooray for Queenie. When Mummy declared she'd have her coffee in the morning room, I decided it was time to tackle Plunkett.

"I need to speak with you," I said. "Come through into the library."

He followed. "My lady?" he asked. His face was placid and showed no distress.

"The household account book you showed me, Plunkett. It was completely false. Don't deny it. I have spoken with the bank manager."

"I don't deny it, my lady," he said. "You're right. It was false and I apologize."

I was taken aback by this. "So what do you have to say for yourself, stealing from your employer?"

"Oh no, my lady. It wasn't like that at all." He seemed quite perturbed. "It was old Lady Anstruther, you see. When you arrived I thought we might be able to keep it from you that she was living here so I cooked the books, so to speak. But she's quite an expense with a full-time nurse and the sort of food she likes. That's where the rest of the money goes."

"Then it is to stop going immediately," I said. "Is that clear? She is not penniless if she is calling someone to appraise her jewelry. And what about the money that was being paid to the home for her care? That can go to pay for her nurse, and she can eat what we eat. Otherwise she goes back to the home again." I looked him straight in the eye. "I leave it to you to sort out, Plunkett, but in future I want to see the real household accounts. Otherwise I shall be forced to write to Sir Hubert."

"Very well, my lady," he said.

I watched him go. Was I being fooled again? I wondered. Would he go down to the butler's pantry with a smirk on his face? I went to rejoin Mummy and to have coffee. "Shall we go to see the gardeners now?" I asked. "Maybe we can do a tour of the grounds first and you can see what is being grown. Although I have to warn you it is horribly neglected. But I have Old Ben starting again this week and with any luck he'll whip the two idle boys into shape."

"You are becoming quite a hard taskmistress," Mummy said, eyeing me with astonishment. "Who would have thought that my awkward and timid Georgie would turn into a replica of her great-grandmother?"

"I'm rather amazed at myself," I said. "But I was so looking forward to living here and then to find that the place had gone to seed was just too much."

"You're right," she said. "It certainly wasn't so drab and dingy when I lived here. There was a lovely painting of a horseman on the wall over there, I remember. What happened to that?"

"Do you think Sir Hubert fell on hard times and had to sell some things?" I asked. "So many people lost money in the crash of twenty-nine. Daddy lost all of his, didn't he?"

"Hubert certainly has enough to go off on his wretched expeditions all the time," Mummy said, "and I think he has plenty of income. The family has sugar plantations in Jamaica, you know."

"I didn't know."

"Oh yes. And some sort of factories in Yorkshire. No, darling, if you are his heir, I don't think you are going to starve."

"Crikey," I said. Then I stopped, my mouth dropping open. "Mummy, I bumped into Lady Mountjoy yesterday morning and she said there had been burglaries in the neighborhood. You don't think this house has been burgled, do you? You've noticed several items missing."

"Ask Plunkett."

"He's only been here for less than a year. It could have been before that."

I rang for him again. He had a wary look now on his face, unsure of what he was about to be accused of this time.

"Yes, I heard about the burglaries, your ladyship," he said. "And luckily they did not come here. I think the master wisely locked away the valuables before he went. There is one small room in his wing that has remained locked and we have no key."

"That's good news," I said. "I would hate to think that Sir Hubert was robbed while he was away."

We both looked up as the front doorbell jangled. Plunkett went to answer it. He was gone quite a long time and came back with a strange look on his face. "It is a police inspector," he said, "and he is asking for you."

"Show him into the library, please," I said.

Mummy and I exchanged a questioning look as I left the room.

Although the man was in plain clothes one could tell immediately that he was a policeman. There is a certain look about them. He held out his hand to me. "Detective Inspector Travers. Sussex Constabulary. And am I speaking to the mistress of the household?"

"I'm Lady Georgiana Rannoch," I said. "The house belongs to Sir Hubert Anstruther and I am only a guest here. Please take a seat. How may I help you?"

"You're only a guest, you say. Is Sir Hubert available?"

"About as unavailable as possible. He is mountain climbing in the Andes." I grinned. His face remained dour.

"I am here because we understand that you had a visit from a Mr. Broadbent last Friday."

"We might have done," I said. "Although I didn't have a chance to speak with him personally. He is the man who was reported missing, isn't he? I saw his photograph in the *Times* yesterday morning."

"That is correct. So you recognized the man but didn't speak with him."

"I only saw him from an upstairs window," I said. As I answered my brain was racing ahead, realizing I'd have to tell him about old Lady Anstruther and he'd have to speak with her and she might well be sent back to the home.

"The butler did not alert you to the fact that there was a visitor?"

"He did not. I reprimanded him for it afterward."

"So you never spoke with the man in person? Never heard what he had to say?"

"The butler saw no reason to call me as the visitor had not come to see me and the person he had come to see was unavailable."

He cleared his throat. "The butler tells me that the man had come to see Sir Hubert Anstruther, regarding transactions for his aged mother. Is that correct?"

Plunkett certainly thought on his feet. "Yes, something to do with his aged mother," I agreed.

"And when he heard that Sir Hubert was not in residence he left immediately." He looked at me for confirmation. "He never came inside?"

"Yes, that is what I was told. As I said, I was upstairs the whole time."

"About what time would this have been?"

I frowned. "About three o'clock, maybe?"

"Yes, that agrees with what the butler told me."

"I was also told that the man said he had other important meetings that afternoon, which was why he was so annoyed at wasting his time with us."

"I see." He nodded. "Yes, we have notes from his agenda at the office indicating addresses in this part of the world. We will be following up on them."

He got to his feet. "So you have no idea why he wanted to see Sir Hubert? Why he came all this way without telephoning or sending a letter first?"

"Absolutely no idea," I said. "I have only been living here a few days myself so I can't verify whether a letter was written in advance or not. As I have said more than once, I was upstairs and the whole encounter with the visitor could only have lasted a few minutes."

He held out his hand. "Thank you, Lady Georgiana. We shall be following up with other addresses he had in his diary. But if you can think of anything else that might be useful, here is my card. Please don't hesitate to call me."

Plunkett had been waiting in the doorway, clearly listening to what had been said. He gave me a quick glance as he led out the inspector. Did I see relief on his face?

Chapter 22

This is getting more confusing by the minute. I don't quite know what
    to believe. Plunkett is covering up for Lady Anstruther. Did she
    really murder that poor man? And why is he so keen to keep her
    here and cover up for her?

I heard the front door shut and then Plunkett hurried up to me as I
was leaving the library and returning to the morning room.

"I want to thank you, my lady."

"For what, Plunkett?"

"For not contradicting me when I told the inspector the man had
come to see Sir Hubert and not his mother. I thought it was simpler,
you see. And of course I was trying to protect her. If he'd seen her in
the state she is now, well, he might have had her sent straight back to
that facility. He might even have suspected—" He broke off. "Now it's
all good. I expect they'll be able to locate the missing man soon
enough."

I went back to Mummy and related my conversation with the inspector. She wasn't exactly displaying much interest. "I told you, darling, the silly man has absconded with funds. It will all come out soon enough."

"How can you be so sure?"

"I know men, darling. Trust me, I know men."

Nobody could dispute that. I looked at her draped on the sofa like a tragic heroine about to die of consumption. I held out my hand. "Come on, get up. Let's go and look at the grounds and you can choose the flowers you want in the rooms."

She sighed. "If we must. Frankly I find it hard to do anything at the moment. I can't believe my life is over."

"I'm sure it's not over," I said. "But Max will have his hands full arranging his father's funeral."

"And comforting that old cow of a mother." She spat out the words. "Why couldn't she have been the one to die?"

"That's not nice, Mummy."

"I know." She sighed again. "I just don't feel nice at the moment."

I tugged at her. "Come on. A walk in the fresh air will do you good."

She allowed herself to be led to the front door. It was a glorious sunny afternoon and the air was fragrant with the scent of flowers as well as new-mown grass. I also caught a whiff of burning wood. Somewhere nearby there was a bonfire. All the familiar smells of the English countryside. We passed the fountain and crossed the lawn to the herbaceous borders. Mummy found rosebushes that she liked and blue hydrangeas and peonies. She quite cheered up. "The grounds here are lovely, aren't they?" she said. "Where is that little gazebo where Hubert proposed to me?"

"A gazebo? I don't remember it."

"For all his rugged appearance and his mountaineering stunts he was a romantic sort of chap." A dreamy look came over her face and I wondered if she was considering the possibility of re-snagging him once he came home (if Max was a nonstarter, that was.)

"So where is this gazebo?"

She stood looking around, frowning; then she pointed. "I think it's in that direction, past that stand of trees," she said. "I know it was in a wild and wooded part of the estate. There used to be a herd of deer."

"I remember the deer," I said. "I wonder if any of them are still here. Come on. Let's go and see if we can find your gazebo."

"It will be sad and neglected and all in ruins and I'll only start to brood about what might have been." She brushed a hand across her face. I noticed that actresses always accompany their words with gestures.

I laughed. "You are always so dramatic. Come on. I want to see it. I don't remember it at all. I suppose I wasn't allowed to wander that far from the house when I was little."

"You had a little pony, but they only let you ride out with the groom. Do you remember your pony? Wasn't it called Squibs?"

"I do remember it. A fat and round little thing. It was almost impossible to fall off." I laughed, but as the laugh faded I found myself thinking. I'd had a pony. This had been a place of luxury. Where had it all gone?

We left the manicured part of the grounds. Now there was uneven meadow grass underfoot and tall oak and beech trees that provided dappled shade.

"There was also a little chapel, deep in the woods," Mummy said suddenly. "The family was Catholic, you know, and mass had to be said in secret in those days. I understand there was a secret passage from the house to the chapel. It was one of those times when being the wrong religion meant having your head chopped off."

"I'm glad it's not like that now, or Darcy and I could never marry," I said. "Let's go and find the chapel too."

"I haven't worn stout shoes," she said. "They'll be ruined in this thick grass."

"There's a path over this way. And I'm sure you have plenty more pairs."

She gave me a sideways glance. "I'm not sure that I like this new assertive daughter. You were always quite a submissive little thing."

"I've had to learn to live on my own. I've had to struggle like you. It makes one tougher."

She took my hand. "It certainly does. Maybe we have more in common than I thought." Then she looked up at me. "I'm so glad I came here. If I'd stayed in London I would have been wallowing in despair."

We had reached a place where the trees grew thicker together and there was tall bracken growing between them. A real wild wood.

"Are you sure it was this way?" I asked.

"Pretty sure," she said. "See, the ground is rising here and the gazebo was on a little hill so that you could look back and see the house through the trees."

We had just ventured into the wood when we heard a loud voice shouting, "Oi. Where do you think you are going?"

Then we heard the sound of big boots crashing through undergrowth. We waited and one of the gardeners emerged, red-faced from having run. When he recognized us he looked uncomfortable.

"Oh, I'm sorry, my lady. I thought it was trespassers."

"No, it is only my mother and I going for a stroll. We're trying to locate the gazebo and the old chapel, Hoskins."

"I don't think you want to go through there," he said. "It could be dangerous."

"Dangerous? Are there wild animals?" I asked, grinning.

"No, my lady, but it's badly overgrown. We haven't had a chance to work on it yet and there are traps."

"Traps?"

"Yes, my lady."

"What are you trapping? Rabbits?"

"No, man-traps, my lady. We've had poachers. There's no game-keeper these days and they think they can help themselves to the rabbits and pheasants."

"Man-traps? How utterly barbaric, and illegal too," I said. "Who gave you instructions to put them out? Surely not Sir Hubert."

"I wouldn't know, my lady. It's just we were told when we got here that there were man-traps to dissuade poachers and we should be careful in this part of the grounds."

"And do you check regularly to make sure nobody has been caught in one of these traps?"

He looked worried now. His eyes darted as if he was seeking an escape route. "No, my lady."

"And if some poor boy is lying there, bleeding to death?"

"Oh no, my lady. We would hear someone yelling."

"Have them removed immediately," I said. "And make sure you go over every inch of this part of the grounds to make sure they are perfectly safe. Old Ben will be joining you and he'll make sure you are doing what I ask."

Now he looked quite scared.

"Go and tell your fellow gardener and then get to work. And if there are rabbits and pheasants to be had, we'd quite enjoy them for dinner occasionally."

Mummy slipped her arm through mine as we retreated carefully through the bracken.

I was still red-faced and fuming. Man-traps, indeed. I knew that village boys might well have dared each other to climb over the wall to an estate like this and steal fruit or even catch the odd rabbit. Still, I reassured myself that none of them had been reported missing or injured. I would surely have heard about it at the fete. But it was only a matter of time. . . . I wondered who had ordered those traps, and why.

"At least my shoes have been saved from utter ruin," Mummy said.

"Your legs have been saved from being broken in a trap," I snapped. "What a barbaric thing to do."

"It must be time for tea." Mummy had perked up already. "Shall we have it on the lawn under the big tree?"

"All right."

We made our way back to the house by the most direct route. This led us around behind the kitchen garden. Here we came upon the remains of the bonfire I had smelled earlier. It was now almost out, just a pile of smoking ashes. A few half-burned bits of wood lay around the edges and out of the pile of ash some straight sticks were jutting out. Not wood, but metal. Thin pieces of metal sticking up. We had walked past before I realized what they were: they were the spokes of an umbrella.

Chapter 23

Monday, July 1, and Tuesday, July 2

Now I'm really worried. Should I tell that inspector?

I was deep in thought all the way back to the house. I wanted to say something, to air my suspicions, but I knew it was no use talking to Mummy. She'd either not be interested or dismiss my worry as imagination. Besides, she had picked up the pace and was striding out ahead of me as we approached the steps, anticipating her tea.

Chairs and table were carried out under the big beech tree and McShea carried out a tea tray. On it was a silver tea set, china cups and saucers and a plate of cucumber sandwiches. It was all remarkably civilized. The presentation was only slightly marred by Queenie tripping over the edge of a flower bed as she carried out a plate of shortbread. She and the shortbread went flying.

"Whoops-a-daisy!" she said, attempting to get up. "Sorry about that, miss. My old dad used to say I'd fall over a crumb on the floor one of these days." And she started to pick up the pieces of shortbread and replace them on the plate.

"I don't think we want to eat them now, Queenie," my mother said in a disapproving voice. "They've been on the ground. They'll have dirt on them."

"Only good dirt," Queenie said. "Ain't nothing wrong with garden soil."

I glanced at Mummy and grinned. "She's probably right," I said, "and you have a napkin to dust it off."

Mummy shook her head in despair but I noticed she did dust off pieces of shortbread and ate them with relish. After she had worked her way through most of the food on the plate she announced that she was quite exhausted after all that way I'd made her walk and was going to take a little nap. I continued to sit in the shade as the tea things were cleared away, alone now with my thoughts.

Umbrellas break all the time, I knew. The wind blows them inside out. The fabric rips. And they have to be thrown away. So it was possible that the remains of this umbrella had nothing to do with the man who had come to the house. But I couldn't get the picture out of my mind of him walking up the drive, red-faced from the heat, with an umbrella tucked incongruously under his arm. If only I'd been downstairs I would have met him and maybe I could have saved him from an awful fate. So the question was whether I should mention this to the inspector or not.

If I did it would mean exposing Lady Anstruther and having her shipped back to the home or asylum or whatever it was. But maybe that would be the best thing for her—certainly if she had become too violent and a danger to others. Oh golly—I wished I could decide whether to send a cable to the embassy to see if they could get in touch with Sir Hubert. I wished Darcy would come home. I wished Zou Zou was still in London. She'd know what was best. She hadn't said how long she planned to stay in Ireland and I supposed I could make a trunk call to Ireland, but it would be hard to explain over the telephone, and horribly expensive too.

My thoughts went to that gardener and the man-traps. Did they really exist or was that his way of keeping us out of a part of the grounds where he didn't want us to walk? And if the latter, what was it that he wanted to keep from us? I certainly couldn't go back there today. He would be watching for me. And I wasn't too keen to put my foot into a trap.

Mummy was in remarkably good spirits after her nap. She knocked back a good deal of sherry before dinner and had two helpings of meat pie followed by poached peaches and ice cream and a good piece of Stilton. I suppose I shouldn't have been amazed at how quickly she bounced back from adversity. After all, she had leaped with ease from one man to another all her life without a moment's remorse. I, on the other hand, found it hard to eat and harder still to be bright and cheerful to her.

"What's the matter?" she asked in a rare moment of noticing anyone else's feelings apart from her own. "You're awfully glum tonight. Missing Darcy, I suppose."

I wanted to tell her but I couldn't. I was conscious that little ears would probably be listening to everything we said. "That's right," I replied. "I am missing Darcy. But I'm awfully glad you are here. It was unnerving being in a house this size alone."

"I felt the same about Castle Rannoch, darling," she said. "I couldn't stand the place. I mean, tartan wallpaper in the loo? And the way the wind howled down those corridors? I thought I'd go mad."

I had to laugh at this. "Yes, it is pretty ghastly, isn't it? But Binky actually likes living there."

"And Fig?"

"Not so much, I suspect."

When I went up to bed I was careful to check the gas tap and to put that chair under my door handle. As I lay in bed, staring at the ceiling, I realized that too many things had happened to be a coincidence. Rogers had fallen down the stairs and been killed. Someone had tried to gas me. A man had disappeared. The remains of an umbrella were sticking out of a smoldering bonfire. And apart from Rogers's death, everything seemed to hint at Lady Anstruther. In one of her moments of clarity had she bribed the servants to keep her hidden here? Had she instructed them to get rid of me so that she'd remain safely hidden from her son? And worst of all, had she killed Mr. Broadbent and made the gardeners dispose of the evidence?

I decided I didn't have enough proof to go to the police yet. It all sounded rather fanciful, especially an old aristocratic lady killing a financial adviser who had come to visit her. But I was determined to get to the bottom of it somehow. I made up my mind to go out early the next morning, before the gardeners were up and working, and I'd find out what they didn't want me to see in that part of the estate. And as for the man-traps, I'd take a big stick and feel around in front of me as I walked, not taking any chances.

I WAS AWOKEN at first light by the dawn chorus. I got up and dressed, putting on my stoutest shoes and a pair of slacks; then I crept downstairs. I heard no sounds coming from the servants' quarters. I selected a strong walking stick from the stand in the hall, then let myself out of the front door. If anyone was watching I wanted to give the impression of going for a morning walk—a perfectly acceptable thing for aristocrats to do. I strode out as if heading for the front of the estate; then, when I reached the first trees, I made directly for the wild forested area where we had been stopped yesterday. There was no sign that either gardener was up yet. Early morning sunlight slanted over the dewy grass. A rabbit bounded out of the long grass in front of me, making my heart do a little flip. I started to move cautiously through the bracken, tapping my stick ahead of me like a blind person. The ground rose gently but steadily ahead of me and through the trees I caught a glimpse of Mummy's gazebo. Ivy now covered its white marble columns and draped over its roof. I decided to wait for Mummy before I went to explore it.

Farther off through the trees I spotted another building. At first I thought it was a garden shed, but as I went closer I saw it was built of gray stone with a pointed roof. The little chapel Mummy had told me about. I was going to explore that when I noticed that the bracken to my left had been trampled down. I followed the path that had been made through the undergrowth and came to a small clearing. And put my hand up to my mouth to stifle a little gasp. The turf had been dug up recently. There was a mound of bare earth.

It looked horribly like a grave. In fact I couldn't think of anything else it could be but a grave. Nobody would have come miles into thick woodland to dig up earth to plant anything. The only reason for it was that something (or somebody) was buried here. Of course then I wished I had brought a trowel or shovel with me. I really didn't want to dig it up, but I knew that I had to. The stick I had carried had a stout rubber tip to it, thus was useless for digging purposes. I looked around until I found a log with the bark peeling off in places. I removed a section of bark and decided it might work well enough as a tool. I wasn't planning to dig up the whole thing. Just enough so that I knew the truth . . .

I squatted down and started to dig up the earth carefully, a little at a time. Something was buried there. I could feel the bark pushing up against something solid. I wasn't at all keen to go on. I've seen dead bodies before, but I can't say I've ever enjoyed the experience. I scraped away earth bit by bit and then stared in disbelief. I was looking at white hair. Now I really was flummoxed. Who might have had white hair? The man I had seen was bald. My heart was racing so violently that I found it hard to make my hands obey me, terrified of what I might see next. I cleared away a little more soil and realized that it wasn't white hair at all. It was white fur. I was looking at the remains of an animal paw. Now I felt rather stupid. Someone's pet had died, some time ago, judging by the lack of flesh attached to the bone. Nothing sinister at all.

I pushed the loose earth back into place and patted it down. It wasn't exactly perfect but if it looked as if the grave had been disturbed, people would assume it was a fox or a badger. Then I stood up, staring down at the grave. It was too small to have been used to bury a human. I should have seen that. I had been letting my imagination run away with me. Since I was in the area I wondered whether I should see if there were any other graves. But if I'd wanted to bury a murder victim, I would have taken care to cover the evidence, not leave it raw and open for all to see.

I had not come upon a single trap as I walked there, and I was inclined to believe that the gardener had wanted to scare us off. So there was something here . . . maybe as harmless as an illicit still, wine stolen from the master's cellar, but something. I peered through the trees in the direction of the chapel. Should I take a look at that? I hesitated. If I were going to hide a body, then I'd leave it on the forest floor, covered in bracken and fallen branches, not put it in a chapel where anyone could come upon it. But it was so close now that I had to make sure.

I moved with extreme caution. The foliage was even thicker here. Ivy twined around trees and threatened to snare my ankles as I walked. I tapped ahead with my stick and came upon the remnants of a flagstone path leading to the chapel. I followed it and came to a clearing with the chapel in front of me. It was indeed tiny. Like a child's version of a church, built in rough gray stone with a steeply angled roof. The door was scarcely taller than me. I opened it with some difficulty, as the latch was very old and rusty, and stepped inside. It smelled damp and musty, the way old churches do, but this one also added the lingering scent of ancient incense. And it was very dark. There was a small window above the altar but a big tree grew right behind it, blocking out most of the light. I held the door open so that I could see inside. It took only a brief look to tell me that there was nothing hidden—in fact nowhere to hide anything. There were four pews—enough seating for about eight people at the most—candlesticks and a crucifix on the altar at the back, statues of the Blessed Virgin and a saint I couldn't identify in the corners. And that was it. Smooth, unadorned walls with niches for long-ago candles. A flagstone floor. I closed the door quietly behind me and started to walk away.

Suddenly I was aware of a silence and watchfulness in the forest. The skin at the back of my neck prickled. I was being observed, I was sure of it. I was conscious of how far I had come into the woods. If the gardeners saw me, after they had expressly warned me about traps, they would know I suspected them. And if something was indeed going on at Eynsleigh, I might find myself taking a tumble down the stairs like poor old Mr. Rogers. Or someone might take the opportunity to finish me off here. If I was set upon now, nobody would see. If I screamed, nobody would hear. I cursed my impetuous desire to find out the truth. I looked around, not even sure which way led back to safety. I had just located a path of trampled bracken and started to follow it back to the outside world when something leaped out, right in front of me. I think I screamed. It took a long moment to realize that it had been a deer, as terrified to see me as I was it. I heard it crashing off through the undergrowth. So there were still deer in the park, I thought. Nobody had mentioned it. Perhaps they didn't even know. Or perhaps they were doing a nice little trade in venison.

I saw bright sunlight and open lawns ahead of me and plunged toward them, coming out of the forest almost at a gallop. It was only when I was walking back across the lawns that I realized—the animal that was buried in that grave had been there for quite a while. And yet the bracken had been trampled down into a path recently.

Chapter 24

TUESDAY, JULY 2
EYNSLEIGH

Oh dear. I really sense that something is horribly wrong, but I have no
evidence, apart from a burned umbrella. I wish I had someone to
talk this over with.

There was still no sign of any activity as I let myself into the house and
returned my stick to its place. I crept back to my room, removed my
slightly muddy shoes and changed into a more suitable skirt and blouse.
One of the advantages of not having a proper lady's maid was that
nobody would notice the mud on my shoes. I waited for a more respect-
able hour to go down to breakfast. Mummy wasn't yet up so I sat alone,
eating smoked haddock and trying to make sense of things. Should I
contact that police inspector and tell him that I hadn't seen the man
leave (although it was quite possible he had done so while I was not
paying attention), that I had seen the spokes of a burned umbrella and
that somebody had recently made trails through the forest, trampling

down bracken? It all seemed too little to go on. I would be seen as a fanciful young lady who was wasting police time.

But apart from going through that forest again, beating down the bracken inch by inch, I didn't see how I could make any progress. Then another awful thought struck me. That bonfire . . . Maybe it wasn't just an umbrella that had burned there. Maybe it was also a body. I wasn't sure about this: could a bonfire of leaves and clippings be hot enough to burn up a body? And then my next thought was: did I dare to go sift through the remains of the fire to see if I could locate pieces of bone?

Crikey, I thought. That really was playing with fire in more senses than one. If I was seen to do that, then whoever was responsible would know.

I was shaken out of my broodings by the arrival of my mother, looking fresh and fashionable in wide navy blue slacks and a white shirt trimmed with navy braid. I noticed she had already discarded her heavy mourning garb but wisely kept quiet about it.

"Hello, Mummy." I managed to give her a bright smile. "Did you sleep well?"

The tragic demeanor returned. "As well as can be expected, given the circumstances." She sighed. "I was just realizing that I have all these new and lovely outfits for my trousseau and now I'll never need them. What a pity you aren't petite and slim like me, darling. I could have given them to you. Now I don't know what to do with them: they were all made to measure so I can't return them. There aren't too many people in the world with my kind of figure at forty."

Since I was now twenty-four and she had been well over twenty when she had me, I disputed forty, but again I just smiled.

"Maybe you can give them to Mrs. Simpson," I said. "She may be needing a trousseau and she is about your size."

"That woman? She is most definitely not my size or shape. She is completely flat-chested, for one thing. No boobs to speak of. Besides, she is so jealous of me that she'd rather run around naked than wear anything of mine." She gave me a wicked grin; then she frowned. "You don't really believe that the prince will marry her, do you?"

"That's what she thinks," I said. "Everyone at the palace keeps hoping he'll shape up and do the right thing, but she has a tremendous hold over him."

"What a disaster that would be. Wallis the queen-in-waiting. They'd never let her be queen, would they?"

"Again that's what she thinks. But I don't see how he can marry her. Twice divorced and he'll be the head of the Church of England, which doesn't allow divorce?"

"Anyway, she's not getting my clothes," said my ever-practical mother.

She had just ordered a couple of poached eggs to go with her smoked haddock when we heard the front doorbell jangle. Post at last, I thought, fighting the desire to jump up and see. Maybe even something from Darcy.

Plunkett appeared with a slim brown envelope. "A telegram for you, my lady," he said.

Telegram? No good news came in telegrams. My heart was thudding. Someone had died. Binky had died. Darcy had died. My hands were trembling as I tried to open it.

"Allow me, my lady," Plunkett said and slit it open with a knife.

"What is it? Read it out loud," Mummy said.

I read: ROMFORD HOSPITAL. NOT LOOKING GOOD. GRANDDAD. We both jumped up.

"The motorcar immediately, Plunkett," I said. "My grandfather is in hospital." I looked at Mummy. "Are you coming too?"

"Of course. He's my father, isn't he? Of course I'm coming."

She ran upstairs to get her purse and give her nose a last-minute powder. Mummy wouldn't ever dream of going anywhere, even to her father in hospital, without looking her best. I was feeling so sick I couldn't even think straight. I knew Granddad's health had been failing, but the thought of him dying was more than I could bear. He had been my own rock through several turbulent years, the one person who loved me and supported me.

The Bentley was brought round to the front door. "Would you like me to drive you to the station, my lady?" Plunkett asked.

It was such an unexpectedly kind gesture that it brought tears to my eyes.

"Yes, thank you, Plunkett," I said. "I had thought of driving up to town, but . . ."

"The train is much quicker," he said. "If you catch the express from Brighton."

"Yes." I nodded. "The express from Brighton. Much quicker." I could hear myself babbling, needing to talk rather than letting my thoughts run riot.

But Mummy had gone horribly quiet. We sat in silence all the way to the station. We sat opposite each other in a first-class compartment as the train sped toward London.

We both stared out of the window, watching green countryside flash past and then the first suburbs, then grimy back gardens, rows of houses, smoke pouring from the chimneys of the newly constructed Battersea Power Station on the south bank of the Thames. We hurried through the crowds at Victoria Station.

"Should we take a taxi, do you think?" Mummy asked.

"It's miles. It would cost a fortune," I said. "Besides, the tube must be quicker than navigating all those narrow streets in the city."

"The tube. How quaint," Mummy said. "Well, if we must, we must."

Any other time I would have laughed. It always amused me when she behaved as if she had always been a duchess when she had been born into a row house, two up and two down, on the eastern fringes of London—a fact she had now conveniently forgotten.

"This way," I said. I took her hand and led her down the steps to the Underground.

The carriage was half-empty, it being now the middle of the day, and I noticed my mother getting a lot of stares. I supposed beautiful women wearing Parisian fashion weren't seen too often speeding toward Romford! It was only after we came up into daylight on the other side of the docklands that Mummy spoke.

"I was a terrible daughter to him," she said. "I kept away when I should have visited. Every time I was in London I told myself I was too busy. But in truth I didn't want my public to see me going to a poky little house like his."

"It's a very nice little house," I said. "And you bought it for him. You should be pleased about that. It was very nice of you."

"I bought off my duty with my money," she said. "But you were such a good granddaughter and went to visit him all the time. I'm glad about that."

"He may pull through," I said. "He's a tough old fellow."

"Yes," she said. "He always was a tough old fellow."

Then we reverted to silence until the train pulled into Romford Station. It was a short taxi ride to the hospital.

I held out the telegram to the nurse who was manning the admittance desk. "I received this from my grandfather this morning. I don't know if he sent it or it was sent on his behalf. Do you know where I can find him?"

The nurse looked at the slip of paper. "Oh yes. Albert Spinks. I helped him send this. He'll still be in casualty, in one of the cubicles there. Down that passage and then to the left."

Our feet echoed as we walked down a white-tiled hallway. There was a strong smell of disinfectant. We came to a waiting room in which a lot of sorry-looking people sat on benches, some bleeding, some coughing. People glanced up and nudged one another when they saw us, or rather saw my mother, I suspected. A harried-looking nurse went past, clutching a clipboard.

"I'm looking for Albert Spinks," I said. "He sent a telegram."

"Oh, yes. I'm sorry, my dear," she said. "Down at the end there. Last one on the right."

Then I heard her call, "Mrs. Jenkins? This way, please," as she moved past me.

We walked down a row of curtained-off cubicles. Moans came from one, the sound of a person being sick from another. It felt like walking into hell. Mummy pulled back the curtain and we both froze. The body on the bed was now covered with a sheet.

Chapter 25

Tuesday, July 2

In Essex at a hospital

I don't want to write anything today. Too emotional to handle.

Mummy let out a great cry, "Daddy! Oh no. Not my dad." I was too shocked to say anything. I don't actually think I was breathing. All I could do was stare at that sheet.

I felt a great sob working upward through my body. I tried to swallow it back but it came out anyway.

"Oh, Granddad!" I gasped.

Mummy and I looked at each other; then we hugged in a way that had never happened before. As a small child I don't remember my mother ever hugging me. I don't ever remember sitting on her knee. When I saw her after I had grown up, we kissed, cheek to cheek, about two inches apart. Now we really hugged, clinging to each other.

"I can't imagine the world without him," Mummy said. "He was such a good man."

"Yes, he was. He was the only . . ." I couldn't finish the sentence.

Mummy released her hold on me and went toward the bed, her hand on the sheet, but hesitated, as if she didn't dare pull it back, as if it might not be true if she didn't see it with her own eyes.

We heard footsteps approaching and the curtain was pulled back. Someone coming to take away the body, I thought, and I wasn't going to let them. Not before I'd said good-bye. I turned to say, "Just a minute, please, we need . . ."

Then a voice behind me said, "Well, blow me down. I didn't expect to see you two here this quickly."

My grandfather was standing there, very much alive.

"Daddy!" Mummy said and reached out to touch his shoulder, as if needing to verify she wasn't seeing a ghost.

"So you got my telegram," he said. "Good of you to come."

"You're alive," I said. "Then who . . ." I looked back at the bed.

"Poor old Hettie," he said. "Her ticker gave out. Must have been all the excitement of planning a wedding. At least she died happy."

I went over to him then and wrapped my arms around his neck. "Oh, Granddad, I'm so sorry," I said. "But you're alive. That's wonderful. When we got the telegram we thought that . . ."

"The telegram said that you were in the hospital and it didn't look good," Mummy said in an accusing voice. "We thought it was you. We worried all the way here."

"I'm glad you finally show some feelings for your old dad," he said. "And I'm sorry if I put you through a lot of worry. I told the nurse what I wanted to say on that telegram but I told her to keep it as short as possible because you have to pay by the word and I ain't made of money."

"So she left out that it wasn't you, it was Mrs. Huggins," I said, laughing through the tears that kept trickling down my cheeks.

"Poor old Hettie," he said. "She was so looking forward to that wedding. Her first wedding, to Mr. Huggins, was a bit of a letdown, she said, on account of no one having any money and Mr. Huggins not being a big one for pomp and ceremony. Just the registry office, then a pint and a sausage roll down the pub. This time she was going all out. She'd got her dress being made and the cake on order and everything. And then we were going for a week in Clacton-on-Sea."

"Oh, Granddad. I'm sorry," I said.

He nodded. "We'll get through it, won't we? We have to soldier on. I remember when we lost your gran it felt like the end of the world. But I came through it in the end."

"Granddad, why don't you come home with us?" I said. "I don't want you to be alone and it would be good for you out in the country with plenty of fresh air."

"I can't do nothing right now, ducks," he said. "I've got to make sure everything is arranged for old Hettie. Of course, I'm not family yet, so it won't be up to me how it's done. First things first, I have to locate her daughter. I know she works at a café down in Southend, but I don't rightly remember the name. So I'll have to go over to her house and break the news. Then I suppose it's up to her what sort of funeral she wants and where she wants her mum buried. Maybe it's beside her dad, although Hettie always said he was a right rotter." He looked up and our eyes met. "I'll offer to help with the expenses, of course. That would only be right."

"I can help with the funeral, Dad," my mother said, sounding for once like an ordinary person and not her famous actress persona.

"Kind of you, love, I appreciate it, but I couldn't take German money. You know how I feel about that. He might be a good bloke, your Max, but he's still a Kraut, isn't he? And they killed my boy, my Jimmy."

"Oh, Daddy, that's all over so long ago. We have to forgive and move on," Mummy said. "Besides, Max wasn't even in the army. And anyway he isn't my Max any longer. It's all off. His father died and he has to take care of his mother."

"All off, eh?" He looked at her with understanding. "I'm sorry, love. So it's back to square one for you as well?"

"It seems that way," she said. "I'm staying with Georgie, who is being so kind. As soon as you have things sorted out you must come and join us."

"I will, ducks. I will." He managed a smile. "I'd like that. Out in the country with my girls. What a treat."

"What would you like us to do now, Granddad?" I asked. "We'll stay with you here, of course, but would you like us to come back to the house with you tonight? I don't want you to be alone."

"Oh, no, thanks, my love," he said. "Kind of you, but I'll be all right. Been on my own long enough, ain't I? And besides, I may be out quite late waiting for Hettie's daughter to come home from her job. She'll be put out, poor thing. Need some comforting, I shouldn't wonder."

Then the decision on what to do next was made for us. Two order-lies arrived to wheel the body off to the morgue. We hailed a taxicab to take Granddad back to his house. I offered to cook him a meal but he said he didn't feel like eating. Then we left him heading to Mrs. Huggins's daughter's place in Grays while we took the train back to London.

"Stubborn as always," Mummy said. "I would willingly have gone with him to look for this woman. I would even have cooked him supper."

"When did you ever learn to cook?" I looked at her, smiling.

"I've had times when I've had to fend for myself, just like you," she said. "I may not be the best cook but I do know how to fry an egg."

When we reached Victoria Station, Mummy declared she wasn't ready to go back to the country yet. She had to visit Claridge's, just to make sure no post was being held for her there. And she needed her special French soap one could only find at a certain little chemist shop. I decided I might visit Belinda and see how my wedding dress was coming along. I suppose I was still a little nervous that Belinda would deviate from the sensible design we had chosen together and revert to some high-fashion experiment. I really didn't want to look like a walking white drainpipe!

So Mummy and I parted company, agreeing to meet for the six o'clock train. I walked up Eccleston Street to Knightsbridge and Belinda's mews cottage. The door was opened by a straight and severe-looking person in black. I asked if Belinda was home. She asked my name, then informed me she would see if madam was available to receive a caller. I heard words exchanged upstairs and then Belinda herself followed the maid (Huddlestone, one presumed) down the stairs.

"Georgie, what a lovely surprise," she said before Huddlestone got a chance to officially announce me, which clearly annoyed her as she stood with pursed lips while we hugged. "What brings you to town? I'm afraid I'm not ready for your fitting yet."

"I had to come up for my grandfather," I said. "The woman he was going to marry just died. Mummy and I were in an awful state because the telegram just said that my grandfather was at the hospital and we thought it was he and not Mrs. Huggins who had died."

"Well, I'm sorry for your grandfather, but what a relief for you," she said. "I know how fond you are of him. So while you're here let me show you where we are up to." She took me up to her bedroom, which now held three tailor's dummies on which pieces of fabric were pinned.

"I've been working up here," she said. "Out of the reach of the dreaded Huddlestone."

She went over and closed the door. "She's pretty grim, isn't she?"

"Terrifying," I said. "I thought you weren't going to keep her because she can't or won't cook."

"I know, but I haven't had time to find anyone else yet. I think she's about to quit anyway. This sort of establishment is so far beneath her. But she has to maintain a semblance of politeness or I might not give her a good reference." She grinned, then turned to the biggest dummy. "This is yours," she said. "I had a brilliant idea. Because the lines are so simple I'm going to do a wide band of pearls around the waist, like this." And she held up a piece of fabric embroidered with pearls for me to inspect.

"Oh yes." I beamed. "That would be splendid."

"And I thought I'd echo that theme for the princesses," she said. "A thin band of pearls at their waists and then random pearls embroidered into their fabric."

I looked at her sketches. "Perfect, Belinda," I said.

"Good." She sounded pleased. "I'll be ready to go to the princesses for a fitting in another week, I think, so I'd really appreciate it if you'd come with me. I'm afraid I'll get nervous and stick a pin into a princess or something."

I shot a glance at her. This was Belinda, who had been afraid of nothing. She who climbed down the roof at school to meet ski instructors. Having a baby had certainly changed her. Secretly I hoped she would gradually get back some of that derring-do personality I had so much envied.

"Of course I'll come with you," I said. "But I wouldn't worry about sticking a pin. Elizabeth would be too polite to tell you and Margaret would let you know instantly! In fact she'll probably hit you. But they are both sweet girls and so is their mother."

Belinda went to say something, then looked up with an expression of delight on her face. "I've just realized: If your grandfather's future bride has snuffed it, then there will be no talk of including the dreaded granddaughter in the wedding, will there?"

"Oh golly, you're right. Thank heaven for small mercies. I was so worried about that."

"So was I," said Belinda. "I didn't think I'd bought enough fabric!"

And we both laughed. It felt wonderful.

Chapter 26

I'm still in shock. I can't get over the awful despair I felt when I
thought that Granddad had died. Now nothing else matters but
knowing that he's alive, and he'll be coming down to Eynsleigh
and I can make everything all right for him. And I'm wrestling
with the feelings of guilt that I'm relieved he's not going to be
marrying Mrs. Huggins. I suppose I should be sad for him, but I'm
really not.

I left Belinda, having planned out with her when I'd come for my fittings and when we'd go to the house on Piccadilly for the princesses
to try on their dresses. Then I decided I still had time to pop across to
Rannoch House and see if any wedding RSVPs had come yet. I was
shown into the drawing room, where Binky and Fig were having tea.

"You're just in time, Georgie," Binky said. "Pull up a chair and
dig in."

There was a big Victoria sponge on the table as well as iced fairy cakes and crumpets. It looked most tempting and I realized that we had missed lunch. "Thank you," I said.

Fig looked rather put out that she'd have to share the meal.

"How is your foot doing, Binky?" I asked as I put a couple of fairy cakes on my plate and poured myself a cup of tea.

"Right as rain, thank you," he said. "In fact you've just caught us. We're taking the Flying Scot back home tomorrow. We won't be back down until a week before your wedding. I'm getting a new kilt made. The old one is a trifle snug these days. I had it made for me when I was eighteen."

I noticed that he was getting a little broader around the middle.

"And we're having a first kilt made for Podge too," Fig said. "He's very excited about being a page boy. So did you decide on having bridesmaids? I'm afraid I can't recommend Addy. She is such a willful child."

"My best friend, Belinda, will be maid of honor," I said, "and the two little princesses are going to be my bridesmaids."

"Elizabeth and Margaret?" Fig sounded either amazed or impressed. "You asked them to be part of your wedding?"

"Actually I was asked, by the queen, on their behalf," I said. "Naturally I was pleased to say yes." I took a satisfying bite of cake.

"And the king and queen?"

"Both coming," I said, "although the king is quite put out that it's not at Westminster Abbey."

"And they will be coming back here, to the house, afterward?" Fig asked, glancing nervously at Binky now.

"I expect so."

Fig's eyes were now open rather wide. "Exactly how many royals will be coming?"

I grinned. "Well, the queen wanted half the crowned heads of Europe, but Darcy and I have kept it down to those that we know personally."

"Half the crowned heads of Europe!" Fig sounded alarmed. "Did you hear that, Binky? Coming to this house."

"There's nothing wrong with this house, Fig," Binky said. "I remember Father used to entertain the old king before the war. He was his uncle, after all. And these are all Georgie's relatives so it's only natural that they come to her wedding."

"Yes, I suppose so." Fig could never get over the fact that I was related to the royal family and she wasn't. It was a constant thorn in her side.

"Don't worry, Fig," I said. "The crowned heads of Europe probably won't come. Have any RSVPs come back yet?"

"I think there are a few letters for you in the front hall," Fig said.

I jumped up and went through to the front hall, where Hamilton, the butler, appeared in that uncanny way that well-trained butlers have.

"You'll be wanting your post, my lady," he said and handed them to me.

"Thank you, Hamilton." I took them.

"And may I say how delighted I am that we'll be having the wedding breakfast here at Rannoch House. You've brought honor upon the family, my lady."

"Thank you, Hamilton," I said. As I walked back into the drawing room I was deep in thought. This was a butler of the old school. He made sure the household ran smoothly. He knew the right thing to say. And when the family was honored, then he shared in that honor. So unlike that dratted Plunkett. I came back into the drawing room still thinking.

"Are either of you acquainted with a Countess of Malmsbury?" I asked.

Binky, as usual, looked blank. "Never heard of her," he said.

"You've never heard of anybody," Fig said scathingly. "You are the most unsocial person in the universe, Binky. If it was up to you you'd stay at that dratted castle in Scotland with your Highland cattle and be quite content."

"You're right. I would, old bean," he said.

"So do you know this lady, Fig?" I asked. "You come from Cheshire, don't you?"

"Derbyshire. Close," she said. "But yes, I do know of her. I think I met the old countess when I was a child. Rather an eccentric old thing. Wore black shawls like a witch."

"You don't remember her butler, do you?"

"Her butler?" She gave me a withering smile. "Who ever remembers butlers? Unless they do something terrible like spill the sherry on one."

I took a seat again and opened the first envelope. "Oh good. Cousin Fergus and Cousin Lachlan have accepted."

"They'll be wanting to stay here at the house, I expect," Fig said, her lips pursed. I knew what she was thinking. They were both large Scottish lads with prodigious appetites, for both food and whiskey.

The next two were from Darcy's list and were delighted to accept. And the fourth bore a crest on the envelope. It said:

His Royal Highness Prince Nicholas of Bulgaria and Princess Maria regret they will be unable to attend.

And then, underneath, in ordinary handwriting Nicholas had written:

Sorry to be missing this but Maria is due to give birth to our first child that same week. Wishing you much joy.

I looked up. "That will be a relief for you," I said. "The Bulgarian royals can't come. Princess Maria is about to give birth."

"Exactly how do you know the Bulgarian royal family?" Fig asked.

"I was at school with Maria, and I was one of her bridesmaids," I said.

"And the Romanian prince? The one there was talk of you marrying?"

"Siegfried? Good heavens. There was no way I was going to invite him," I exclaimed. "He was beyond awful. No, Darcy and I decided we would only invite people we actually liked."

"And where is Darcy now? Not down in the country with you, I should hope?" Fig said.

"No, he's off on some assignment. But my mother is with me at Eynsleigh. Max's father has just died so they've had to postpone their wedding plans. Naturally she's rather upset."

"I shouldn't think your mother would stay upset for too long." Fig gave a malicious smirk. "Plenty more fish in the sea."

"Oh, that's not nice, Fig," Binky said. "I like Georgie's mum. She's a good sort. She was kind to me when she was at Castle Rannoch."

"Thank you, Binky," I said. I glanced at the clock on the mantelpiece. "I really should be going. I'm meeting Mummy at six at Victoria."

"So all is going well at your new home, is it? Everything running smoothly?"

"Oh yes," I said. "Couldn't be better."

I managed to keep up that bright face until I was safely out of the house.

MUMMY ARRIVED AT Victoria with only minutes to spare, a porter following her with arms full of packages.

"I decided I didn't have enough clothes suitable for mourning," she said. "I was going to give it up but I decided that I do look rather stunning in black veils. And I also wanted to make sure I enjoyed that bank account in case Max decides to close it."

We were loaded into a first-class compartment and off we went. Mummy was quite chatty, having recovered, as Fig had predicted, from her latest tragedy.

"I wonder if Max would buy me a little flat in London, near the park," she said. "He does owe me something for breaking my heart. Or maybe in Paris."

"You don't speak French," I reminded her.

"I manage perfectly well with my dress designers," she said. "And you have to admit Paris is more civilized."

"I think you are jumping the gun, aren't you? I mean, Max might decide he can't live without you once he's taken care of his mother. And if you don't marry and continue to live in sin—well, it's not the first time you've done that, is it?"

Two elderly ladies, typical village spinsters, overheard some of this, even though I spoke in a low voice. I saw their eyebrows go up and they leaned as far forward as they dared, determined not to miss anything.

"I don't even know if I want to marry him now," Mummy said. "I mean, it is tiresome living in Germany and not understanding most of what is going on around me." She sighed. "We'll just have to see. In the meantime I can help my darling daughter plan for her wedding! Have we got the catering taken care of?"

"The reception is being held at Rannoch House and Cook is going to supervise."

"You're not going to have the reception there, are you? What's wrong with the Dorchester or Claridge's?"

"Money, for one. And also I think it's nice to hold the reception at the family home."

"But your poisonous sister-in-law will limit everyone to one glass of champagne and one smoked salmon sandwich each!"

I grinned. "I'll get Zou Zou involved. She'll make sure there is enough champagne. And I want to keep it simple. A few nibbles, a few toasts, we cut the cake and off we go."

"You go where?"

"I'm not sure yet. The queen has offered us Balmoral."

"Good God! If any place would put a dampener on your sex life it would be Balmoral. You'd be haunted by your great-grandmother saying she wasn't amused every time you wanted to take your clothes off."

I laughed. "I'm hoping Darcy has other ideas. Actually I'm hoping Darcy comes back soon because I really want . . ." I broke off. All day I had managed to keep my worries at bay. Now, as Haywards Heath came closer, they flooded back into my brain.

"Of course you really want!" Mummy said, giving me a nudge and a giggle, completely misinterpreting what I had been about to say. "I don't know how long I care bear to go without sex myself."

This time the two elderly ladies looked well and truly shocked.

As the train slowed for the station Mummy grabbed my hand. "I've just had an awful thought," she said. "I was all set to marry Max and his mother died. Your grandfather was all set to marry Mrs. Huggins and she died. Good God, Georgie! I hope we're not cursed as a family. I hope someone's not going to die and prevent your wedding."

I wished she hadn't said that, because the same thought had crossed my mind as we had stood with my grandfather waiting for Mrs. Huggins's body to be removed. Now that was one more thing to worry about. I was living in a house of unexplained threats. Darcy was away probably doing something dangerous. Please keep him safe, I prayed silently.

We alighted at Haywards Heath and Mummy decided on a taxi rather than wait for Plunkett to drive out to fetch us. No servants appeared to greet us as we entered the foyer. The house was eerily silent.

"I don't know what's the matter with your servants," Mummy said. "Anyone could just walk in here and burgle the place."

"There's not much worth taking, is there?" I asked.

"Those family portraits in the long gallery. But they are rather big to tuck under one's shirt." She looked around her. "I wonder where Hubert has stowed the good stuff."

As she talked I had spotted a letter, addressed to me, bearing an impressive coat of arms, lying on the hall table.

"It's from the Earl of Malmsbury," I said excitedly. "Now maybe we'll know more."

"About what?" Mummy asked, always disinterested in things that were happening to other people. "Shall we ring for sherry and cheese straws? I'm famished."

She went off to locate the nearest bell. I opened the envelope.

Dear Lady Georgiana:

With regard to your query about Charles Plunkett. He was a good and faithful retainer who served my mother loyally for many years. When she died last year we were sorry to let him go.

> *Yours faithfully,*
> *Malmsbury*

Chapter 27

I am really confused about Plunkett. Fig said that old Lady Malmsbury
was eccentric. Perhaps he deliberately seeks out eccentric elderly
ladies and is able to manipulate their finances or pocket some of
their jewelry, which is why he was so hostile when I arrived to spoil
things.

I heard Mummy ordering sherry and Queenie's reply, "Bob's yer uncle."
She'd never make it in a proper stately home, I thought. She was quite
incapable of learning how to behave toward members of the upper
class. Or perhaps she simply thought that she was as good as any of us
and thus could address us as equals. Who knew what went on in her
head? At least she was pleasant and willing, and she did bake the most
divine cheese straws!

But as for Plunkett, he was only just civil to me. Quite unlike
butlers I had known. And yet apparently elderly ladies adored him. I
wondered if he'd even had a hand in helping Lady Anstruther escape

from her old people's home or clinic or whatever it was, so that he could look after her here and get his hands on her money. In which case he would have had every reason to get rid of Mr. Broadbent, who might have come because he was concerned about her finances. But I still needed some kind of proof before I went to the police.

I looked down at the letter I still held in my hands. The thing that bothered me was that the earl described Plunkett as a faithful retainer. That implied someone who had been with the family for many years. Plunkett was not old. He was fifty at the most, probably in his forties. Yet one more thing that didn't make sense. Was this man maybe not Charles Plunkett at all, but had somehow stolen Plunkett's letter of reference? In which case, where was the real Plunkett now?

I looked around me. The house still appeared deserted, apart from Queenie, who had gone back to the kitchen. I went through to Mummy, who was piling her packages on a chair in the foyer. "I've told Queenie to carry those up to my room after she's delivered the sherry and cheese straws and ask Claudette to put them away."

"You are trusting," I said, unable to resist a smile. "You know Queenie. She's likely to fall and sit on your hat box."

"Nonsense. I think she's doing splendidly here. I must say her cooking is remarkably good. And if she has disasters in the kitchen where we can't see them, then nobody is the wiser."

"Will you do something for me?" I asked. "If Plunkett appears, will you keep him talking for a few minutes?"

"What are you up to?" she asked.

"Just a little snooping," I said. "I'll tell you later."

I crept to the door leading down to the kitchen and servants' part of the house, pushed it open and listened. I could hear nothing, but I hesitated to go down to the butler's sitting room. He might well be taking a snooze in an armchair. But I could check out his bedroom. I went up the main staircase at the back of the west wing, then along the hall and through the door in the wall that led to the servants' staircase. This stair was steep and uncarpeted and I had a moment's compassion for poor little maids who over centuries had had to carry jugs of hot water or scuttles of coal up these every day. And this was the stair where Rogers presumably fell to his death. I could understand how an elderly man, doddery on his feet, had lost his footing. But there was a good banister on one side he could have grabbed on to. I thought it more probable that someone had crept up behind him and given him a shove. What didn't quite make sense was that he was planning to retire. He had already contacted the agency and presumably they had recommended Plunkett. But Plunkett wasn't already in the house at that time. Then who?

Now my suspicious mind mulled this over. What if Rogers knew the real Charles Plunkett and this one was an imposter? Butlers did sometimes know one another. And Rogers had recommended him to take over because he was a good butler of the old school. Then he fell down the stairs, something happened to Plunkett and this man came to assume the role. It seemed possible. I reached the top-floor landing, where the servants' bedrooms were situated. When I peeked into the first one I was struck by how bleak and spartan servants' bedrooms were. A narrow bed, a chest of drawers, a couple of hooks on the wall for an overcoat and hat. Almost nothing personal, nothing to brighten up the room. This one had to belong to a woman because there were dainty slippers beside the bed. I worked my way along the hall. I could tell Queenie's instantly because it was already messy, with her awful overcoat hung on the peg.

Then, at the end was the biggest room. Obviously Plunkett's. I looked around, then entered. This room was not spartan. He had a big, comfortable bed, a satin eiderdown, lace-edged pillows, a rug on the floor, velvet curtains at the window. All pilfered from down below, I thought. I went over to the chest of drawers. There was a mirror over it and on top of it a polished wood box containing a set of silver-handled brushes, such as one is given for a twenty-first birthday. And on it were initials: EP. So not Charles Plunkett but maybe a relative? I started to go through the drawers, but they didn't seem to contain any papers.

Anything of a sensitive nature would probably be in his desk in his office down below. I'd have to find a way to occupy him while I snooped in there. I was just about to leave the room when I heard footsteps coming up the stairs. I looked around desperately. Should I hide behind the door? Behind the curtains? I realized I had left the door slightly ajar. That would give me away. I closed it as quietly as I could. Then I decided to take no chances and dived under the bed. Just in time, it would seem. I heard the footsteps coming along the hall; then the handle turned and someone entered this room.

I held my breath as feet crossed the floor. All I could see was the lower portions of brown trouser legs and beneath them a pair of brown suede shoes with crepe soles. The man moved swiftly and silently, opened a drawer, closed it again and then retreated, closing the door quietly behind him. I lay, not daring to move, for quite a while. Who wore brown suede shoes, I wondered? Certainly not Plunkett or Mc-Shea, who wore polished black shoes with their uniforms. Had I noticed Fernando's feet? But then his shoes didn't have crepe soles. I remembered hearing the tap of his footsteps as he approached me. One of the gardeners, perhaps? But suede shoes with crepe soles were quite a luxury and the gardener who had run toward us yelling had definitely been wearing big boots. Besides, a gardener would never be allowed inside the house, and most definitely not up to the servants' bedrooms. Unless . . . Unless something funny was going on.

I had led a sheltered life and it had been a shock to me to find that people crept between bedrooms at night, that men had liaisons with other men. Was Plunkett like that? Was this a secret lover leaving him a note? My first thought was excitement that I now had something to hold over him. I hadn't yet had to resort to blackmail, but one never knew. . . . I hauled myself out from under the bed, brushing off copious amounts of dust. Really, the housekeeping at Eynsleigh left much to be desired! Then I crept across to that chest of drawers and opened the top drawer. The note had been tucked between folded pairs of underpants. I took it out. It read:

Put forward. Boat Thurs now. Watch what you say. New maid is sharper than she looks.

I folded it and slipped it back into the drawer. What could it mean? Boat Thursday? Was Thursday Plunkett's day off? Was he planning a tryst on the river or a boat ride at Brighton? And what had to be kept from the new maid, presumably referring to Queenie? Whoever it was had taken a big risk creeping into the house in broad daylight. I hurried down the stairs and into Mummy's bedroom. The sun was setting, the trees along the driveway casting long shadows. But it was still light enough to see anyone leaving the house. I watched for a long while but saw nothing. Was the intruder maybe hiding out in one of the unused rooms, waiting to slip away after dark? Or was it possible it was one of the gardeners?

As I went to join Mummy in the drawing room I passed Joanie carrying a load of folded linen up the stairs. "Has anyone just gone out of the house, Joanie?" I asked. "I'm sure I heard the front door close."

"Not that I know of, my lady," Joanie replied in that tone that implied she couldn't care less. "But then I've just come from the laundry room, where you can't hear anything."

I waited until she had gone up the stairs and then let myself out of the front door. I walked around the house but saw no sign of anyone. The Bentley was parked outside the garage. As I passed it I smelled that hot-oil smell. I went closer and I realized that the motor was still warm. Someone had used it recently. Would the motor be as warm as that if Plunkett had merely driven it out of the garage, ready for us? I wondered. Or had someone taken it for a joyride and that was why there was a distinct absence of servants when we came back from London? I sighed. I was tired of suspecting the worst. I wanted a house that ran smoothly and happily. I went back to join Mummy.

Plunkett appeared almost immediately. He seemed rather breathless. "I'm sorry, my lady. I did not realize you had returned home."

"Ah, there you are, Plunkett," I said in a pleasant voice. "We wondered where you'd got to when we arrived home and nobody was there to greet us."

"I apologize, my lady," he said. "I was down in the pantry, polishing silver. I thought it was about time you had proper candlesticks out on the table again, now that Her Grace is living here. And we expected you to telephone from the station to send for the Bentley."

"We took a taxicab," I said. "It seemed simpler."

"Was it indeed bad news, my lady?" he asked. "Your grandfather's health?"

"Is perfectly fine, thank you, Plunkett," I said. "It was his bride-to-be who unfortunately had a heart attack and died. So naturally he is most upset and I've asked him to come and stay here to recuperate."

"My condolences, my lady," he said. "When will the gentleman be arriving?"

"I'm not sure. He has a funeral to plan first. But I should like a bedroom to be made ready for him."

"Of course, my lady."

"Do go and find out what has happened to my sherry and cheese straws, Plunkett," Mummy said. "I'm positively famished. And tell Cook that we'd like dinner in half an hour."

Heaven forbid that we put her father's well-being before food!

Chapter 28

I'm so happy that Granddad will be coming soon. He'll know what to
do. Maybe I'm worrying over nothing. The police will have located
Mr. Broadbent and all will be well. But not quite . . . there is still
the matter of Charles Plunkett and my intuition that something is
definitely not right at this house.

The night passed without incident. Mummy and I breakfasted together.
She seemed to be more cheerful by the minute. "I'm glad that your grandfather is coming here. It will be just like old times, won't it? The family
all together." She popped a piece of toast, laden with Cooper's Oxford
marmalade, into her mouth. "The food is much nicer here than in Germany," she said. "All that stodge and cream. So bad for the waist and the
complexion, but then the Germans like their women plump, don't they?"

"You are beginning to sound relieved that you are not marrying
Max," I said.

"Oh no. Not at all. I adore Max. I'm just not wild about living in

Germany." That wistful look came over her face again. "Shall we go and see if the gardeners have done what you asked and removed those awful traps? I would rather like to revisit that little gazebo. Those were such happy times. . . ."

"All right," I said. "You'd better go and put on your stout shoes. It's horribly overgrown in that part of the grounds."

It was a brisk morning with a strong wind from the west and we both were wearing jackets over our summer frocks. Mummy complained immediately that she should have tied up her hair in a scarf. "Now Claudette will have to spend hours getting my curls back into place," she said.

"There's nobody to see except me," I pointed out.

As we came around to the back of the house I was pleased to see Old Ben striding out toward the kitchen garden.

"Ben," I called. "Welcome back."

He touched his cap to me. "Morning, my lady. Lovely day, isn't it?"

I made sure we accompanied him until we located the two gardeners. They had been stacking crates of lettuce and looked guilty as they saw us approaching.

"Are those heading for the village shop?" I asked. "You've made sure you've left enough for the house?"

"Yes, my lady," Bill muttered, shooting a swift glance at Ted.

"And I've brought in an expert to supervise you," I said. "Do you remember Ben? He's worked in this garden all his life. Under his supervision we'll soon have it looking splendid again. And he'll be reporting directly to me."

I could tell this didn't please them. "Oh, and about those traps." I gave them a long, hard stare. "Ben says that Sir Hubert would never have used man-traps and would be horrified to know about them. So did you do as I asked and remove them all?"

"We couldn't find any after all, my lady," Ted Hoskins said, looking down so that he didn't meet my gaze. "It must have been a prank played on us by the last gardeners who were here."

"Well, that's a relief, isn't it?" I said. "I would have worried that one of you would wind up losing a foot to his own trap."

They both managed a weak smile. My gaze went down to their feet. Both had on heavy boots, the sort that countrymen wear. And they didn't look the sort to consider wearing suede shoes. So the mystery intruder remained a mystery.

"Well, we'll leave you to get started, then," I said, giving them my brightest smile. "We are going for a walk around the grounds. My mother is anxious to see the gazebo she remembers."

"You want to watch out for them deer, missus," Bill called after us. "They can be quite fierce if startled."

"I'm glad to know there still are deer in the grounds," I said. "I always loved to see them when I was a child. But thank you. We shall be careful where we walk."

As we moved off I heard Ben's voice, "Right, you two. First things first. Herbaceous borders. They're a proper disgrace."

I wondered how long they'd stick with it here under his supervision. I steered our course deliberately toward where the bonfire had been. It was no use. A new pile of branches and garden waste had been dumped on the site, ready for burning. So on we went, into the wood, heading for the gazebo. This time we located it easily enough, but it was in such a sorry state that Mummy gave a little sob of despair. Ivy had enveloped the columns and great tendrils hung down from the roof as if ready to grab anyone who tried to enter. The marble floor was piled with layers of dead leaves and the steps leading up to it were cracked, with saplings shooting up between the stones.

"My lovely gazebo," Mummy said. "It would break Hubert's heart to see it like this. We must get those gardeners working on it right away, Georgie."

"It's really not a top priority," I said. "We need the lawns mowed and the beds weeded first. It seems that they've put all their energy into the kitchen garden so that they could sell the produce."

"But that's disgusting," Mummy said. "I'd dismiss the pair of them."

"The problem is that I haven't exactly been given authority to sack anybody," I said. "Believe me, Plunkett would have gone by now if it were up to me. And Fernando. And Joanie, for that matter."

"They aren't the best lot of servants I've ever seen," Mummy agreed. "Nor the most willing. It comes to something when one is thrilled to have Queenie, doesn't it?"

That made me laugh and we giggled as we left the gazebo. "I tell you what," I said. "When Granddad gets here we can tackle this as a family project. We'll come here with clippers and rakes and we'll have it back to its former glory in no time at all."

"Yes. That's the ticket. It will give me something to do. Take my mind off what I have lost." She looked pleased. "And what about that little chapel?" she said. "I wonder if that is similarly taken over by the forest? It was not too far from here."

"No, it was quite all right," I said. "I found it yesterday, by accident."

"You came here yesterday? Before you knew whether they had removed the traps?" She shook her head. "Georgie, what were you thinking?"

"I was thinking that I didn't really believe there were any traps in the grounds. I think we were told that because those gardeners didn't want us to come here."

"Why would that be?"

"I don't know. Another of their little moneymaking schemes perhaps."

"So you went in the chapel?"

"I did. It was in quite good condition. A little dusty but everything in place."

"And what about that awful crypt? What did you think of that?"

"Crypt? I didn't see a crypt."

"Didn't you? Absolutely gruesome."

"I didn't see any doors or stairs in the chapel."

"Oh, now I come to think of it, the entrance was round at the back.

Hubert only took me there once. I found it quite alarming: all those Anstruthers stacked on top of each other around the walls."

"What do you mean?"

"Their coffins, darling. Vaults. All the Anstruthers buried there."

"I have to see this," I said.

"Well, I'm not coming down with you," she said.

"You can keep watch and let me know if anyone is coming," I told her.

We located the chapel quite easily and this time we went around to the back, where there was a small door in the wall, only about four feet high. It was made of solid oak with impressive wrought-iron decorative bars across it. I opened the latch to see a flight of steep steps descending into darkness. I had to agree with Mummy that it did not look inviting.

"Don't let the door close," I said and started downward. The wall felt cold and damp to the touch. Luckily the staircase was not long. Eight steps and I was in a low underground area. Even in the gloom I could see what Mummy meant. All around the walls were vaults, one above the other, each with an inscription on it. HENRY WILLIAM ANSTRUTHER, 1745–1789. JULIA MARIA ANSTRUTHER, 1648–1720. And on the floor were what I presumed were more elaborate tombs: a sleeping knight; a black marble slab. It really was awfully creepy.

I didn't want to go any farther, but I had to make sure that there was nothing hidden behind one of the tombs. I was about to step down onto the floor when I noticed something. The floor was dusty and covered in remnants of old leaves that had blown in over the years. And one new leaf, still green although starting to curl up now. And near the steps was a footprint. A big boot had been here recently.

Chapter 29

Things are becoming rather frightening. Please hurry up and get here, Granddad!

I tiptoed forward and peered over the black marble slab but saw nothing. But now my suspicions were truly roused. What better place to dispose of an unwanted body than in a place where many bodies were buried? I wondered if I could see whether one of the vaults had been recently opened, but it was too dark and frankly I wasn't keen to try this on my own. The thought of reaching my hand into a recess and touching goodness knows what did not appeal! And it was no good asking my mother for moral support. She'd shied away from anything unpleasant her whole life. I'd just have to wait until Granddad got here and we could explore together. And if we found what I suspected we might, then we'd go straight to the police with proof.

In the meantime, however, I had to face the thought that I was in a house with at least one murderer. If Mr. Broadbent was indeed entombed in this crypt, then it must have taken a couple of stout men to carry him this far. So if Lady Anstruther had accidentally killed him in one of her rampages, then she needed the assistance of other members of the household to hide the body—as that big boot print proved. I came out of the crypt again, shut the door behind me and gave Mummy my brightest smile.

"I can see why you didn't want to go down there. Horribly macabre!" And I shuddered.

"Hubert didn't think so at all," she said. "He was awfully proud of having all his ancestors here in one place. He's even selected his own vault already."

We walked away quickly, both wanting to get back to the safety of open lawns. I caught sight of both young gardeners working on a flower bed along the front drive. Ben was snipping away at one of the overgrown topiary hedges. His expert cutting had already returned it to the shape of a bird. He nodded to us as we went past.

"Had a good walk then, my lady?" he asked me.

"Very nice, thank you, Ben."

We passed on into the house.

I then checked that a suitable room had been made ready for my grandfather: on the sunny side of the house and near enough to the bathroom. Then I opened all the windows wide to let in the fresh air. I remembered that this was the room I had come to on the first night when I had heard the scrunch of tires on gravel. And I had discovered that it contained nothing but bedframes with cloths draped over them, when I had been sure that it had been full of furniture. I stood, staring out of the window, thinking. So many things that didn't make sense. Why had the furniture been moved out of the room in such a hurry and why make it seem that it was still full of stuff?

The day seemed to drag by, with me pacing restlessly. What if Granddad decided he had to stay in town for a week to organize the funeral? Should I perhaps go to the inspector right now? But the worrying thought in my head whispered that if the police found nothing, then the servants would know that I suspected them. And if the body was hidden somewhere else, if there was something underhanded going on here, then I might just be the next to tumble down those stairs or to find the gas tap turned fully on while I slept.

Queenie appeared just after six, asking if I wanted her to dress me for dinner.

"It's a casserole tonight," she said. "And I've left Fernando to do the potatoes and veg. Even he can't mess that up."

"Is he really that bad?" I asked as I pulled my cotton frock over my head.

"Bleeding hopeless, if you ask me," she said. "I don't know where he's cooked before, but he don't half leave the kitchen in a right state."

"And what about the rest of them?"

She pursed her lips. "I tell you one thing, miss. They wouldn't last five minutes in a proper house like your brother's. No respect for the butler. Sloppy dress. Her what's supposed to be the maid, Joanie. She smokes in the kitchen. Did you ever hear anything like it?"

This would have been priceless, coming from the world's biggest disaster of a maid, if it hadn't been so worrying. Who had hired these people? Surely Sir Hubert's solicitor would have made sure that replacement servants were competent and trustworthy?

Queenie finished doing up the buttons at the back of my dress, still chatting away. "That Joanie. She don't half give herself airs too," she said. "Told me she's too good to be a servant and the only people who become maids are those not smart enough to get a proper job." She looked up, her eyes meeting mine in the mirror. "I asked her why she was a maid, then, and she said it wasn't for long, trust her."

"Interesting," I said.

Queenie finished dressing me without a hitch, except that the hairbrush got caught in my hair somehow, needing a long and painful session as she tried to pull it free.

"Sorry, miss," she said, red-faced from exertion. "I tried to make the pageboy go under nicely and it wouldn't. I can't seem to get it out now. Every time I pull it gets more tangled." She tugged again. "Should I get some scissors and cut it out?"

"Absolutely not," I said. "I don't want a big patch with no hair at the back."

"Then how about we leave it and put a bow over it for now?"

"Oh, let me do it," I said, reaching up to feel the back of my own head. "Queenie, you should go back to the kitchen, where you are less of a disaster."

"Sorry, miss," she repeated with a hangdog expression. "I do try. I just ain't very good at some things."

As she retreated to the kitchen and I finally extracted the brush from my hair, I realized I was glad she was still the same old Queenie, prone to mistakes. She probably did drop the chicken on the kitchen floor, where we couldn't see it. But at least I felt comfortable with her. I wondered if I should keep her on as my maid when a better cook was hired or whether I should let her be assistant cook. Anyway, that was all far in the future. I had the present to get through first.

I had just joined Mummy for sherry when Plunkett appeared.

"There is a person asking for you, my lady," he said.

"A person? What sort of person?"

"A rather lower-class sort of elderly male person, my lady. I sent him around to the servants' entrance at the back. He wasn't too pleased about this on account of carrying a rather large suitcase."

I leaped up while he was still speaking, pushed past him and rushed to the front door. It had started to rain and he was just disappearing around the corner of the house.

"Granddad!" I yelled and tried to sprint after him. Unfortunately one of my satin evening shoes went into a particularly muddy puddle and got stuck there. I left it behind and ran on in a stockinged foot. "Granddad, wait!"

He heard me, stopped and waited.

"Come back, you silly old thing," I said, opening my arms to him.

"But that bloke said to go around to the back."

I reached him and picked up his suitcase. "And I say you come in through the front door. Come on. We're getting wet."

"He obviously thought I was the new boot boy," he said, chuckling now.

"Why didn't you tell him you were my grandfather?"

"He never really gave me a chance," he said. "He took one look and said, 'Round the back. The servants' entrance.'"

"Bloody cheek!" I exclaimed, making him chuckle even more.

"I never thought I'd hear a lady like you say those words," he said.

"This is the right time and place for them, don't you think?"

I had taken his arm and led him up the steps. Plunkett had just fished out an umbrella and was coming down the steps to meet us. "I'm sorry about that, my lady. I thought, you see . . ."

"Plunkett, this is my grandfather," I said.

"Your grandfather?" His jaw dropped a little.

"That's right. And you are to treat him with the same respect you give to me and my mother, is that clear?"

"Oh yes, my lady. Absolutely," he said.

We entered the front hall. Plunkett put away the umbrella. "May I help you with your coat, sir?" he said to my grandfather. "And, my lady, you are rather wet, I fear. May I suggest you go and change before you catch cold?"

"I will," I said. "Tell Cook there will be one more for dinner. And send someone to retrieve an evening shoe I left in a puddle."

Granddad's coat was taken from him and I led him up the stairs to his bedroom. He looked at it with dismay. "Oh no, ducks," he said.

"You don't like it?" I asked. "I chose it especially for you because it's nice and sunny and not too fussy."

"Oh, don't get me wrong," he said, looking around with a worried expression. "It's a smashing room, all right. It's just that I wouldn't feel right here. It's too good for someone like me."

"Rubbish!" I said. "You're my grandfather and this is my house so I want you to have one of the best rooms."

"If you say so, my love," he said.

I took his hand and squeezed it. "I want you to be happy here," I said. "And don't take any nonsense from the servants—especially not from Plunkett."

"That podgy bloke? He's the butler, is he?"

"Yes, and I'm having a bit of trouble with him. But I won't bore you with that tonight. Tomorrow we might take a stroll and I'll tell you everything."

He looked at me. "You're shivering," he said. "Go and take that wet frock off."

"All right," I said. "Don't bother to unpack now. I'll take you down for some sherry with Mummy."

He nodded. I left him staring out of the window. He was sitting on the bed looking like a lost boy on his first day at a new school when I came back for him, wearing my silk tea dress because I had only brought one long evening gown. I hoped Clotilde had remembered to send on my trunks and wasn't waiting for me to ask for them.

"Come on. Let's go down," I said.

He looked around him in awe as we went down the staircase. "Nice place you got here," he said. "Big, ain't it? Are you going to enjoy living here?"

"Eventually, when Darcy and I are married. Right now I'm glad you and Mummy are here. And you're welcome to stay for as long as you want."

I saw that Mummy had worked her way through most of the cheese straws as I led Granddad into the drawing room.

"Sherry?" I asked him as he stood in the doorway, looking uncomfortable. "Or would you rather have a whiskey? I'm sure there must be some."

"I'm not much of a drinker, love," he said. "A little swig of sherry would go down a treat, I suppose. We only ever had sherry and port in the house at Christmas."

I poured him a glass. He perched nervously at the edge of the sofa beside Mummy.

"How are the funeral arrangements progressing?" I asked.

He shrugged. "Her family has taken over everything. Her daughter wants her buried with the late Mr. Huggins. I didn't think she'd like that, seeing as how she told me what a rotten husband he was, but it seems they bought a double plot and the daughter's not about to waste it. Well, it leaves me out, don't it? I told them I'd come back for the funeral on Saturday."

"I'll come with you," I said.

"No need for that."

"You won't want to go alone." I patted his hand.

"You're a good girl." He gave me a beaming smile.

We were summoned to dinner, which was a good, if humble, steak and kidney pie. Granddad nodded with approval. "Good cook you've got here."

"This is Queenie's work, I expect."

"Queenie? You mean Hettie's great-niece? The one what burned down her family's kitchen?"

"The very same. She has turned into quite a good cook. Amazing, isn't it?"

"Her family will never believe it when I tell them. They couldn't wait to be rid of her."

I realized as we were speaking that I hadn't told Queenie about her great-aunt's death. I always forgot that she was related to Mrs. Huggins, which was how I'd acquired her in the first place. "She'll want to come to the funeral on Saturday too, I expect. Maybe we should all drive up in the motorcar," I said.

I sent for her after dinner. She came into the drawing room, drying her hands on her apron. "Is something wrong, miss?" she asked. "Was the pie not good enough?"

"The food was perfect, thank you, Queenie. But as you can see, my grandfather has come to stay with us because your great-aunt Hettie has unfortunately died."

"Yeah, I heard about that when Plunkett told us that your grandfather was coming to stay." She grinned. "He obviously thought it would be some grand old duke or something. He said we all had to be on our best behavior."

"What a shock, eh?" Granddad grinned. "And he finds out it's only me."

"Not only you!" I said. "You are just as important as any duke. They had still all better be on their best behavior." I turned back to Queenie. "So, Queenie, I expect you'll want to attend the funeral with us on Saturday. We'll drive up in the motorcar."

"Yeah, I suppose I'd better come," she said. Obviously not too keen to see her family again.

"You can tell them you are a cook in a big house now," I said.

She brightened up. "I can. How about that, eh? And you'll be there to tell them I'm not fibbing either. And I ain't burned down no kitchens."

I silently added the word "yet."

Chapter 30

THURSDAY, JULY 4
EYNSLEIGH, SUSSEX

I feel so much better, knowing that Granddad is here. After all those years' experience in the police force he'll know if something is really wrong here or I'm imagining things.

I was up early the next morning and relieved to see it had stopped raining. A mist hung over the parkland and seemed to somehow magnify the birdsong. A cuckoo rang out loud and clear, above the cacophony of wood pigeons, thrushes, blackbirds. On other occasions I would have enjoyed just standing there at the window, admiring the view, but today I was too tense. I wanted to show Granddad that crypt as soon as possible. I wanted to put things right.

As I came out of my bedroom my grandfather poked his head around his door.

"Oh, you're up, ducks," he said. "I was wondering when anything got going around here."

"Not normally as early as this," I said. "Are you already washed and dressed?"

"That's right. I've always been an early riser."

"Then let's go down and get a cup of tea."

"That would go down a treat," he said.

"You know, you can always ring the bell in your room if you want something," I said. "One of the servants will come. You can ask them to bring you up a cup of tea."

"Oh, I couldn't do that," he said. "I'm not used to your way of life, ducks. Always done everything for myself."

I rang the kitchen bell and eventually Fernando appeared. There was no sign of Queenie yet and I suspected she slept in late. I ordered tea and it came, looking like dishwater. My grandfather sniffed at it. "What's this stuff, then?"

"It's the way Fernando makes tea. I'll have Queenie make you a proper pot later."

"What was this Sir Hubert bloke doing hiring a Spanish cook in the first place?" he asked.

"I wish I knew. All the staff seem to be brand-new, so it's quite possible that Plunkett hired him. Maybe Plunkett has a taste for Spanish food, or maybe the old lady does."

"Old lady?"

I told him about Sir Hubert's mother. His face brightened up. "Maybe she'd like a visit from an old geezer like me. We could chat about old times."

"She doesn't chat. She throws things and has birds that fly around and land on your head." When he looked puzzled, I laughed. "She's quite dotty, Granddad."

"Oh, I see. Blimey. I don't envy you living here with a bunch of strange servants and a barmy old lady."

"I don't envy me either," I said. "Which is why I wanted to talk to you." I looked around. The house still seemed quiet, but I knew how well servants managed to overhear most things that went on. "Shall we go for a walk?" I asked. "I'll show you the grounds and introduce you to Old Ben if he's here today. You two would get along famously."

We put on jackets, as the wind was quite brisk. Rooks rose cawing from a big yew tree as we passed behind the house. There was no sign of the two gardeners.

"Nice grounds. Like a ruddy Kew Gardens," Granddad commented.

"They really are lovely and I'm going to get them back to the way they were. I've already got the fountain up and running again. But the lawns need mowing and the beds need tidying up."

"Growing some good-looking beans, I see. And marrows? Nice little kitchen garden."

"That's the only part of the garden that is flourishing," I said. "The gardeners have been growing extra produce and selling it."

"Go on! Is that normally done?"

"Not as far as I know. Sir Hubert told them they could sell any excess, so I suppose they had the right. But I've now made the village shop send the proceeds straight to the household account. And I'm going to be checking the books weekly. Plunkett has been dipping into the funds, I'm sure."

"A rum ruddy lot you've got here," he said.

"I know. And frankly I'm worried." And I told him everything that had happened since I arrived. Now he looked worried too. "Someone turned the gas tap on? I don't reckon that was no accident, love. And this finance bloke? Why would anyone have killed him?"

"I thought that maybe Lady Anstruther killed him by accident. If she threw something heavy and it hit him on the head perhaps?"

"And the staff were willing to cover up for her? That's loyalty for you, knowing they could all go to prison as accessories to murder."

"I know. It doesn't quite make sense." We had reached the edge of the lawns and the wild part of the estate stretched ahead of us. "That's why I wanted you to come with me and see this." I led him down a narrow path into the woods. We didn't speak until the chapel appeared in a clearing ahead of us.

"Well, blow me down," Granddad said. "It's a ruddy little church."

"Yes, it's the family chapel. They were Catholics and had to hold their services in secret in the old days when being a Catholic got you burned at the stake."

I opened the door and let him peek inside; then I led him around to the back. "Mummy told me about the crypt under the chapel where all the family members are buried," I said. "And someone had been there recently. There was a footprint of a big boot in the dust on the floor. And a leaf. So I wondered if one of the vaults had been opened and a body hidden inside. What better place to hide someone?"

"Blimey," he said. "Didn't you think of going to the police with this? Rather have them poke around in old vaults."

"I did think of it," I said. "But what if I was wrong? What if nobody was hidden here, but they'd buried the body somewhere else? Then they would know that I suspected and something might happen to me. I might be pushed down a flight of stairs like Rogers."

"I think maybe we should all go back to London for the time being," he said. "Wait until your Darcy gets here. He'll sort things out."

That was the last thing he should have said. Wait for the damsel to be rescued by the handsome prince? Darcy had had to rescue me from difficult situations before and I was very grateful to him. But I wanted to start this marriage as an equal partner, not as a helpless female needing to be protected.

"I want to see it through," I said. "The moment I have any proof of wrongdoing I'll go to the police, I promise."

We stood outside the door to the crypt and I took a deep breath before I turned the knob to open it. "There's no light down here," I said. "We should have brought a torch. That was silly of me."

"We can prop the door open," he said and picked up a stone that was lying nearby.

"Careful on these steps," I said. "They are quite steep."

We went down, holding on to the wall. At the bottom step I halted. "Look, see the footprint?"

"That could have been there for ages," he said. "It's pretty much sealed off down here, isn't it? Like a walk-in tomb."

I shivered. "It's awfully cold. Come on. Let's get this over with."

We went around the walls, examining each of the vaults, seeing nothing strange or suspicious. Then Granddad stopped by one of the marble tombs on the floor. "Hello, hello," he said. "Look here."

My heart was beating so loudly I thought I could hear it echoing from the vaulted roof. "What?"

"See this. It's been moved recently. Look at the floor. And there's no dust on the marble."

It was a white marble sarcophagus against the far wall, smaller than some of the other tombs, its top carved with a sleeping lady in medieval costume. Granddad and I looked at each other.

"We wouldn't be strong enough to lift the top off, would we? It's solid marble."

"No, but we might slide it sideways, just enough to see."

I swallowed hard. I wanted to see, but I didn't. "All right. Let's give it a try."

We pushed with all our might. Finally we felt it give an inch or two.

"Hold on," Granddad said. "I'll go up and get a bit of wood." He went up the stairs with impressive agility for one of his age and returned with a fallen tree branch. He stuck the thinnest part into the narrow gap and then pulled down, using it as a lever. As the marble moved we both recoiled at the horrid smell.

"Oh goodness." I covered my nose with my hand.

"It's not too bad," he said. "Recently dead bodies smell much worse. I'd say this one had been in here for some time."

"Really?"

He nodded. We both moved closer. I was expecting to see a bald head, a black suit. Instead the first thing I glimpsed was long white hair. This time it really was hair, not animal fur. And it surrounded a face . . . a face with the flesh shrunken back but not yet gone. Mouth open in a grimace showing yellowed teeth. And below the face a white nightgown.

"It's an old woman," Granddad said.

I peered down at her, trying to make sense of what I was seeing. "How long do you think she's been dead?" I asked.

"A few months, maybe? Not that long."

"Golly," was all I could find to say.

"Who do you reckon it is?" he asked.

"I've no idea. An Anstruther relative, I suppose. But if Sir Hubert was away, who would have arranged for her burial here? Another Anstruther relative, maybe? And were people buried in a nightgown?"

I broke off as I heard a movement outside the door. In the next instant the door had slammed shut, plunging us into total darkness.

Chapter 31

At least I know I was right to sense that something suspicious is going
on at Eynsleigh. But maybe I should have gone to the police
immediately with my suspicions. Now we're in a bit of a pickle.

For a second I was too terrified to move. Then I stumbled forward,
feeling my way over the cold marble of the tombs until I reached
the wall. I moved along the vaults until eventually I located the stairs
and went up them. I ran my hands over the smooth wood of the
door. There was no latch that one could open on the inside. We were
trapped.

"We can't get out, Granddad," I said. The seal around the door
was almost perfect. It didn't seem to let in a single chink of light.

"Hold on, love. I'm coming." I heard him mutter as he bumped
into things on the way to me; then I heard the exertion in his breath
as he felt his way up the steps.

"Move over. Let's have a look," he said, reaching out beside me to
touch the door.

"You can't look, that's just the point!" I heard my voice quiver. "There's absolutely no light."

"You're right," he said after a while. "I can't feel any kind of latch. Why would you need one? The dead don't want to get out."

"Someone will come looking for us," I said. "When we don't turn up Mummy will wonder where we've got to."

"Your mother is so wrapped up in herself that she probably won't notice we're gone for hours," he commented.

"But she will eventually," I said.

"I'm just wondering how long we can hold out," Granddad said.

"What do you mean?"

"I mean how much air we've got."

"Oh crikey, Granddad. That door does fit snugly. Do you think it's possible that we'll run out of air?"

"Don't worry. We're bound to be all right," he said, patting my shoulder. "Like you said, your mum will wonder where we are."

Horrid thoughts were going through my head. Whoever was behind this—whether it was the gardeners or Plunkett or whoever—might be wily enough to say that we had gone up to London. And Mummy might just believe them. And she wouldn't worry about us until we hadn't returned this evening.

I sank to the top step and sat hugging my knees. Granddad eased himself down just below me. "So what do you make of it?" he asked.

"I don't know what to make of it," I said. "I brought you here because I thought they might have hidden Mr. Broadbent's body in here. But I never expected to find an old lady. You say she's been dead for months, but not years?" As I said it, I was conscious of the horrid smell that surrounded us.

"Oh no. Not that long."

"Even in a place that's airtight and dry like this?"

"I really don't think so."

"Then the only old lady we know about is Sir Hubert's mother.

And she is supposedly alive and living in the west wing. But what if she did escape from the retirement home and came back here and was murdered and someone has taken her place?"

"Why?"

I thought about this. "Money? She collects an allowance, maybe? She has investments that the imposter is selling?" I touched his shoulder. "Yes, that must be it. Maybe they weren't expecting Mr. Broadbent to come in person and they realized he'd know that the imposter wasn't the real Lady Anstruther so they had to kill him."

"Could be," he agreed.

Another long pause; then I said, "So if Lady Anstruther is in this coffin, then who is impersonating her in the house?"

"We need to go to the police the moment we get out of here," Granddad said.

"Yes." I didn't change his words to say what I was thinking. *If we get out of here*

We sat in silence. In spite of wearing a jacket I felt horribly cold. I eased myself down a step and snuggled up against my grandfather. He put an arm around me. "It will be all right, my love. Don't worry."

After a while I said, "Those hinges on the door are really old. Do you think we could kick the door open?"

"Can't hurt to try," he said. "It's just we don't have much room here to move. We don't want to fall off the stairs."

"I'll try. You support me," I said.

He held on to me and I kicked with all my might. I shoved at the door with my shoulder as I have seen policemen do in films. It hurt my shoulder horribly and the door didn't budge. I tried kicking again.

"Should we shout, do you think?" Granddad asked.

"It wouldn't do any good. We're miles from anywhere. And the only people who could hear are the gardeners and we have to think it was one of them who closed the door. Unless—" I broke off, sensing a small glimmer of hope. "Unless Ben is working today. He's the old gardener I told to come a couple of times a week. But he was here yesterday so I don't think . . . But maybe he came anyway. Okay, let's bang and yell."

We did. Our voices echoed alarmingly in that vaulted chamber. The silence seemed more stifling after we stopped. I could almost sense that the dead were angry we had disturbed their peace.

"It's no use," I said. We sank back onto the steps again. I rested my head on Granddad's shoulder. Mummy will come eventually, I told myself. Even she will start to get worried if we've been gone long enough. She'll remember I said yesterday that I wanted to show Grand-dad the crypt. But then I had to admit that Mummy was not an early riser. What if she decided to stay in bed all morning? How long did we have before we couldn't breathe? Of course the moment I had that thought it seemed as if breathing was already harder. I thought about Granddad and his compromised lungs.

"Are you all right, Granddad?"

"What? Oh yes, love. Right as rain. Don't you worry about me."

But I did worry.

"This is stupid," I said. "Can't we pick that lock somehow? Do you have anything in your pockets like a penknife?"

"I left everything up in my room," he said. "And it's a simple latch, not a lock. Not the sort of thing you can pick with a hairpin."

"I don't use hairpins," I said, half laughing. "We could try that piece of wood you used to open the coffin."

I eased myself past him down the stairs, felt my way around and located the branch. It was sturdy and too thick to slip into a lock. I tried breaking it or splitting it but it was no use. I came back to Grand-dad. "It's too thick to be any good. But I could try battering the door with it. Maybe there's one weak spot in the wood after all these years."

I rammed the branch against the door again and again. *Crash, crash, boom* echoed around the vault. The door didn't yield.

Then suddenly I heard a far-off voice. "Hold on. Hold on. I'm coming."

The door opened. I blinked as daylight flooded in and looked up as a great shape blocked the doorway. Queenie stood there.

"Bloody 'ell," she said. "They really are in here. Stone the flippin' crows."

"Oh God. Are they all right?" It was my mother's voice behind her. Queenie held out a hand and pulled me to my feet; then we helped Granddad up. He came out gasping.

"Blimey, love," he said. "I thought I'd had my chips then."

"You are so clever to come and find us," I said to Mummy.

"It wasn't me, darling. It was your girl Queenie."

"How did you know, Queenie?" I asked.

"You're lucky your granddad liked the runner beans last night," she said. "I went to see if the gardeners had some more. I spotted the beans and decided to pick some myself. And while I was standing among the bean poles I heard two blokes talking. And one sounded really upset and he was yelling, 'I can't believe you did that. Are you crazy? Someone's bound to find them before it's too late. They'll know it was us and we'll get caught.'

"And the other voice said, 'Not if we scarper right now. We'll be long gone when they come looking for us.'

"And then the first bloke said, 'You mean get out now and meet up with the others later?' And he says, 'No. I mean we ditch the others. Save ourselves.' And the first one says, 'Phil will kill us when he finds us.' And the other replies, 'It's all over anyway, isn't it? I'm not going to swing with them.'"

She looked from one face to the next as she talked. "So I waited until they walked away and then I came back to the house. I knew it was something dodgy but I didn't know quite what they were talking about. Then your mum came up to me and asked if I'd seen you this morning. So I told her what I'd overheard and she said we had to go and look for you. So we looked all over the house and she said we should try this place. And Bob's yer uncle."

I had never been happier to hear that expression.

"Queenie, you are a marvel," I said.

We started to walk back to the house. As we approached I motioned the others closer to me. "We must be very careful what we say and do," I said. "From what Queenie overheard we know maybe all the servants are involved. They are all in this together, whatever it is."

"We must go straight to the police," Granddad said. "It's quite possible that they'll find your bloke hidden down in that vault."

"Which bloke are you talking about?" Mummy asked.

"The missing man. Mr. Broadbent," I said. "I think someone here on the property killed him and hid his body."

"Don't be silly," Mummy said. "I told you he absconded, didn't I? Well, it was in the *Times* this morning. His body was found at the foot of Beachy Head last night. A popular spot for suicides, so the paper says."

"Are you sure?"

"It's the *Times*, darling, not the *Daily Mirror*. They don't get things wrong."

"Golly." I couldn't find anything else to say. My whole theory was now shattered. I realized if we went to the police we had nothing to go on now. Maybe I had leaped to the wrong conclusion. Maybe Mr. Broadbent did go to Beachy Head and throw himself over. Anyway, there wouldn't be enough left of him after that drop to prove that he wasn't murdered first. So what could I say to the police? That we felt something suspicious was going on at the house? That Lady Anstruther might be buried in the vault and an imposter taking her place? That we were shut in that vault when we went to investigate and left to die?

I could just see the police smiling politely and suggesting that maybe I had an overactive imagination and it was the wind, not criminals, that blew the door shut on us. So how did I prove that the body in the coffin was Lady Anstruther? How could we possibly go back to the house and act as if nothing had happened?

"We could start by going to the retirement home where Lady Anstruther was living," I said, frowning as I thought this through. "They'll be able to tell us more."

"And where is that?" Mummy asked.

"I'm not sure."

"We can't check out every old people's home in England," Mummy said.

"I'm just thinking . . ." I paused. "The old housekeeper, Mrs. Holbrook, might know. She lives nearby. Let's go to her. She'll be a good person to talk to anyway."

We approached the house. I looked at Queenie. "Queenie, can I ask you to be very brave and stay here?" I said. "That way things will seem normal and they won't know we're onto them. It's clear the gardeners didn't tell anyone else what they'd done and that they were about to abscond. So you act as if nothing has happened and if you are asked you can say that you overheard my mother saying that she wanted to go shopping and it would be good for my grandfather to have an outing."

"Right-oh," she said. "I can do that. And I can listen for anything else they might say." She broke off. "Which of them do you suspect of something, my lady?"

"That's just the problem. I don't know. All we have to go on is that all the servants are new. The old servants either died or were let go. So what if they are all in some kind of scheme together?"

"It would be quite an ideal setup for criminals," Granddad said thoughtfully. "Master's away. One of them gets hired, brings the rest in and they have a nice little place to carry on their criminal activities where nobody would ever suspect them."

"Lady Mountjoy did say there had been burglaries in the neighborhood," I said. "I wonder if they have anything to do with that."

"A gang of burglars? Quite possible." Granddad nodded.

"Maybe they started by helping themselves to Hubert's good stuff," Mummy said. "Remember I commented how many things had gone and Plunkett said that Hubert had locked them away? What if he hadn't? What if they have filched them?"

"This is all supposition," I said.

"I've got a friend at Scotland Yard," Granddad said. "If we go to him he'll listen. I trained him when he was a young recruit, green as grass he was, but I licked him into shape and now he's a detective chief inspector. So he won't give us the brush-off."

"Then we'll find that home and go straight to Scotland Yard," I said. "Come on. Let's get the motorcar."

"Hold on a minute," Mummy said. "I think it might be a good idea if I stay here too."

"Why would you want to do that?" I asked. Mummy was normally the first to shy away from any unpleasantness, and staying in a house full of criminals was about as unpleasant as possible.

She gave a delightfully elegant shrug. "Create a semblance of normalcy," she replied. "I'll be my usual self, quite demanding. Wanting things brought to me. Nobody will suspect that anything is up."

"But, Mummy, you could be in danger. What if they do suspect?"

She gave me a withering glance. "You forget I am one of the great actresses of our age, darling. I can convince anyone of anything. They will believe that you've taken your poor old grandfather out for a spin in the motor to cheer him up."

"If you are really sure, that would be brilliant," I said, giving her a hug. She looked rather pleased with herself.

"And Queenie and I can watch out for each other," she said.

We reached the point where they would go back into the house and we'd turn toward the garage. At that moment we heard tires scrunching on gravel and the postman came toward us on his little motorbike.

"Letter for you, my lady," he said. Then he tipped his cap and was off again.

I turned the envelope over and saw the crest. "It's another letter from the Earl of Malmsbury," I said and tore it open.

Dear Lady Georgiana,

After I sent the first letter to you my wife pointed out that you might have been inquiring about Charles Plunkett because you were thinking of employing him. She felt that I should let you know that we were sorry to learn that he had died last year.

Yours faithfully,
Malmsbury

Chapter 32

THURSDAY, JULY 4
ALL OVER THE PLACE

Things are getting more complicated by the minute. If only Granddad's policeman can finally intervene . . .

As we were ready to drive off in the Bentley, Mummy stood on the steps, waving. "Oh, and don't forget to buy me that special soap I asked for, darling. That chemist in Haywards Heath should have it," she called in that voice that had charmed millions. She really was quite remarkable at times.

Granddad and I drove on. No one answered when we knocked on Mrs. Holbrook's front door, but we found her in the back garden, taking sheets down from the clothesline. She looked flustered at seeing us and tried to smooth down her hair. "Sorry, my lady. You've caught me at a bad moment," she said. "I was just taking in the washing. It looks like it could rain later."

"Here, let me help," Granddad said and started to take the pegs off the next sheet on the line.

"Oh, no need. That's very kind of you, sir," she said, even more flustered now.

Between us we put the sheets into the laundry basket and carried it into the house.

I introduced my grandfather and before I could let Mrs. Holbrook rush to make us a cup of tea I said, "I'm sorry to bother you again, but there is something at Eynsleigh that is not right and I need to know some facts before we go to the police."

"The police?" She looked worried. "Goodness me. What has been going on?"

"I'm not sure," I said. "Maybe something criminal."

"I never liked that new chap," she said. "I always thought there was something funny about him. And the way he got rid of the old servants. Turned them out without a thank-you."

"I wanted to ask about Lady Anstruther," I said. "Were you still working at Eynsleigh when Sir Hubert put his mother into the retirement home?"

A grin crossed her face. "I was indeed, my lady. And she wasn't too anxious to go, I can tell you. Made an awful fuss. But he said it was for her own good. He said he was going to be away for quite a while. She'd had a fall, you know. Broke her hip. He thought there wouldn't be enough servants to take good care of her and she'd be much happier being properly looked after and having other people to chat to. So off she went."

"Do you happen to know the name of the place?"

"It was called Downsview, I believe, and it was just outside Lewes."

"Mrs. Holbrook, you're a lifesaver," I said.

She beamed at me. "Always glad to help, my lady. And very nice to meet you too, sir."

I noticed she gave my grandfather an encouraging smile.

"I think you've got yourself a new female admirer," I commented as we drove off again.

"No more lady admirers, thank you," he said.

"I'm sorry, that was tactless of me. Obviously you're still grieving about Mrs. Huggins," I said. "It must have been an awful shock for you."

He took a deep breath. "Between you and me, ducks, I'm rather relieved. Oh, don't get me wrong. I'm sorry poor old Hettie kicked the bucket, but I wasn't at all sure I was doing the right thing getting married to her. It all started harmless enough with her coming to cook for me and before you know it she's talking about us getting hitched and her moving in with me. And for a while I thought it might be nice to have company after so long. But when it finally struck me that I was going to be stuck with her and that she'd drive me round the bend, it was too late to back out. So now I'm feeling guilty that I'm actually relieved."

I glanced across at him and smiled. "Oh, Granddad. You made her happy; that's the main thing. She was really looking forward to her wedding."

"Wasn't she just!" He had to laugh. "Talk about going to town! Pulling out all the stops, she was. It's a wonder she hadn't invited the chorus line from the Palladium to come and dance. And Gigli to sing for us!"

His laughter faded and we drove on for a while in silence.

"You know, you're more than welcome to come and live with Darcy and me at Eynsleigh," I said.

"Oh no, ducks. The last thing that newlyweds want is some old geezer getting in the way."

"But it's a huge house. You wouldn't be in the way. You could live as privately as you want."

"It's kind of you, my love," he said. "But I quite like my own little house and I'm used to my own routine. Although I won't say no to coming to stay sometimes and enjoying your good country air."

We exchanged a smile.

We headed south toward the coast. Ahead of us was the graceful sweep of the South Downs. We drove into the old town of Lewes with its impressive castle and quaint town center and stopped to ask for directions at the police station. They were most helpful and gave me directions to Downsview, about a mile out of town. I wondered if we should ask them to put through a telephone call to Scotland Yard, but Granddad seemed unwilling to introduce himself and have to explain our situation, so we went to a telephone box instead. After being passed along a series of ever-more important people, finally Detective Chief Inspector Garland came on the line and I handed the receiver over to Granddad. The result was that the DCI suggested that we shouldn't come up to London but that he'd meet us at Haywards Heath station at about two o'clock.

"Couldn't be better," Granddad said, smiling as we left the telephone box. "Always was a good bloke. Steady as a rock, that one."

"He clearly thought a lot of you too," I said.

Granddad nodded. "Well, I did teach him a thing or two, I suppose," he said modestly.

We got back in the motorcar and drove out along country lanes, between fields in which sheep or cows grazed, until we came to an impressive gateway with a discrete brass plaque on the brick post. Downsview. We continued up a long drive. There were manicured lawns on either side. Some residents were playing croquet. Others were strolling or sitting on benches, enjoying the fresh air. Ahead of us was a handsome Georgian house and we came to a halt outside a pillared entrance. It certainly didn't look like an asylum! The front door was open and we entered a marble-tiled foyer. A lovely display of flowers stood on a low table. From one of the rooms came the sound of soft chatter and then laughter. A piano was being played somewhere. It all seemed very civilized.

As we looked around, wondering where to go, a woman in a crisp white uniform came out, stopping in surprise when she saw us. "Can I help you?" she asked.

"Can you tell us where we would find the matron?" I asked.

She looked amused. "The matron? We're not a hospital, my dear. We are a home for retired gentlefolk."

"Oh, I see. So you're not . . ." I sought the right word. "You don't have people who have to be—looked after?"

"No, we're really not equipped for complete invalids," she said. "We do have some who need help walking up steps, but that's about it."

"And those who have become . . . confused?"

She grinned. "Some of them do live in their own little worlds, I admit. We have one lady who still thinks she's in India. Keeps asking for her elephant. But on the whole I'd say most of them are as normal as you and me. We have a director of residents' services who is in charge, but I think she had to drive someone to a doctor's appointment. She shouldn't be too long."

"Maybe you can help us, then," I said. "I understand that Lady Anstruther was a resident here."

"She most certainly was." Her face betrayed her feelings on the matter.

"I gather she wasn't the easiest person," I went on.

"You can say that again, my dear. Oh my goodness. I don't think there was a person here she didn't pick a fight with. Nothing was right for her ever. Didn't like the food. Didn't like the activities. And those cats of hers . . ."

"Cats?"

"Oh yes. We let residents bring their pets. She came with these two enormous white Persian cats. Rajah and Rani. They were the bane of everyone. I don't think there's a member of staff here who doesn't bear the scars around the ankles of being attacked by one of the monsters when we went into Lady Anstruther's room. I can't tell you how glad we were when they left with her." She stopped abruptly as she realized she had no idea who we were. "Oh, that was tactless of me, wasn't it? You're not a relative, are you?"

"No, we're not," I said. "No, we just wanted to verify that Lady Anstruther had been a resident here and to find out when she left."

"She left in the New Year. She had complained about our Christmas and New Year merrymaking and said she wanted peace and quiet and was going home."

"And nobody tried to stop her?"

"Of course not. This is not an institution. It's more like a high-class residential hotel. Residents may come and go as they please. I believe our director did try to talk her out of it, knowing that her son was keen to have her here, but she wouldn't listen."

"And how would you say her state of mind was at the time?" I asked. "Would she have been competent to make such a decision?"

"Competent?" She shook her head. "She might have been difficult to deal with, but she knew exactly what she was doing. Sharp as a tack. Did the *Times* crossword every morning." She glanced down at her wristwatch. "Now, if you will please excuse me, I have to see that the room is set up correctly for this afternoon's piano recital. We have a resident who is a famous classical pianist. So if you'd like to go into the sitting room and wait for our director?"

"No, thank you," I said. "We have learned all we need to know and we have an appointment later in Haywards Heath."

$\mathcal{C}$hapter 33

THURSDAY, JULY 4
HAYWARDS HEATH, SUSSEX

Now we are getting somewhere! Now we know that they murdered
Lady Anstruther and brought in someone to impersonate her. The
only question is why they needed to do that. I hope we get some
answers soon. This whole thing is just too suspenseful.

We came out of the house and I paused to admire the green grass of
the Downs rising in front of us. At last a house that actually merited
its name!

"Well, now we are getting somewhere," I said to my grandfather
as we drove away. "We know that Lady Anstruther was completely
sane, if highly objectionable. Obviously this person impersonating
her wanted me to think that she was not only mad but dangerous
so that I kept well away from that part of the house. And those birds
flying around the room—well, that was a giveaway that she's a fraud,
isn't it? Nobody who adored two big cats would ever keep birds!" I
turned to him triumphantly. "And I know where those cats are buried

too. They must have killed the cats when they murdered Lady Anstruther."

"We'll get 'em," Granddad said. "I wouldn't be surprised if we found stolen goods stashed in that part of the house."

We were feeling rather pleased with ourselves when we arrived at Haywards Heath railway station. We were a little early so we fortified ourselves with a sausage roll and a cup of tea at a café opposite. The sausage roll was surprisingly good, so we followed it up with an iced bun each.

There was no mistaking Chief Inspector Garland. He was tall, sandy haired and broad shouldered, and he strode out with an air of authority. He spotted my grandfather immediately and came toward him, hand outstretched. "Sergeant Spinks, so good to see you again after all this time."

I was introduced and if the chief inspector was surprised that a lowly sergeant from the East End had a granddaughter who was a lady, he didn't show it. Maybe he had done his homework before setting out!

"I'm sorry to call you out here," Granddad said, "but I think we've got a very serious matter on our hands and it may be beyond the local boys here."

"I assumed it would be a matter of importance or you would never have gone over heads," Chief Inspector Garland said. "You always did have sound judgment."

Granddad gave a modest grin.

"Is there somewhere we can sit?" the DCI asked.

We suggested the café where we had eaten and soon we were sitting in a quiet corner, drinking more tea while we told the chief inspector our story.

"So let me get this straight," he said. "You know that the person who is acting as your butler is not who he claims to be and that the real person bearing that name is dead? And that someone is impersonating a lady who is also dead? And you suspect that whoever is behind this might have a hand in the disappearance of the city financier whose body was found at the foot of Beachy Head?"

I nodded. "I know it sounds farfetched," I said. "I'd find it hard to believe myself but I've seen the body in the coffin. I know where her cats are buried and my own life has been threatened twice now."

"Really?" He looked genuinely concerned.

"When I first came to the house someone turned on the gas tap in my room. Luckily I sleep with all the windows open, having been brought up at Castle Rannoch. And then this morning my grandfather and I were locked in an underground vault, fortunately rescued by my maid and my mother."

"So what do you attribute this to?" he said. "Why go on a killing spree?"

"I was told there has been a spate of burglaries in this part of the world recently," I said. "And my mother commented that items were missing from all over the house we are staying in. She used to be married to Sir Hubert and lived in the house, so she remembered it well."

"Ah," he said. "So you think that maybe a gang of burglars might have set up shop while the master was away and used it as a head-quarters?"

"It would be very convenient, wouldn't it?" I said.

He nodded. "A perfect situation, I'd say. Who would ever suspect a stately home as a place where burglars were operating?"

I thought for a moment before I went on. "What I don't understand is why one of them had to impersonate the old Lady Anstruther. I mean, I didn't even know she had been living in the house. They could just have kept quiet about her instead of that ridiculous charade of pretending she was quite mad and having birds flying all over the place."

"Birds?" he asked.

"Yes. I was taken into her room at night. She wore this shawl over her head, so that I couldn't see her face properly, I presume. And this large parrot came and landed on my head, and another bird was flying around. They were quite alarming, actually."

A strange look had come over the DCI's face. "It's funny you should say that because it brings somebody to mind." He turned to my grandfather. "I think this might have been after your time, Sergeant Spinks, but there was a highly successful burglary ring in London led by a chap they called the Birdman. Phil 'Birdman' Vogel."

"Oh yes. I remember reading about him." Granddad nodded. "He was never on my patch, but the name is familiar."

"Did they call him Birdman because he kept birds?" I asked. As I spoke I remembered Queenie had overheard the gardeners mentioning someone called Phil.

"Three reasons, actually," the DCI replied. "They called him Birdman not just because his last name was Vogel, German for 'bird,' but because he kept birds as pets and he was such a successful cat burglar that people wondered if he could actually fly. He managed to scale walls and get in through windows on upper floors that might have seemed impossible. So the rumor had it that he flew." He grinned at us. "We caught him eventually and put him away for ten years." A thoughtful look came over his face. "That was quite a while ago now, so it's possible he's already been let out early for good behavior."

"Golly," was all I could think of saying.

"What about his former gang?" Granddad asked.

"I think we nabbed most of them. He had a woman who worked with him. Skinny little thing. Actually I believe he used her to climb in through some of those windows. What was her name? Parsons . . . Joan Parsons. Yes. That's right."

"Joanie!" I exclaimed. "We have a maid called Joanie who fits that description. And she told my maid that she thinks herself above working in service and won't be a maid for long. And she was the one who must have turned on my gas tap that night."

"Fascinating," Chief Inspector Garland said, nodding to me. "I wonder if you've got the whole gang there at the house. You're quite lucky you weren't all murdered in your beds."

"We have a Spanish cook who can't cook," I suggested.

"Looney Lopez." He waved a finger in delight. "Remember him, Albert? Yes, that might well be him."

"And an Irish footman. McShea," I continued.

He shook his head. "No, that doesn't ring a bell. Maybe he's legit."

"And a scared little mouse of a kitchen maid called Molly."

"She's probably not one of them either," he said.

"We had two gardeners who didn't seem to know much about gardening and were selling the produce," I said.

"Maybe local lads with no idea what's going on," the inspector said.

"No, they knew very well," I said. "It was one of them who locked us in the vault. At the very least they must have helped to bury Lady Anstruther's cats and possibly Lady Anstruther herself." I paused, considering. "And then there have to be two people impersonating Lady Anstruther and her nurse."

"I wouldn't be surprised if it wasn't Phil himself who was impersonating the old lady. I believe he had dressed up as a woman before when he robbed a swank home during a party."

"Maybe that was why she spoke in a whisper. So that I wouldn't recognize a man's voice," I said, and then asked, "And the nurse?"

"Not sure about that," the inspector said. "There have been other gang members—hangers-on."

"And what about Plunkett? Or at least the man who calls himself Plunkett. Chubby fellow, about forty. Parts his hair down the middle. Bit of a Cockney accent he tries to hide."

DCI Garland frowned, thinking. "No, he wasn't part of the gang that I remember."

"The initials on his case were EP," I said.

Garland shook his head. "No, doesn't ring a bell. Maybe he's a legitimate household servant who got himself roped into this."

"I have found out that the real Charles Plunkett is dead and this man was impersonating him if that's any help."

DCI Garland looked at me, long and hard. "You have been an enormous help, young lady. I'm impressed."

I had the grace to blush.

"So what happens next?" my grandfather asked.

DCI Garland sucked in through his teeth. Then he said, "I have to square things away with the local boys. Can't tread on toes, you know. Then I'll assemble a team and we'll stake out the place and pounce."

While he was talking I had remembered something important. "You might not have time to do much," I said. "I intercepted a note that was meant for the butler. It said something about a boat on Thursday. At the time I thought perhaps it was a place for a lover's tryst."

The DCI now looked alarmed. "Phil Vogel's old gang used to ship stolen silver and antiques to the Continent and America. If he's up to his old game, then he could have a boat lined up ready for the latest shipment. And it's Thursday today." He stood up. "I better get onto it right away. There may be no time for protocol. We must get them before they escape."

"What do you want us to do?" I asked.

"Stay well away," he said. "Find an excuse to go out this evening. Say you're going to the pictures or out to a concert. I don't want you to run the risk of being hurt."

"Do you think they'd try to kill us before they left?" I asked, trying not to sound too concerned.

"I think they might want to take one of you as a bargaining chip, just in case," the inspector said. "Anyway, that's a risk we won't take, will we? I'm pretty sure they won't leave until it's almost dark, and we'll be waiting for them. You just make sure you are well clear, understand?"

"Yes, absolutely," I said.

Chapter 34

THURSDAY, JULY 4
BACK AT EYNSLEIGH

Things are finally coming to a head. I am so relieved that the police are going to catch these people. Imagine sharing the house with a gang of thieves! We are lucky that nothing worse happened to us!

Neither Granddad nor I spoke much on the way home. I think we were both going over the full ramifications of what we had just learned. And both realizing that we had to go back into that house and act normally until we could make our escape. I thought about Mummy, still there, and Queenie stuck in the kitchen with a man who might be Looney Lopez. I put my foot down and the Bentley sped through the narrow lanes.

"Steady on, old love," Granddad said. "It won't do anyone no good if we wind up in a ditch."

I slowed a little. The drive home seemed to take forever and my heart was beating very fast when we drove through the gateway and up the drive. Even as we pulled up Plunkett came down the steps to meet us.

"Oh, there you are, my lady," he said, opening the door for me. "We wondered where you had got to. Your mother was getting concerned. She said you had only gone into town to do some shopping."

"That was the original intention," I said. "We bumped into someone who used to know my grandfather and went to have a bite of lunch with him."

As Plunkett helped me from the motorcar my mother appeared at the doorway. "There you are, you naughty girl. I was worried about you. I wondered if you could actually drive that powerful motorcar."

"I'm perfectly all right, Mummy," I said. "Granddad bumped into an old colleague from London."

"Who has retired down here in the country and is now growing orchids," Granddad said. "He invited us to have lunch with him, and let me tell you, there is nothing more boring than listening to a talk on growing orchids." He laughed. I did too.

"Did you remember my soap?" Mummy asked.

"Of course. Number one priority," I said, and reached into my purse. We had remembered to purchase a few items before we left Haywards Heath to prove we had been on a shopping trip. Mummy's so-called French soap had come from Boots.

Mummy smelled it. I expected it smelled disgusting but I had grabbed the first one. "Ashes of roses, my very favorite, you clever thing," she said with a look of rapture on her face.

"I will put the motorcar away for you, my lady," Plunkett said, almost pushing past me to get into the driver's seat.

"That won't be necessary, Plunkett," I replied. "We saw that there is a comedy playing at the Gaumont in Haywards Heath and I thought it might cheer us all up to have a good laugh. So we'll have a high tea and then go to the cinema tonight."

"Tonight, my lady?" A spasm crossed his face before he regained his composure, and it dawned on me that perhaps they were planning to use the Bentley as part of their escape.

"Yes, Plunkett. I can't see any reason why not tonight, can you?"

"It's just that Cook and your girl were already working on the meal. I don't know if it will keep."

"Then we'll eat late when we get home," I said. "So please let Queenie know that we'd like tea in half an hour, and maybe something like a boiled egg to sustain us."

"Very good, my lady," he said. He went to say something more, but then walked away. If it hadn't been so alarming I would have grinned.

"Did you buy anything fun and exciting you want to show me?" Mummy asked, pretending to peep into the bag I carried.

"Mummy, it's Haywards Heath, not Oxford Street," I said, laughing. "I bought some new face cream, that's all. But come up and see if you approve, if you like."

"Darling, I've always told you that English cosmetics will destroy your face," she said loudly as we went up the stairs with Granddad in tow. "One has to buy them in Paris. Next time I'm there I'll have some made up for you. . . ."

We passed out of Plunkett's hearing and made a beeline for my room, shutting the door behind us. Mummy's eyes widened as we told her everything we had found out.

"We could have all have been killed," she said.

"Quite possibly."

"That explains why Plunkett was so concerned where you had disappeared to. He quizzed me several times and actually asked when I thought the motorcar would be back."

"I wonder if stealing the Bentley was part of their plan," I said.

"Terrible people," she said. "I bet they've stolen all the good stuff from Eynsleigh. I jolly well hope those policemen nab them before they can send it overseas. Hubert would be furious if he found out." A look of alarm crossed her face. "You don't think there will be a shoot-out, do you? Will we be safe?"

"Mummy, it's Sussex, not Chicago," I said. "But just to be on the safe side the inspector wants us out of the way. That's why we are going to the cinema this evening."

I managed to keep calm as we went down to tea. It looked most inviting, with dainty little watercress and cucumber sandwiches, boiled eggs with fingers of bread beside them and little iced cakes, but I didn't feel that I'd be able to swallow a morsel. Mummy, ever the actress and sure of her lines, tucked in with relish. Granddad met my gaze across the table.

"It's a bit soon after that large lunch for Georgie and me," he said. "I told her we shouldn't have had that second helping."

We had almost finished eating when Queenie came in. "I was told you ain't wanting your dinner tonight on account of going to the cinema," she said. "But don't worry. We'll keep it hot until you get back. It's a shepherd's pie and I made it. That Fernando bloke is bloody useless. Hasn't done a thing for days." She paused, then said, "Are you going to finish them sandwiches?" She reached across the table to grab the plate. As she leaned closer to me she muttered, "There's something funny going on, miss. I went to pick some chives for the sandwiches and I saw a strange bloke come out of the French windows on the other side of the house carrying a ruddy great painting."

"A painting?" I asked.

"Yeah, you know. One of them things in a frame. And he took it into the stables. Why would he be doing that? I just thought you should know."

"Thank you, Queenie," I said. "Very observant of you." I was tempted to invite her to come to the pictures with us this evening, but that was so against all protocol that I simply couldn't. I had to assume that she'd be safe, that nobody would have reason to harm a servant and that nobody would want to take a girl of her stature hostage. She'd be too big to lug around. But I wanted her to know what was going on. "Queenie," I said, "I'll need you to come up and dress me at six o'clock. I want to wear my black dress to the cinema and it has all those buttons down the back."

She went to say something, then changed her mind. "Bob's yer uncle, miss," she said and she gave me a wink. Sometimes, I realized, she wasn't as stupid as I had always thought.

"It's turned into a nice afternoon," I said. "Shall we take a walk around the grounds?"

"Good idea," Mummy said. We went out of the front door and paused, admiring the fountains. The pattering of water masked our voices.

"I'm going to take a look in the stables," I said. "You two keep watch and let me know if you see anyone coming."

"How do we do that?" Mummy asked. "Hoot like an owl or something?"

"Owls don't come out during the daylight," I said. "Try a wood pigeon. They are easy enough to imitate."

"Hoo-hoo," Granddad made the noise. It was so funny that we laughed.

"Hoo-hoo?" Mummy tried.

"You are both hopeless." I was still laughing. "Mummy, why don't you just call my name? What could be more natural than our taking a stroll in the grounds?"

"Yes, that's better," she agreed.

Granddad was frowning. "I don't want you to do this, ducks. It could be dangerous."

"But we need to know, Granddad."

"But what if they've got a bloke stationed in the stables?"

"I'll bluff. After all, it is my house, and it would be quite natural that I visit the stables, wouldn't it? I'll say something like 'Oh, hello. Are you one of the new gardeners?' And I'll smile sweetly and then babble on about buying a new horse and checking out the facilities."

"I still don't like it," Granddad said. "What if they want a hostage?"

"It's a risk I'll take. Come on." We started to walk around the house, giving the west wing a wide berth. We paused on the other side of the yew hedge, where we had a clear view of the French windows and the stable yard beyond. Nothing moved. A real wood pigeon was cooing mournfully from the copper beech tree. Bees buzzed around the roses. It felt like any summer afternoon.

I took a deep breath. "Here goes, then," I said and I set off in the direction of the stables. It was hard not to move too quickly or to look around. I reached the stable block that had now been converted into garages. The door of the first was open and waiting for the Bentley. Then I opened the second door and took a step back in amazement. A van was parked there. Its back doors were open and it was crammed full of crates and packages. Several smaller crates were stacked against the wall. It struck me that they were ready to leave and that maybe my telling them I was taking the Bentley that evening might have pushed their departure forward. I would have to try to warn DCI Garland.

I was just about to come out of the garage when I heard my mother's voice, "Georgie? Are you out here?"

And then the answer in a good imitation of my voice, "I'm over here, Mummy. Come and see. There is a deer and a fawn."

At the same moment I heard the crunch of footsteps heading my way. I had no alternative but to duck behind the van. If they decided to drive it out now I'd be well and truly caught. The footsteps came closer.

"You left the garage door open, you idiot," said a voice I didn't recognize.

"I pushed it to. It wouldn't latch properly," replied a second strange voice. "And did you hear—those people are out in the grounds. You don't think they've been snooping?"

"Don't worry about them. They're heading for the woods. With any luck we'll be gone before they get back."

"How are we going to get this lot into the motorcar without anyone seeing if we leave soon?" the second voice asked. "Why don't we wait until dark?"

"Something to do with the tides; that's what the skipper said."

A van door slamming made me jump.

"Might as well lock this right now. If we have to leave stuff behind that's just too bad." The second door slammed shut. "I'll drive the car around to load it up when we're ready to leave. And for God's sake shut the bloody garage door this time."

I was suddenly plunged into darkness. I felt my way around the van, located the door and was pleased to find it was a simple latch that could be pushed up from the inside. At least I wasn't locked in this time. I waited what I felt was a suitable amount of time, then let myself out, hugged the shadow around the stable yard and then made my way back to my mother and grandfather. They were both looking sick and worried.

"I told you it was a bad idea," Granddad said. "We were just about to go and call the police."

"We have to call the police right now," I said. "They've a van packed with stolen goods in the garage there and they are planning to leave soon."

We made our way back to the front door. Plunkett was hovering. "Been out for a walk, my lady, Your Grace?" he asked.

"We have, Plunkett. I saw a baby deer in the woods. Isn't that amazing?"

"Oh yes. Quite amazing," he answered. "What time will you be leaving for the cinema?"

"Well, it starts at seven so we should probably leave just after six. All right, Mummy?" I turned to her.

"Fine with me. I'll go and get changed." She started up the stairs.

"And Queenie is going to help me change. Would you send her up right away, Plunkett?"

"Very good, my lady." He gave a little nod and off he went.

I glanced at Granddad, then picked up the telephone. I had to assume there was still an extension in the other wing and that someone might overhear what I was saying. But I also had to hope they weren't close enough to pick up the receiver immediately.

"Number please?" said the operator's calm voice.

"Haywards Heath police station. It's an emergency." I tried to keep my voice as low as possible.

I waited; then a gruff voice said, "Police station. Sergeant Willis speaking."

"Oh, hello," I said in my brightest voice now. "I'm calling for Uncle Garland. I know he's visiting you from London. I don't suppose he's home at the moment, is he? No, I didn't think he would be. So please give him this message. It's his niece Georgiana and it's about the party we were planning. We have to move the time forward, I'm afraid. I really want to have the treasure hunt in the grounds and we can't do that in the dark, can we? So please ask him to come over to discuss details as soon as he can. And tell him I do look forward to seeing him very soon."

"Have you got the wrong number, miss?" the sergeant asked.

"Oh no. Absolutely not. And you will tell him the moment you see him, won't you? It means a lot to me." Then I hung up. I had no idea whether he would work out that I wasn't a babbling idiot or not, but it was the best that I could do.

Chapter 35

**I'm not sure what to do. I can just pray that the policeman at the
station didn't think I was batty. Otherwise we've no way of
stopping them if they decide to leave early.**

I met Queenie up in my room and tried to think how much to tell her.
Then I decided, Damn protocol. I wanted her safe.

"Look, Queenie," I said. "I want you to come with us. It may be
dangerous to stay here this evening."

She shook her head. "Oh no, miss. That wouldn't look right. If
they are intending to scarper they'd get the wind up right away if I
went with you. So I'll stay put. But don't worry, I'll keep well out of
the way."

I looked at her with a fondness I'd never have believed. "You are a
brave girl, Queenie, but I don't want you to get hurt."

"Don't worry about me," she said. "If things get too hot around here I'll slip out into the grounds and hide. They won't bother about someone like me."

"Are you sure . . ." I started to say when Mummy poked her head around my door.

"A strange van has just pulled up outside the front door."

"Not a police van?" I asked hopefully.

"Not an ordinary tradesman's van. And a chap got out. He seemed to be heading for the front steps. I couldn't see much because it was in the shadow of the building."

"Come on," I said, already heading out of my room. "If he's one of them he's going to regret it."

I ran down the stairs. Anger had now taken over from common sense. This was my new home and these people had spoiled it for me. And they had stolen Sir Hubert's lovely things. I snatched a silver-topped cane from the umbrella stand in the front hall.

Mummy was right behind me. "Georgie, you can't," she said. "What if he's an ordinary tradesman?"

"He would go around to the tradesman's entrance, wouldn't he?" I took up a position behind the front door. If he was a bona fide visitor he'd ring the front doorbell. If he had come to help them get away with another van, then I was ready for him. I didn't stop to think that the whole rest of the gang was still here and outnumbered us. My grandfather appeared at the top of the landing. "What's going on?" he asked, coming down the stairs. I put my finger to my lips as the front door started to open, slowly. No ordinary visitor, then. I had been right. I raised the heavy cane above my head. Brilliant sunlight flooded in, silhouetting a dark man. He came in, closing the door quietly behind him. Just as I stepped out with my cane poised to hit him, he looked around and called out, "Hello? Anybody home?"

It was lucky that he did this or he would have been lying on the floor, struck with my silver-headed cane. Instead I dropped it to the marble floor with a loud clatter and flung myself at him.

"Darcy!" I exclaimed and burst into tears.

"Well, that's what I call an effusive greeting," he said, wrapping his arms around me. "I wanted to surprise you. I hitched a ride from the station in a plumber's van. And I can see that I've surprised you, all right, but you don't need to cry every time I come home."

"You don't understand," I managed between sobs. "I nearly killed you, or at least knocked you out."

"No," he said, "I don't understand." He held me away from him and looked at my tear-stained face. "Come on, old thing. This isn't like you. What's going on?"

"Morning room." I took his hand and led him down the hall. There was no sign of Plunkett. I wondered if he had got away while the going was good, like the gardeners. I dragged Darcy into the morning room. Mummy and Granddad followed. Granddad stood at the door, ready for action. Trying to be coherent, I told Darcy everything. His expression became more and more incredulous. "Are you sure?" he asked.

"Of course I am. Quite sure. And the Scotland Yard detective recognized immediately who they are too."

"Why on earth didn't you leave the place and go back to London?" he asked.

"Because we've only just put two and two together," I said. "Until now we thought it was all about a deranged old woman living here. The police will be arriving this evening. I just hope they are not too late. It looks as if the gang is all ready to leave and I suspect they plan to take our Bentley with them. I left a message for the inspector in charge but I don't know if he'll get it. I had to make it sound as if I was calling my uncle, in case anyone was listening in."

Darcy! looked at me with concern, but then he smiled. "How do you manage to get yourself mixed up in things like this, Georgie?"

"I certainly didn't intend to," I said. "I was looking forward to enjoying my first real home, not being gassed in my bed or left to die in a vault."

"So what do you plan to do now?" Darcy asked.

"The inspector wanted us all to go to the pictures and be well out of the way."

"Good idea. We'll go now, before they can steal the motorcar."

"But what if they leave before the police get here?" I asked. "What if they get away with all the lovely things they have stolen?"

"You certainly can't stop them," Darcy said. "We certainly can't stop them. They may be armed."

"We could slow them down," I said. "Mummy, you and Granddad can drive off in the Bentley, can't you? That will make them think that we've all gone. And maybe Darcy and I can do something to their van."

"Such as what?" Darcy asked. "I've read in books about removing the rotor arm or the distributor but I've never had to do it myself. Besides, if they are coming out to load up, I think they'd notice that someone had raised the bonnet, don't you?"

"I know!" I said excitedly. "The birds!"

"What birds?"

"Listen," I said. "They call him Phil the Birdman and he keeps birds as pets. Maybe he's fond enough of them to go hunting for them if we steal them."

Darcy was frowning as he looked at me. "You want to steal birds from a known criminal?"

"Yes. It's the only thing I can think of that might slow them down."

"You're crazy."

"No. If he's as passionate about his birds as they say, he'll come looking for them. With any luck they'll be in cages ready to be transported."

"With any luck?" Darcy asked. "You mean you may want to catch flying birds?"

"If they are flying we don't need to catch them. We simply open the French doors and shush them out. And we leave a note to say we've taken his birds. Come and find them in the forest."

Darcy shook his head. "Georgie, this is not a good idea."

"It could be. We could try at least. We presume the French doors are unlocked because they've been coming and going." I reached out and touched Darcy's sleeve. "At least let's try. And if we're spotted they'll be confused to see you. They may not know if more reinforcements have arrived." I didn't wait for an answer. I went over to the writing desk, took out a sheet of paper and then wrote in big black letters: WE HAVE YOUR BIRDS. COME AND FIND THEM.

Darcy shook his head. "This is stupid, Georgiana."

I think it was the first time he had called me by my whole name, and it did make me pause, but I was not about to be deterred. "I'm going to try it. You can come or not, as you choose. At the very least you can keep watch for me."

"And you think you can carry a blasted great birdcage to the forest by yourself?" he asked.

"I won't know until I try," I said.

He sighed. "Very well. I'm certainly not going to let you do it alone. Come on, then, show me where we are going."

"And you and I will drive off, Daddy," my mother said.

We all walked to the front door together, talking among ourselves about going to the cinema and how long it had been since we saw a film. Then Mummy and Granddad got into the motorcar and Darcy and I crept around the front of the house, hugging the deep shade. Fortunately the lowest windows were above our height. We came around the corner and stopped. Fernando and McShea were coming out of one set of French doors, carrying an ornate clock. I heard a woman's voice call from the direction of the stables, "Hurry up. We haven't got all day." And Joanie came out of the shadows. She was no longer dressed as a maid but in a smart frock and hat. "Is that the last of it?"

"A couple more bits and pieces," McShea replied. So much for not being one of them, I thought.

"But they just drove off in the motorcar," Fernando shouted.

"Already? Damn them!" Joanie said. "I thought they weren't supposed to be going until after six. Well, we'll just have to leave the rest of the stuff, then. I don't think we can cram any more in the van."

"To hell with the stuff," Fernando said. "What about us? We can't cram six of us into the van."

"Two of you may have to make your own way to the boat."

"Hey, listen, I've stuck with Phil through all this. I'm not going to be ditched now," McShea said. "Leave Plunkett behind. He never was much use anyway."

"Of course we're leaving him behind. He's played his part. We don't need him anymore," Joanie snapped.

"You're not leaving us," Fernando said, his eyes flashing angrily. "You take some of the stuff out of the back to make room for us, okay?"

"Okay. Keep your hair on." She turned and walked back to the stables.

"What about this clock?" McShea called after her.

"Bring it. I like it. I'll carry it on my knee," Joanie said.

"Where's Phil?" Fernando asked.

"He's with Plunkett. Sorting things out."

As they headed for the stables, Darcy and I crept toward the French doors. I thought that the room with the birds had been at the far end of the corridor, therefore the one now closest to us. I turned the handle and the glass door swung open. I peeked inside and pointed with glee. Two birdcages now sat on the table, each covered with a cloth. The birds were indeed ready to travel. Darcy moved past me to pick up the biggest one. I put the note down and picked up the smaller cage, and we made a quick exit. It was all too smooth. We had a brief sprint across a piece of lawn where we could have been seen, but then we were behind the yew hedge and worked our way around to the first of the woods. We had not gone far enough into the trees when we heard the sound of someone coming toward us, footsteps crashing through bracken. Darcy put down his cage and darted behind a tree, only just in time, as the man I presumed was Birdman Phil caught up to me.

"You stupid bloody girl," he shouted. "What did you think you could gain by this? Did you think I wouldn't find you? And what did you think I'd do to you when I caught you? This isn't a bloody kid's adventure story, you know. Now you're to be sorry . . ."

"No," I said. "You're going to be sorry." And I whipped the cover off the largest cage, opened the door and tipped the bird out. It did just what I had hoped. It flew off, up into the trees with a noisy flapping of wings. Birdman Phil gave a cry of part rage, part despair. "Charlie!" he called. "Come to Daddy, Charlie. Here, birdie, here." And he held up his wrist. Darcy stepped out from behind his tree, put his hands around Phil's neck and gave what looked like a little squeeze, and Phil collapsed to the ground like a rag doll.

"A little something I picked up in Argentina once," Darcy commented with a satisfied little smile.

"Is he dead?" I asked nervously.

"No. He'll regain consciousness soon." He started to remove his belt. "I just hope my trousers don't fall down without it," he added as he turned Phil over, brought his hands behind his back and bound them tightly with the belt. Then he straightened up and reached into his pocket. "Ah yes." Again he looked pleased. "My old nanny always told me never to go out without a clean handkerchief. She was right." And he gagged Phil's mouth with it.

"What do we do now?" I asked, looking down at the figure in the bracken.

"We make ourselves scarce before the others have time to find us or Phil," he said, "and hope that the police get here in time to catch them. If not, at least they should be able to intercept them on their way to the port. Come on." He took my hand and led me away from the scene. Above us in the tree the parrot called out, "Hello, bird! Give Charlie a kiss."

"Should we try to catch that parrot and put it back in its cage?" I asked. "It will alert everyone to where Phil is."

"We'll have to risk that. I'd rather we put a good distance between us and them. Let's find a good spot to hide out where we can watch the front gate."

We moved as silently as possible through the woods, then crept around the perimeter of the estate, keeping to the shade of the wall and moving from tree to tree. We chose an old oak with a good view of the house and the gate and stationed ourselves behind it. And waited. And waited. From time to time we heard voices, shouts, the squawk of that bird. We glanced at the gate, but no police cars arrived. I wondered if Chief Inspector Garland had ever received my message and what time he had planned to stop the getaway.

"If the police don't come in time, is there anything we can do?" I whispered.

"What were you thinking—stepping out in front of the van and saying 'Stop, you naughty boys'?" He shook his head. "We have to let them go, but we can telephone the police the moment they leave."

"Don't you think one of us could go to the house now and make that telephone call?"

"Too dangerous. We don't know how many of them are still in the house. They will probably be armed." He put his arm around me. "There is a line between bravery and recklessness." Then he looked at me, his face inches from mine. "I'm not going to risk anything happening to you. I intend to marry my bride!" And he kissed me. We broke apart at the sound of a motor. It came from behind the west wing. They had started the van. We held our breath as it came into view. I couldn't see how many people were in the cab because the sun was now in our eyes. I felt so helpless and angry, knowing that they were escaping with so many treasures. Darcy's grip on me tightened as if he suspected I might rush out and try to stop them.

As they reached the front gates I noticed for the first time that the gates were closed. Usually we left them open, not having a gatekeeper in residence. I didn't have time to work out who might have closed them. Perhaps it was Granddad's brilliant idea after they drove out. The van screeched to a halt. Fernando jumped down and rushed to open the gates. He pulled one heavy gate open, then the next, and was about to get back into the cab, when suddenly figures in blue poured into the driveway.

"Going somewhere, Birdman?" Chief Inspector Garland asked.

Chapter 36

Thank heavens. I can't believe the nightmare is over. Darcy is back and
everything is wonderful.

When the police had departed with Phil's gang, we went back into the
house.

"I think you deserve a stiff brandy," Darcy said. "But I'd better
find it myself. There are no servants to ring for."

"Queenie!" I exclaimed. "Oh gosh, Darcy, I hope she's all right."
I didn't wait a second longer but pushed open the baize door and ran
down the steps to the kitchen. It was empty. I went through to the
butler's pantry and stopped in horror. Plunkett was sprawled at his
desk with his throat cut, quite dead. So that's what Joanie meant when
she had said Phil was sorting things out with Plunkett. I realized he
might have been brought into this scheme against his will. Poor Plunkett. I never thought I'd feel sorry for him. But that made me all the
more anxious for Queenie.

"Queenie?" I shouted, my voice echoing around the cavernous kitchen. "Are you here?"

Slowly the pantry door opened and Queenie's face peeped out. "Blimey, miss, I thought I'd had my chips," she said. She emerged brandishing a large kitchen knife. Behind her, terrified little Molly came out.

"Oh, my lady, thank the good Lord," she said. "That Fernando, he was the very devil himself. He took a knife to Queenie."

"He did?" I looked at Queenie.

She shrugged. "He told me he was very tempted to cut me to shreds for being such an annoying woman and if I ever breathed a word he'd be back for me. So Molly and I hid in the pantry and I had a knife ready in case he came back."

"You don't have to worry anymore," I said. "The police have got them all, except for Plunkett, poor fellow. They killed him first."

"We heard something nasty going on, didn't we, Molly?" Queenie said. "Some kind of fight and a nasty cry."

"Well, he's in the butler's room. Don't go anywhere near it."

"Oh, don't worry about that. I ain't touching nothing," Queenie said. She looked up as Darcy stood in the doorway. "Well, blow me down, it's Mr. Darcy. Luckily I made plenty of shepherd's pie. Shall I pop it in the oven?"

Darcy looked at her and burst out laughing. "Queenie, you are a treasure," he said. "You've just escaped death and you calmly talk about shepherd's pie."

"Well, we have to eat, don't we?" she said. "But I'm afraid you'll have to make do with marrow. I ain't about to go down the garden to pick more beans."

Mummy and Granddad returned and were both excited and horrified to learn all the details of what had happened.

"Poor old Plunkett. How horrid," Mummy said. "I can't say I was too fond of him, but he must have found himself trapped in a situation he couldn't escape from. But thank God that's all over and we can start looking forward to your wedding."

"What about your own wedding?" Darcy asked. "And your grandfather's wedding? Surely they come first and you're looking forward to them?"

"There will be no wedding for me or my father," Mummy said in true dramatic fashion. "Death has robbed us both of our chance for happiness."

"Max died?" Darcy asked.

"His father died. He doesn't think it appropriate to marry me at the moment."

"And poor old Hettie Huggins died of heart failure," Granddad said. "The excitement was too much for her."

"So many deaths," Darcy said, glancing at me. "I hope that's not an omen for us. I'm going to keep a watch on you every second until our wedding, Georgie."

"And I on you. No surprise jaunts to foreign parts, Darcy."

"None, I promise." A strange look came over his face. "Actually I've been offered a proper job, by the foreign office. It's a desk job. Safe as houses. No more getting the odd summons to far-flung places."

I hugged him. "Oh, Darcy, that's wonderful. What good news."

"Yes, isn't it?" he replied. "You'll be stuck with me for dinner every night."

Then we ate the shepherd's pie with a bottle of a rather good Beaujolais. And we chose to ignore the police who were coming and going, removing Plunkett's body and combing the house for clues.

Later that evening Darcy and I took a stroll together outside. The fountain was pattering gently and the last of the daylight glowed in the western sky. It felt so peaceful, and it was hard to believe that our lives had been in danger a few hours before. It hadn't been until I found Plunkett dead that I realized just how much danger we had put ourselves in. Anyone who had calmly cut a colleague's throat would certainly not have thought twice about finishing us off.

"I'm so glad you came back just in time," I said to Darcy.

"So am I. I rather think you'd have gone off to face that Birdman character alone and you'd probably be lying dead in the woods at this moment."

I shuddered. "Don't. It's been so horrible, Darcy. I was so looking forward to making this house into a lovely home by the time you arrived. Now we won't be able to touch any of the items that were stolen until Sir Hubert can come and identify them. And they'll have to be exhibited as evidence."

"Is someone going to tell Sir Hubert?" he asked.

"I don't know how to find him. We can't cable Sir Hubert Anstruther, somewhere in South America." I laughed, but Darcy said, "I'll cable the embassy in Buenos Aires. We have a special connection. They'll track him down for us."

"You are quite useful in your way," I said, gazing up at him adoringly.

"Yes, I suppose I do have my uses." He smiled at me and took me into his arms. "I can't wait for this wedding to be over and us to be off on our honeymoon," he whispered, nuzzling at my ear.

"Neither can I. Oh, I want to enjoy the wedding first, but I am rather looking forward to the honeymoon part."

He laughed and kissed the tip of my nose. "I always suspected you were a hot little piece," he said.

"But speaking of honeymoons . . . The queen has offered us Balmoral."

He drew away from me, giving me a horrified look. "You didn't accept, did you?"

"No. I thanked her kindly, but I said I was sure you were planning our honeymoon."

"Thank God for that. I can't imagine anything worse than sleeping in a room with tartan wallpaper and being woken by bagpipes at dawn."

I laughed. "And having all those servants creeping around," I added. "So what do you have planned for us?"

"I can't tell you; it's a secret."

"That's not fair. How do I know what to pack if I don't know where I'm going? It would be rather different if it's Brighton or Beirut." I looked up at him. "You don't know, do you? You haven't planned anything yet."

"I have several options," he said. "I haven't yet decided on one. But it will be fantastic wherever we go. And I have the first part in place. A friend has offered me his houseboat on the Thames. I thought you and I could go there after the ceremony. Just the two of us on a boat. No servants. No hotel."

"Oh yes," I said. "That does sound heavenly."

"Good. And don't worry about the rest. It will all fall into place."

"I'd be happy on a houseboat," I said. "I don't need to go anywhere else."

"We'll see." His arms tightened around my waist. "And in the meantime . . ." And then neither of us spoke for quite a while.

As we walked back to the house Darcy said, "I'll stay until everything is sorted out here with the police, but then I'd better go back to Zou Zou in London."

"You prefer her company to mine?" I teased.

"I don't want any talk before the wedding," he said. "No nasty rumors about the groom's impropriety and the bride's honor. We're doing things properly."

We were heading back to the house when a police motorcar arrived and Chief Inspector Garland got out.

"Well, that's that," he said, striding out to catch up with us. Then he noticed Darcy. "Hello, who is this?"

"My fiancé, the Honorable Darcy O'Mara," I said. "Darcy, this is Detective Chief Inspector Garland of Scotland Yard."

The men shook hands. "You've just arrived, have you?" he asked.

"Just in time, so it seems," Darcy said. "My bride-to-be was about to run off into the woods with the gang leader's birds."

"Was she, now?"

"We had to slow them down somehow," I said. "They were about to leave before you arrived. And it worked, didn't it? Darcy helped me carry the birds into the forest. And Phil followed us and Darcy knocked him out and tied him up. And by the time the others found him they had wasted at least half an hour."

DCI Garland looked at me, shaking his head. "You take risks, young lady."

"I know. I don't always stop to think things through."

"Luckily it all ended well for you," DCI Garland said. "What a nasty business, eh? We've got them all under lock and key and the stolen goods are all in our possession. Very astute of you, by the way, Lady Georgiana. If you hadn't made that telephone call, they'd have been on a boat by now. We apprehended the boat too, as it was docking at Newhaven."

"I wasn't at all sure that the police sergeant wouldn't think I was batty," I said, "but I couldn't risk anyone listening in on the extension."

He grinned. "As luck would have it, I was passing his desk when he put the phone down and said, 'Some barmy girl wanted to speak to her uncle Garland.' And he was laughing until I said, 'I'm her uncle Garland. What did she say?'"

"Would you like to come in for a drink, Chief Inspector?" Darcy asked.

"No, thanks, but good of you," he said. "I've a couple of things to check on where the body was found. It won't be a few years in prison this time; it will be the rope for Birdman Phil."

"So you don't think that Plunkett was part of their gang?"

"We've no record of him. I suspect he arrived as butler and they either bribed or threatened him to turn a blind eye."

The inspector accompanied us into the house and popped in to talk to my grandfather.

"So I suppose you'll have to go back to a London house for a while, won't you?" he asked us. "I'm afraid we've robbed you of all your servants, and places like this don't run themselves."

I thought for a moment, realizing I didn't want us to go. I certainly didn't want Granddad to have to go back to his own home yet, and Mummy to have to find a hotel. "You know, I think we can muddle through," I said. "Queenie can cook for us and Molly can help her."

"And I can muck in and help keep the place tidy," Granddad said.

"Certainly not," I said. "You're my guest. And the women from the village come in to clean anyway. We'll just ask them to come more often. Old Ben can take care of the kitchen garden and I bet Mrs. Holbrook wouldn't mind coming back as housekeeper until we get things sorted out."

I saw nods of agreement all around.

Chapter 37

Counting down the days until my wedding! I can't believe it's finally
going to happen. Everything is finally going smoothly.

And so it was just us at Eynsleigh. As I suspected, Mrs. Holbrook was
delighted to come back to work for a while and in turn she brought
back two local maids who had been let go. Old Ben brought in a
couple of village lads as undergardeners and the place ran like clock-
work. I was beginning to think that I didn't want another butler. They
were always so impossibly snooty and I didn't think they contributed
much!

We all accompanied Granddad to Mrs. Huggins's funeral on Saturday. Queenie came too and I heard her boasting about her prowess
as cook in a "bloody great house. Ever so posh." Having seen Mrs.
Huggins's family together, en masse, I was truly grateful that Granddad had not married her. He was extra quiet all the way home and I
suspect he was thinking the same thing.

And a few days after that DCI Garland paid us a visit. He told us we would be called upon as witnesses but suggested we leave out any mention of the death of Mr. Broadbent when we were questioned. Although he suspected I was quite right in my deduction, he saw no way of proving it, and it would just confuse a jury. As it was we had a clear case of murder, and one was enough. All he had to ascertain was who actually did the deed and whether the others could be charged as accessories to the crime.

"And what about Lady Anstruther?" I asked. "Can you prove murder there?"

"Unfortunately not. There is no sign of trauma to her body, but she could have been suffocated or poisoned really easily and we'd never know about it now."

"I can understand why they wanted her dead," I said. "If she arrived back at Eynsleigh unexpectedly and found them in residence, she would have made an awful fuss about the state of the house and the quality of the servants. Clearly she'd have to go. But why pretend she was still alive and impersonate her?"

DCI Garland grinned. "I'll give you one reason. Money. The old girl was getting a sizable allowance while she was alive, and she had plenty in bonds and securities and jewelry, which they were busy selling off. Her adviser Mr. Broadbent must have sensed something was wrong, which was why he paid her a visit."

"Poor Mr. Broadbent," I said.

"And I'll give you another reason," the inspector went on. "While neighbors thought a batty and difficult old woman was living at the house, they'd stay well away."

"I don't suppose we'll ever know if Mr. Rogers was pushed down those stairs or it was a simple accident," I went on thoughtfully. "And what about Plunkett? Have you found out who he really was?"

The chief inspector nodded. "We have. His name really was Edward Plunkett. He was the nephew of the Charles Plunkett who had been a butler. Edward Plunkett had been a footman and then went to jail for some petty pilfering. When he came out he stayed with his uncle, who then died. We don't know if young Plunkett aided the death. It may just have been old age. But Edward Plunkett found the letter of recommendation and used it to get himself a plum job. However"—he looked up and wagged a finger at us—"one of Birdman's gang recognized Plunkett from jail and held that over him to move in and take over the house."

"I see," I said. "And the gardeners? Were they part of the gang?"

"No, Plunkett hired them. They were both petty criminals and I think they soon found they were in over their heads. Now they'll be tried as accessories too."

"So they all deserved each other," I said. "What a relief that they are gone. Everything is going wonderfully smoothly now."

"And your wedding is coming up."

"It is."

"And your young man?" He looked around.

"He's gone back to London. Propriety, you know."

DCI Garland laughed. "Of course. It's all right to have a gang of thieves in the house as long as there is no hanky-panky." And I laughed too.

After I watched him drive away I stood at the front door, watching the fountain playing in the late afternoon sunlight, thinking about the strangeness of what had just occurred. Four deaths within a week. Two weddings canceled. I had been breezy and optimistic, but deep inside I really did worry that it might be a bad omen for my wedding. I wished that Darcy was still with me. And more than that I wished the wedding was safely over and I was happily married and on my honeymoon. I gave a sigh, closed the door and went back into the house.

THE NEXT WEEK I went up to London for another fitting for my dress. Belinda had surpassed herself! It really was going to look stunning, and so right for me. Not too girlish but with classic lines that made the most of my slim figure and height. I actually felt quite glamorous with that train swirling out behind me.

"Belinda, you are a genius," I said.

"And you wait until you see the bridesmaids' dresses," she said.

We took them over to the home of the Duke and Duchess of York at 145 Piccadilly and the princesses tried them on. Elizabeth twirled around in hers. "I really feel like a princess in this," she said.

Little Margaret looked at her with scorn. "You already are a princess, silly!"

※

A WEEK BEFORE the wedding we were sitting at tea at Eynsleigh when there was a thunderous knock at the front door. Mrs. Holbrook went and I heard her shriek of delight. Curiosity got the better of me and I went to the sitting room door. Sir Hubert, looking tanned and healthy, stood in the front hall.

"The master is home!" Mrs. Holbrook exclaimed. "He's come home!"

He held out his arms to me and I ran toward him. "What a lovely surprise," I said.

"Well, I couldn't miss your wedding, could I?" he said, enveloping me in a big bear hug.

"But how did you manage it? All the way from South America?"

He gave a deep rumbling laugh that tickled my cheek. "It's a wonderful little device called an aeroplane. Or rather quite a few aeroplanes. I flew from Buenos Aires to Rio, from Rio to Miami, from Miami to New York, from New York to Newfoundland, from there to Shannon, on to London and here I am."

"Golly," I said. "How brilliant. I am so happy to see you," I said.

"Everything going well at the house?" he asked. "Are you enjoying country life?"

"Now I am," I said.

He gave me a questioning look.

"You didn't get a cable from the embassy in Buenos Aires?" I asked. "They tried to locate you."

"No, I didn't. I left the Argentine three weeks ago. So what's been wrong?"

"Come and have some tea and I'll tell you."

I led him through to the sitting room. He paused in the doorway, frowning. "Where's the picture of the man on the horse?" he asked.

"Long story," my mother said.

Sir Hubert noticed her for the first time. "Claire?" he said.

"Hubert." She stood up, a radiant smile on her face, her arms extended to him. "How absolutely lovely to see you." She came toward him and they hugged. I have to say that my suspicion was confirmed that she might be hedging her bets, in case Max did not return!

He pulled up a chair. Mummy poured him a cup of tea and he heard the whole story.

"My dear girl." He reached out and put his hand on mine. "What an ordeal. And what a fiendishly clever scheme. Thank God it's all over now. We'll find a new lot of servants—and double-check their references—and we can start afresh."

Then, of course, I remembered his mother and tried to tell him as tactfully as possible. He was silent for a while. Then he shook his head. "Silly old thing. I don't know why she wanted to come back here in the first place. She never liked this house. And I imagine she would have been a big shock to the gang who were holed up here. She was never very tolerant." He managed a smile. "But I suppose I can't regret her passing too much. She was eighty-five after all."

THREE DAYS BEFORE the wedding I left Mummy and Granddad and went up to Rannoch House, taking Queenie with me. I was pleasantly surprised at the way my family had thrown themselves into the task with enthusiasm. The house positively sparkled. There were flowers everywhere (and lots of interesting packages sitting on the table in the drawing room). Given the large number of attendees, the ballroom at the back of the house had been opened up, the chandeliers glittered and little groups of white-clothed tables and chairs had been hired for the occasion, both in the ballroom and in the garden beyond if the weather was fine. It all looked very grand.

Fig was being almost civil to me. I suspect she was glad that I'd finally be off her hands once and for all. She came into my bedroom bearing an old leather box. "Here you are, Georgie. The family tiara. It was given to your grandmother on her wedding day by Queen Victoria."

She opened the box and I saw the sparkle of diamonds. We tried it on and decided it went well with my hair. It was also rather heavy, but I didn't think I'd notice on the day. I'd be worrying too much about not tripping over my train.

"Now that you will be a married woman, you are entitled to wear it on formal occasions," she said. "You might as well put it in the bank down here. God knows I have few enough occasions to wear it in Scotland."

Then we went up to the nursery, where Podge and Addy greeted me with whoops of delight.

"Auntie Georgie. I'm going to be a page boy," Podge said. "Come and see my new kilt."

"I page boy too!" Addy insisted.

"You can't. You're a girl. And there is no such thing as page girls," Podge said with scorn.

"You will wear a pretty dress and flowers in your hair," I said. "You'll be like Cinderella."

"Oh yes. Me Cinderella." She looked very pleased.

Then it was down to the kitchen, where Mrs. McPherson showed me the wedding cake. It looked amazingly professional. "You are a miracle worker, Mrs. McPherson," I said.

"I added plenty of brandy to the fruit for good measure," she said, blushing with modest pleasure at my praise. "And we're going to put real gardenias on the top, along with the statues of the bride and groom."

Zou Zou came over with two cases of Veuve Clicquot. "In case you run short of bubbly, darlings," she said. "And I have to tell you, Georgie, I saw Darcy trying on his morning suit today and he looks absolutely gorgeous in it. I almost wished I'd snapped him up myself."

"When is his father arriving?" I asked.

"He's here, darling. Arrived yesterday. And he looks rather yummy in his suit too." She gave me a little smile. "In fact, we'll make a handsome couple—as long as Mrs. Simpson doesn't wear the same dress as me!"

"We didn't invite her," I said. "Not with the king and queen in attendance. He's been so ill, poor dear, that the sight of her might give him a stroke."

Zou Zou chuckled. Then she said, "What's this I hear about Darcy taking a desk job?"

"Yes. He seemed quite pleased about having a regular schedule for once."

"Do you really think so?" she asked.

No more was said, but I realized how perceptive she was.

Two days before the wedding we had to have a complete rehearsal with Her Majesty's secretary. There was so much protocol involved about when and how Their Majesties should enter, where they should sit, how I should curtsy as I passed them. All quite alarming and fraught with opportunities for things to go wrong. After an exhausting hour, Darcy and I escaped across Park Lane and walked together in Hyde Park.

"Did you ever think it would turn into a three-ring circus?" Darcy asked.

"Don't blame me. I didn't invite them; they invited themselves," I said. "I am still wishing we had eloped." I took a deep breath. "So about this new job . . ."

"It won't start until we return from our honeymoon," he said.

"Have you definitely accepted it?"

"Not exactly," he said, staring straight ahead.

We paused in the shade of a spreading chestnut tree. "You don't want it, do you?" I asked. "You enjoy your life as it is. You like never knowing where you'll be sent and what you'll be doing."

"Georgie, I'm going to be a married man with responsibilities," he said. "We need a steady income. And you've said yourself that I can't go flitting off around the world and leaving you for long periods of time."

"I can't say I'm thrilled about it," I said, "but I don't want you to take a job where you'd be miserable, just because of me."

He took me into his arms. "You're very sweet, do you know that? Let's not talk about it until after the wedding; then we'll decide."

I nodded.

"I won't see you again until you walk up the aisle to me," he said. "It's my stag night tomorrow and God knows what the boys have planned."

"Don't you dare come to our wedding with a hangover, Darcy O'Mara," I said.

He laughed. "It takes a good deal of drink to leave me with a hangover. Just as long as we don't wind up in jail."

"Darcy!" I exclaimed in horror.

He gave me a little kiss on the forehead. "Don't worry. My father will be coming along. He'll make sure I behave myself."

"Your father drinks more than you do!"

Darcy merely grinned.

Chapter 38

SATURDAY, JULY 27

My wedding day! At last.

The day arrived. Mummy and Granddad came up from the country with Sir Hubert. I noticed that Mummy had given up any pretense of mourning and instead had a stunning sheath dress of pale blue silk with a sweeping ostrich feather in her hat. I noticed Sir Hubert giving her some stealthy and appreciative glances. Granddad looked distinguished in a morning suit, hired for the occasion. Mummy came up to my room to help with my hair and makeup.

"I can't believe my little girl is getting married," she said, looking quite misty-eyed. "I'm so glad everything worked out for you."

"I'm sure it will for you too." I squeezed her hand.

"Blimey, miss, you don't half look a treat," Queenie said as Mummy helped me arrange my veil and then secure the tiara.

"Now I just need the white satin shoes," I said.

"Bob's yer uncle." She fished around; then she said, "I can find one of them." She held it out to me.

I felt a shiver of alarm. "Then find the other."

"It don't seem to be here," she said.

I tried to stay calm. "Queenie. You can't have lost one of my shoes. How am I going to walk down the aisle? I can't hop."

She and Mummy rummaged around, opening drawers, looking under the bed, but to no avail. "Where can it be? It can't just have vanished. You couldn't have thrown it away, could you, Queenie?"

"I wouldn't do no stupid thing like that," she said hotly; then a strange look came over her face. "Remember when we went over to Miss Belinda's for the final fitting? We took the shoes, didn't we? So she could get the hem right. I reckon we must have left one there," Queenie said.

"We must have? Queenie, I brought you to look after my things for me. You were supposed to pack everything up."

"Sorry, miss. It was a bit higgledy-piggledy in that room. I suppose it's a bit late to pop over there and see if I can find it?"

"She'll have already left for the church," I said. I was nearly in tears. "I can't walk down the aisle in ordinary day shoes."

"Don't worry, darling," Mummy said. "Let me see if I have something." She darted along the hall to her room, then came back with white leather pumps. "The best I can do, but at least they are white."

I tried them on. They were very tight on me but better than nothing. "Now I'll have to hobble up the aisle," I said.

Queenie looked quite crestfallen. "I'll go over to Miss Belinda's, find the shoe and bring it to the church," she said. "Then at least you'll have it to wear afterward."

"Yes. I suppose her maid will be there, if she still has a maid, that is." I was still fighting back tears. "Take a taxicab. Here." I handed her some coins from my purse.

Queenie departed. Mummy and Granddad left in their car. Now it was just Binky and me. I tapped on his door. "Binky, are you ready yet?"

No answer.

Cautiously I opened his door. The room was empty. Golly—Binky couldn't have gone without me, could he? I knew he was a trifle absent-minded but . . . I rang for a servant. Hamilton appeared. "You rang, my lady?"

"You haven't seen His Grace, have you, Hamilton? We are supposed to be leaving for the church."

"I haven't seen him for a while, my lady. I'll go and look for him."

Now I was really worried. Surely Binky wasn't clueless enough to have gone off in one of the other cars.

"Binky?" I called, my voice echoing around the hallway and up the stairs. Then I thought I heard someone knocking. I followed the sound up the stairs, walking with great caution with my train and veil behind me and shoes that hurt.

"Binky?" I called again.

"In here!" came the voice from the third-floor bathroom. I made my way up the next flight of stairs.

"What are you doing in the bathroom up here?" I shouted through the closed door. "Are you all right?"

"The one on our floor was busy all the time so I popped up here for some peace and quiet," he said. "A bit nervous, you know. And when I tried to come out I went to turn the blasted key and it dropped out of my hand and down a crack in the floorboards."

"Oh crikey." I tried to turn the knob on my side of the door. It wouldn't move. It was well and truly locked.

"If I pass you some tweezers under the door could you retrieve the key?"

"I don't think so. I heard it land quite a way down. It's a bloody rum do, isn't it?" he said.

"A bloody rum do? It's a disaster, Binky. We should have left by now. We'll be keeping the king and queen waiting and you know what they are like about being on time."

"Sorry, old thing. You know I get clumsy when I'm nervous."

Obviously that ran in the family. "I'll get Hamilton."

Hamilton came. "His Grace has dropped the key down the floorboards, Hamilton. Do you have an extra key?"

"I will bring all the keys I have, my lady," he said, betraying no sense of alarm in good butler fashion.

He returned with several footmen. A couple of maids stood on the stairs, looking on with interest. None of the keys worked. "I think we need a locksmith, Your Grace," Hamilton said.

"Bugger the locksmith," Binky yelled through the door. "Get a hammer. Break down the bloody door!"

⁂

"Don't worry about it, old thing," Binky said as we finally drove off. "Brides are supposed to be fashionably late."

"That's fine if the king and queen aren't in attendance," I said. "You know what he is like about time. He'll be fussing and fuming that I'm keeping everyone waiting."

"Let him fuss." Binky patted my hand. "This is your day. Enjoy it."

We pulled up outside the church. There was a large crowd on the pavement. I hadn't expected that, but then I realized that the royal family does always draw a crowd. There were cheers when I was assisted from the car, and flashbulbs popped. I tried to look serene and elegant in my too-tight shoes. Mummy and Belinda were waiting for me just inside the church.

"Don't worry. Queenie's got the other shoe," Mummy whispered, and we did a quick-change act.

"Sorry that I didn't notice it before," Belinda said. "It was under some fabric and I've been so busy trying to get my own dress finished in time." She looked awfully glamorous in figure-hugging off-white with a cape trimmed with feathers.

"Ah, there you are at last." Fig stepped out of the shadows with Podge and Addy at her side. "We were worried something had happened. Off you go, Podge. Don't let us down." She pushed her son forward. He was dressed in a kilt and blouse with a white frilled jabot and he looked worried.

I gave him an encouraging smile. "Just follow us, Podge," I said. "You'll be splendid, I know."

He nodded solemnly.

The two little princesses were standing with their nanny, looking absolutely adorable. They had fresh gardenias and orange blossom in their hair to match my bouquet. Elizabeth looked very solemn but Margaret was twirling around, watching her skirt go out. "You behave yourself, young Margaret," the Scottish nanny said severely. "You'll not be letting your cousin or the family down."

"You look lovely, Georgie," Elizabeth said. "I'd like a dress just like that when it's my wedding."

Binky held out his arm. "Are you ready, old thing?"

I took a deep breath. "I think so. As ready as I'll ever be." I slipped my arm through his. He patted my hand. "Between ourselves I think you look spiffing and I think that O'Mara chap is a lucky devil."

The organ had been playing softly. Now the melody changed to "Here Comes the Bride." The congregation rose. We started down the aisle. "Just don't let me tread on your train," Binky whispered. We exchanged a grin.

Faces passed in a blur, all smiling at us. We reached the front pews, where the king and queen and the other royals were seated. I stopped, turned to face them and curtsied. I didn't fall over. Binky didn't tread on my train. The princesses didn't drop the veil. Queen Mary was giving me an encouraging smile. So were the ancient great-aunts and various cousins. And a thought came to me: I might no longer be in the line of succession, but these are still all my relatives. I turned to face the altar again and walked on, and then he stepped out from the front pew on the right. My Darcy, looking so handsome that it took my breath away. And he looked at me and he winked.

I don't remember much about the ceremony. I think I said the right things at the right time. I know I said, "I do." We went into the sacristy to sign the marriage register and as we came out the church was suddenly filled with an awful din. The bagpiper was waiting at the foot of the altar steps. He piped us all the way down the aisle and out to the waiting car.

"Well, Mrs. O'Mara?" Darcy said as we drove away.

"Oh, Darcy, I'm so glad that's over," I said.

The reception went smoothly enough. The king and queen were seated in places of honor and smiled politely at the speeches. Binky managed to get through his with a couple of awful jokes. Darcy's best man, a dashing-looking fellow, told some frightfully witty stories about Darcy's misdeeds. We cut the cake and toasted with champagne, then Belinda and Mummy took me up to change into my going-away dress.

"So you're going to a houseboat with no servants?" Mummy said with horror. "Who is going to cook for you? Who will clean up?"

"We'll manage," I said. "It's what we want. To be on our own, completely."

"And you still don't know where you are going for your proper honeymoon trip?"

"I still don't know. Maybe now Darcy will tell me."

"So how will you know what to pack if he doesn't?"

"Don't worry about it, Mummy. We'll face that when we come to it."

"Just one word of warning," Mummy said. "Don't let Queenie pack for you."

༈

WE CAME DOWN the stairs. I threw my bouquet and Zou Zou caught it. Now that was auspicious, wasn't it? I saw her glance across at Darcy's father. I also did not miss my mother glancing at Sir Hubert. As we came out onto Belgrave Square, we had to dash through a barrage of rice and rose petals. The car was waiting and we drove away, watching the waving hands vanish in the rearview mirror.

The houseboat was outside the city, on the Thames near Henley. There were no signs of civilization, just the river, meandering along at a sedate pace between lush green meadows. Weeping willows trailed branches into the water, where ducks and swans were swimming. We had to walk along the towpath with cows watching us curiously over a fence. Then I spotted it, moored beside a willow tree. It was an old canal longboat, brightly painted. Darcy put down my suitcase, swept me up into his arms and carried me aboard. On the deck a table had been set up with two chairs and a bottle of champagne, sitting in a bucket of ice.

"Good show. Exactly as ordered," Darcy said as he put me down on the deck, "And I think we'll find the makings of a good dinner down below." He took my hand and led me down the steps into the cabin. The table was well stocked. Darcy gestured like a magician. "Oysters. Smoked salmon. Lobster. Salads. Crusty bread. Do you approve?"

"Brilliant." I couldn't stop smiling. "I'm absolutely starving. I couldn't eat a bite all day, and there wasn't a moment to eat at the reception."

"So you want to eat now?" Darcy's eyes swiveled from the table to the bedroom beyond. "Because I thought of a better way to whet that appetite. . . ."

I was suddenly embarrassed and hesitant. "Oh, I see."

He laughed and came up to me. "We're married, you silly old thing. We're perfectly legal. Finally you don't have to fight with that Queen Victoria conscience of yours." And he started undoing the buttons on my dress. There were many of them. "I suppose this is your good dress, is it? You wouldn't like it if I tore it off you?"

"I certainly would not, Darcy. You know how few good dresses I own. And you're not ripping off my new silk underwear either."

"We'll see about that." He laughed, swept me up into his arms and carried me through to the bedroom, the romantic effect being marred only by the fact that he banged his head on the low doorway.

And as to what happened after that, I'm afraid that modesty prevents me from going into detail, except to say that it was frightfully nice.